THE WHISTLE STOP CANTEEN

Barb Warner Deane

Enjoy !

Barb Warner Deane

AUTHOR'S NOTE

While The Whistle Stop Canteen is a work of fiction, many elements of this story are based on real people, places, and historical facts.

North Platte is a real town in Nebraska, and during WWII, it had, and still has today, the largest railroad yard in the world, known as Bailey Yard, although the population of North Platte in WWII was about 12,000. While all Union Pacific passenger trains crossing the northern part of the United States in WWII stopped in North Platte, passenger service ended in 1971, and the depot was torn down in 1973. There is a monument commemorating the North Platte Canteen on the spot where the depot stood and a wonderful exhibit at the Lincoln County Historical Museum in North Platte. A fascinating collection of mail sent by servicemen and women who stopped in North Platte are among the memorabilia at the museum.

The North Platte Servicemen's Canteen was real, very real, to the 6 million servicemen and women who spilled out of their troop trains that made ten- to fifteen-minute stops in North Platte for service and often replacement crews. Rae Wilson and Helen Christ are the actual names of the women who started and ran the Canteen, with the help of 55,000+ volunteers from 125 communities for fifty-one months—from December 25, 1941 to April 1, 1946. Fred Astaire, Liberace, and Fred McMurray were among the celebrities who stopped in North Platte. President Roosevelt actually sent a $5 bill to the Canteen, and Eleanor Roosevelt wrote to show her support. And a young Gene Slattery did raise money for the Canteen by auctioning off his shirt. These and many other little-known facts are included in the story. The other names in the book are fictional, as are the characters they represent. I wove in the culture and news of the day, but the story came entirely from me.

Thank you to the wonderful people of the Lincoln County Historical Museum in North Platte, Nebraska, the Dennison Depot Railroad Museum of Dennison, Ohio, and the National World War II Museum in New Orleans, Louisiana.

Thank you to Wendy Byrne, a very talented writer and an extremely patient critique partner, for her unfaltering support, terrific suggestions, and wholehearted support. Thank you to all of my beta readers: Patty Kehe, Kate LaMoreaux, Jane Klenck, and Jan MacLeod, for their support and suggestions. And to my wonderful developmental editor, Jill Welsh, for her help in best telling Maggie's story. Thank you to my daughters, Elizabeth, Samantha, and Miranda, for listening to me talk about each book for months and years before they actually saw it in print and for never telling me, "Enough, already!"

And, as always, my sincere thanks to my husband, Chris, for his love, support, brainstorming sessions, and willingness to drive to Nebraska, Ohio, and all the other places where there might be a museum or exhibit I wanted to visit. I will continue to try and time my research trips with the dates of state fairs or sporting events so we can both be entertained.

I hope you enjoy this glimpse into the lives of American women during WWII. If so, may I please ask you to write a review for The Whistle Stop Canteen on Amazon and/or Goodreads. You can also check out On The Homefront, my first published novel of women during WWII, or attend a presentation of one of my historical programs on Women of WWII: "On the Front Lines & the Home Front" or "At the Whistle Stop

Canteen," where I explore the many ways in which American women helped win WWII. You can find more information, join my mailing list, or contact me to request one of my presentations at a library or for a book club or other organization near you by visiting my website www.barbwarnerdeane.com.

Thanks, and I hope you enjoy the story – Barb

PROLOGUE

"Canteen Here Is Suggested For Soldiers
Following the visit of the troop train here yesterday
afternoon Miss Rae Wilson, sister of North Platte's Captain
Denver Wilson, suggested that a canteen be opened here to
make the trips of soldiers thru [sic] the city more
entertaining. She offered her services without charge. Her
public-spirited and generous offer is contained in the
following communications to The Bulletin:

December 18, 1941
To Editor, The Daily Bulletin:
I don't know just how many people went to meet the
trains when the troops went thru our city Wednesday, but
those who didn't should have.

To see the spirits and the high morale among those
soldiers should certainly put some of us on our feet and
make us realize we are really at war. We should help keep
this soldiers' morale at its highest peak. We can do our part.

During World War I the army and navy mothers, or
should I say the war mothers, had canteens at our own

depot. Why can't we, the people of North Platte and other towns surrounding our community, start a fund and open a Canteen now? I would be more than willing to give my time without charge and run this canteen.

We who met this troop train which arrived about 5 o'clock were expecting Nebraska boys. Naturally we had candy, cigarettes, etc., but we very willingly gave these things to the Kansas boys.

Smiles, tears and laughter followed. Appreciation showed on over 300 faces. An officer told me it was the first time anyone had met their train and that North Platte had helped the boys keep up their spirits.

I say get back of our sons and other mothers' sons 100 per cent. Let's do something and do it in a hurry! We can help this way when we can't help any other way.

-Rae Wilson"

CHAPTER ONE

December 22, 1941 – North Platte, Nebraska
When a few raised eyebrows greeted me in the fellowship hall of the First Methodist Church, my left hand touched the back of my victory roll to ensure my hair was not coming undone. Everything seemed in place.

Women filled the room, from Rae Wilson in her mid-twenties to Gertrude Zimmerman, who was pushing eighty. The North Platte Canteen committee had a lot of work to do in just three days to serve the first trains, and the group assembled looked ready to roll up their sleeves and get to it.

Nothing could stop a Nebraska woman on a mission to help her neighbors.

As the town librarian, it had always been my responsibility to ensure an accurate history of North Platte, including this endeavor, be maintained for posterity. It would be important for me to keep a complete historical account of the Canteen, starting from the beginning.

What we were gathered here to plan might not be world peace, but it could make a difference in the lives of soldiers heading off to save the world.

"Why, Margaret," Rae Wilson rose to greet me, taking my arm. "How lovely of you to join us."

I nodded and followed her lead. "Of course, Rae. I'm only too happy to be the Canteen historian and do what I can to help."

When we stopped in front of an empty chair, she motioned for me to sit. "What a smart idea, Margaret. I'm sure we need a historian to keep track of Canteen events for us." She smiled at me and then looked around the circle at the other women.

"Precisely," I said, as I took the seat she offered. "I will do my best to ensure we have clear and concise records of the servicemen who come to the Canteen." No one should expect any less of me.

Trudy Bellows cleared her throat. "I thought I was going to be in charge of the guest books and making sure we have as many soldiers sign them as possible." Her lips formed a slight pout, as if someone had taken her candy.

"Well, Trudy," Rae started in a quiet voice, "I'm sure it will be helpful to have all the volunteers ask servicemen to sign our guest book. Margaret can be in charge of tracking the servicemen, units, and divisions that come through, and you can make sure we have enough guest books and pens. And please make sure, as part of your hospitality duties, the guest books are located in an easy place for servicemen to see and access."

What was all the fuss was about? "I think it would be helpful if I communicated with some of the servicemen who come through the Canteen and find out where they go after they leave us and what becomes of them, as best we can."

Dorothy Schmidt, next to me, was nodding. "Oh, what a wonderful idea! I'm sure we'd all be interested to know where the boys go once they leave our Canteen."

Several other women murmured their agreement.

Rae looked from me to Dorothy. "The news won't always be good, ladies. You understand that, right? This is a war, after all."

Rae took her seat and started outlining her vision for the servicemen's Canteen. Volunteers stepped up to take on various roles, but the discussion seemed to center on how to get enough volunteers and supplies. "We don't have any funding from the government," Rae was explaining, "so, I'm thinking of asking towns in the area to each take on a day, say for Grand Island Lutheran Women's Club to cover the third Thursday of the month, or something similar. Each organization will be in charge of supplying or purchasing the food needed for their day, although we'll raise our own funds here at the Canteen to help cover the milk, coffee, bread, and supplies needed."

Dorothy spoke up. "And we can ask local businesses for donations. I bet Mack over at the Sunshine Dairy would be willing to give us milk at a substantial discount."

Surely the local businesses would want to support such a worthy cause.

Rae nodded. "Good idea, Dorothy. And we'll ask for donations of money, of course. I'm sure some of the local groups would be happy to host fund-raisers for the Canteen."

Everyone seemed to be in agreement, and very enthusiastic, about the work to be done and the way to get started. We agreed the first day our North Platte Servicemen's Canteen would be officially open would be Christmas Day, which was only three days away. We had a lot of work to do and quickly.

****

December 25, 1941

Rae came rushing over to the Cody Hotel from the train depot. "The train is coming. Let's hurry, ladies."

I picked up a basket of cookies and cigarettes and followed the line of women rushing across the street to the station platform. Lucy Cook raced by me carrying her own basket, lined with white linen cloths, full of sandwiches.

"This is so exciting," she said, smiling at me. "Our first troop train. I wonder where they are headed."

I looked at her. "Surely you understand the men cannot tell us, even if they know."

Lucy tilted her head. She was either about to trip or drop the basket. "Of course they can't tell us, but doesn't that make you wonder even more?"

Where they're going was hardly the point. They were going to war. "Certainly not. All I want to do is offer them the food and gifts we have prepared, wish them well, and send them on their way. They must concentrate of winning the war and getting home safely, not satisfying our idle curiosity."

She made some noise like air releasing from a tire and must have slowed down, as she was no longer walking next to me. Perhaps she needed more exercise in her free time in order to be fit enough to carry supplies for the troops.

As the train came to a stop, the Union Pacific employees jumped to work, relubricating the train locomotive's large driving wheels and refilling its water tender. We had to hurry, as the men would have no longer than it took to service the locomotive and possibly switch out the crew before the train would be on its way again.

The steam escaping from the train mixed with the smell of the exhaust, creating a dank, bitter sting in the air. As I approached the passenger cars, the first men were stepping off the train. They appeared to be Army officers and seemed confused as to why we were there to meet their train. No other soldiers came off the trains, however, and as we moved toward Rae and the officers, we learned why.

"This is a train of Negro troops, ladies." Rae had a very serious expression, as if she'd said prisoners of war instead of Army troops. "The soldiers won't be allowed off the train, nor can we board it." She gestured to the white officers. "So we'll spread out the length of the train and pass our baskets through the windows. Try to cover each train car with at least two volunteers."

The men would be hungry, regardless of their skin color.

I walked up to the open door at one end of the third train car, and Dorothy walked to the door at the opposite end. Soldiers were crowded in the doorway.

The men were young and thin, but seemed happy to see us.

I handed my basket to the young man at the front of the line. "Merry Christmas and welcome to North Platte, Nebraska, soldier. Here are some cookies and cigarettes for you all. Mrs. Schmidt is at the other end of this train car with a basket of sandwiches. Please help yourself and pass my basket down to Mrs. Schmidt and her basket back up to me."

"But how much does this cost us, ma'am?"

I smiled at the soldier, who looked worried.

"Not a thing, young man. These are gifts to you from the people of North Platte to help you on your way to fight. We wish you good luck, blessings, and a speedy return."

His eyes became large and he opened his mouth long before he actually spoke. "Thank you, ma'am. And to everyone here who brung these things to us. This is very kind of y'all."

While I waited for Dorothy's basket to make it back to my end of the train, I used the time to speak to the soldiers in the doorway, pulling paper and pencil from my pocket.

"Do you mind telling me your name and what town you're from, or even what your unit is? We hope to keep track of the troops coming through our Canteen, if we can."

Several of the men crowded the doorway and stuck their heads out of the open windows.

"I'm Julian Clements, ma'am, from Tuscaloosa, Alabama."

"Jeremiah Moody, Maplesville, Alabama, ma'am."

"Benjamin Jackson Watkins, ma'am. From Jasper, Alabama."

I might not be able to read my notes later, I was writing so quickly. It would be so much easier when the troops could come to the guest book, but maybe I could come up with a better method of tracking soldiers unable to get off the train.

The soldier at the front of the crowded doorway, his uniform read "Clements," handed me the empty basket that Dorothy had sent through the train as the call All Aboard rang through the platform. I grabbed the basket and made to step back, but young Mr. Clements grabbed my hand.

"We can't thank you enough, ma'am, all of you nice ladies of North Platte. We'll never forget you for your kindness."

I shook his hand, and he released mine as the train started to move. I found myself unable to speak, but nodded and smiled. There may have been a tear in my eye.

The rest of the volunteers and I stood, waving and calling after the train as it pulled away and didn't move a step until long after the train had chugged out of sight.

A wave of exhaustion swept over me, as if I had run after the train or carried a heavy load for miles. The walk back to the hotel was exhausting in a way that couldn't be explained by the empty baskets we carried. Knowing many—or even most—of the young Negro soldiers on that train, wherever it was headed, would never make it back to their homes in Alabama or elsewhere hung heavy on my mind the rest of the day.

If we could comfort them, make them smile, and fill their stomachs for the briefest of moments in this wide world war and unknown future, what a powerful thing this was going to be. It might well be the most important work I would ever do.

****

December 30, 1941

Rae called out, "Put the coffee on," and we all rushed to our spots to meet the incoming train. I walked to the serving table, assuming I should help with sandwiches or something, but there didn't seem to be an open spot.

Someone ram into my shoulder and I turned to find Dorothy Schmidt pushing past me. "Oh, I'm sorry, Margaret…trying to get to the kitchen so we're ready for the troops."

"Of course. I was…"

Rae walked up then, cupping my left elbow in her hand. "Margaret, would you please manage the periodicals table for us?" She was walking toward the far side of the room, and I had little choice but to accompany her.

"Well, I…"

She smiled, gesturing with her other hand to the long table of plywood set up on four saw horses along the wall. "You would be so much help to any of our soldiers looking for reading material. This is basically our Canteen library."

I couldn't argue with that. "Of course." The magazines seemed to be arranged in a rather haphazard fashion among the stacks of books, although mostly Bibles, and current newspapers. There were no other volunteers working behind the periodicals table. "But am I to work this long table alone?"

Rae shook her head. "Certainly not…," she glanced around the room. "Rose dear," she called to a slender, redheaded teenage girl standing at the doorway to the platform. When the girl turned around, her expression was not necessarily one of helpfulness. She rather looked like she'd been caught doing something untoward.

"Yes, Miss Wilson?" The young woman turned and walked to where Rae and I stood in front of the table.

"Rose, I'm sure you know Miss Parker, our town librarian. Would you please help her work the periodicals table? The train should be stopping any moment, and I'm sure there are many young men who are interested in finding something to read on their trip."

While disappointment was clear on her face, the girl nodded.

Rae turned back to me. "Margaret, this is Rose Nelson. Her mother is Trixie Nelson, who runs a boarding house over on Cottonwood Street."

I nodded. "Yes, I know Mrs. Nelson. It's nice to meet you, Rose."

She smiled, nodded, but didn't return my greeting. Perhaps the girl was a simpleton…

"Here comes the train," Rae cried out, finally releasing my elbow and pushing me toward the table before turning to face the rest of the volunteers. "Stations, ladies."

Several teenagers rushed out to the platform with baskets full of apples, cigarettes, popcorn balls, and newspapers. Rose watched them go. Rae and three other volunteers followed the girls outside to act as greeters and direct the soldiers inside to the Canteen.

I turned to Rose. "Please stand there." I motioned to the end of the table closest to the food tables. "I will stand at this end," motioning to the end of the table nearest the door to the platform, "with the hopes of both helping servicemen intent on obtaining reading material and encouraging them to sign our guest book."

"Yes, ma'am." She scurried behind the periodicals table, walking to the far end. I took my spot and turned to face the impending onslaught of soldiers.

"And Rose?"

She turned toward me. "Yes, Miss Parker?"

"Please be sure to direct our servicemen to the books and newspapers as well as the magazines."

She nodded. "Yes, ma'am."

My stomach skittered with tension, but in a good way. I only hoped we were able to help the troops heading off to war know that people at home were thinking of them.

The servicemen started flooding into the Canteen, rushing from one table to the next with shouts of excitement. Many raced immediately to the food tables along the back wall of the depot lunchroom. Thank heavens Rae had obtained Mr. Jeffers' permission to use the lunchroom. The more trains that we met every day, the harder it would have been to carry over supplies from the Cody Hotel.

"Please help yourself to some magazines, newspapers, and books. Feel free to take along something to read." I motioned to the tables, speaking generally to the throngs of servicemen flooding the depot. Many smiled and nodded at me and might well stop by for reading material after filling their stomachs, but most couldn't seem to believe their good luck in finding all this delicious food waiting for them.

A skinny young man, probably not even nineteen yet, stopped in front of me. He might never make it to twenty. I had to swallow hard and sure up the smile on my face. "May I help you, soldier?"

He nodded, and his Adam's apple bobbed a bit before he spoke. "Excuse me, but where do we pay, ma'am?"

He was looking around, clearly anxious to get to the food before he had to get back on the train.

My heart melted a bit at his earnest young face. "There's no charge, son. Help yourself to whatever you want."

His eyes went wide, and he didn't speak for a moment. "It's free?" He looked at the food tables behind him and turned back to me. "The food and everything?"

"Yes, it's all free of charge to servicemen. It's our way of saying have a safe trip, good luck wherever it is you're going, and God bless you all."

He took off his hat, sort of bowed to me, and reached for my hand. Shaking it heartily in his own, he smiled at me. "And God bless you, ma'am, and the good people of…well, wherever we are."

I withdrew my hand before it got crushed, touched by his enthusiasm. "You're in North Platte, Nebraska, soldier. Once you get your food and whatever reading material you might like, please take a moment to sign our guest book and tell us where you're from."

He nodded. "Yes, ma'am. I'm from East Longmeadow, Massachusetts, ma'am. Thank you, ma'am." He nodded, sort of bobbed a bow again, and raced off to the table full of sandwiches and cookies.

At the other end of the table, Rose was smiling at a small group of soldiers who were browsing the magazine selection. Of course, we wanted her to be friendly and helpful, but her gaze seemed to contain something a little more predatory. The child couldn't be more than fifteen, or she'd probably be distributing popcorn balls out on the platform. Rae and the hospitality committee had decided young women had to be at least sixteen to work as platform girls. This girl seemed more taken with the soldiers looking at the reading material than she was with helping them, so I'd need to have a talk with her before the next troop train arrived.

When I turned back, hoping to help more servicemen myself or at least encourage some to sign the guest book, I found myself drawn into the gaze of an officer leaning casually against the lunchroom doorway, staring at me. He was tall and broad shouldered with a twinkle in his eye.

"May I help you?"

He smiled, his gaze filled with bits of mischief and insolence, and sauntered toward my end of the table. I had never seen a man in uniform saunter before, but he was clearly in no rush, in contrast to nearly everyone else around us. "Oh, I certainly hope so, Miss…?"

I ran my hand along the belt of my pale-green dress, smoothing nonexistent wrinkles. "Miss Parker, North Platte town librarian and Canteen historian." I motioned to the magazines in front of me, but found I was unable to tear my gaze from his. "Can I interest you in some reading material for your journey?"

He walked to my end of the table and came around to the side, so he was standing inches from me. He was tall and muscular, his hair a dark sandy brown and his eyes a crystal-clear blue with a few crinkles etched into soft lines around them. He leaned back against the brick wall of the depot, his hands deep in his pockets. What happened to those smart young soldiers with ramrod straight spines who stood at attention? I'd never seen such a relaxed and somehow feline-looking military man.

"You interest me, Miss Parker."

His nearness gave me goose bumps, and I became uncomfortable in a tingly way. A feeling of instant familiarity overwhelmed me, even with his formal address. He may have sensed it, because he sobered and backed off, a bit.

Even with slightly more distance between us, his pull was electric.

Looking up, he gestured toward the tables of food, desserts, and drinks. "What's the story behind all of this?"

I swallowed, my mouth suddenly dry. "We, I mean the town of North Platte, want to offer what we can to help our servicemen and women as they head off to parts unknown in the service of our county. We don't have munitions factories in North Platte; we are far from the coastline or even a big city. But this," I said, gesturing around the Canteen, "this we can do."

The twinkle in his eye, so recently more of humor or even ardor, became a strong look of respect and gratitude. "I thank you all for this. My men have been on this train for nearly three days already, and the food has been terrible or nonexistent. This is an oasis in the desert of a crowded, cold, and unpleasant train ride."

I nodded. "Where did you start your journey, if I may ask, Captain?" I couldn't pull my gaze away from him.

He smiled. A world of possibility filled his gaze again. "Captain Tom Carter at your service, ma'am." He bowed slightly. "Most of the men just completed basic training at Camp Benning in Georgia. It's been a long train ride from there."

"These men are not new recruits, then? If they completed basic training, they must have signed up before Pearl Harbor was attacked."

"True," he nodded. "They've been away from home since late summer, so the sight of pretty young girls and…" For some reason, he smiled at me and added, "Lovely women and home cooking are all very welcome to them."

"I'm sure." I was fidgeting with the magazines in front of me, somehow lost in his gaze. I'm not a fidgeter, but I couldn't still my fingers. "And you, Captain, how long have you been in the Army?"

He crossed his arms across his broad chest, the cocky smile back on his face. "Forever." He laughed.

I nodded and motioned toward the guest book. "Would you please sign our guest book, Captain? Or at least sign in for your unit?"

"Sure," He turned to sign the guest book. When he turned back, he had that Cheshire-cat grin on his face again.

"Don't you want some food or drinks before you get back on the train? I only have reading material at this table."

"Worried about me, Miss Parker?" He placed his hands lightly on the table and leaned toward me.

My skin seemed to tingle, although we hadn't even touched. "I don't know where you're going, but it could be a long time before you have the chance to get more cookies or pheasant sandwiches."

He laughed. "Pheasant sandwiches? You're right, I don't know when I'll get those again."

I motioned toward the line of soldiers, trying to pull off an air of nonchalance. "Well, this is your chance. They're really quite delicious."

His gaze met mine. "You're quite delicious, Miss Parker, if you don't mind me saying so."

More flutters tickled the pit of my stomach. I'm sure my surprise showed on my face, as he chuckled. "Well, perhaps you do, but it's the same, nonetheless."

Being somewhat nonplussed, I didn't answer, but that didn't seem to deter him.

"Do you volunteer at this Canteen often, Miss Parker?"

"I, uh…" Why was I having trouble forming full sentences? I took a deep breath and started again. "As the town librarian I'm usually at work, but try to come to the Canteen every evening. It's important I ensure that the records, correspondence, and history of this Canteen are preserved." I took a deep breath. "And I enjoy being able to serve our troops."

He smiled, but somehow it seemed as if he might be mocking me.

When the conductor called, "All aboard," Captain Carter nodded to the sergeant I hadn't noticed standing near the doorway. The sergeant placed two fingers between his lips and blew out a shrill whistle. Conversation stopped, and the sergeant called to the soldiers, "Move it out, men."

I looked with some dismay back to Captain Carter. He still hadn't picked up any food, although he now stood with a couple of newspapers folded under his arm. "May I know your given name, Miss Parker?"

"My name is Margaret, Captain."

"I see you have no wedding ring and your name is Miss, but is there a soldier somewhere or a lucky man here in North Platte who holds the keys to your heart, Miss Margaret?"

This foolish man was going to be hungry if he didn't hurry up and grab a sandwich. Why could he possibly care if I was married or engaged? "No, but Captain, you are going to miss your train and your chance to grab a sandwich." I walked out from behind the table.

He smiled and then had the audacity to wink. "You're right, Miss Margaret." He started backing out of the depot. "Think of me when I'm away. I know I'll be thinking of you."

What could I say to that? The man had talked to me for about fifteen minutes in the middle of a war. "Good luck, Captain Carter. I'll be praying for you and your men."

As he walked to the train, I quickly grabbed a couple of sandwiches, an orange, several cookies, and a half pint bottle of milk. I hurried after the captain, calling to him. He turned, smiling. The sparkle was back in his eyes, and his smile made me flush.

"Already thinking of me, are you, Maggie?" He reached for the food and placed a quick kiss on my cheek. I stopped in my tracks.

He laughed at my surprise and jumped into the open doorway of the train car. "I'll see you next time I stop in North Platte. Don't forget me!"

I stood among the many Canteen volunteers, waving and calling good-byes to the servicemen as the train pulled away. My face was warm and I felt a slight buzz in my head.

Even as the train pulled further away, and his face started to fade, I felt his irresistible tug holding my gaze to the spot where he was standing.

What an incredibly peculiar man. When he left, it felt as if he'd pulled all of the air from the depot and left us all in a bit of a vacuum. How was it possible to make such an impression on me in such a short amount of time?

I found myself smiling for no perceptible reason. It was a good thing the train was getting farther away. If he'd seen the smile, it might have encouraged him, although, really, what difference would it have made as the man was off to war. Even from this distance, I could tell he was still staring at me, smiling, and waving. Surely he was too far to have seen my smile.

CHAPTER TWO

January 2, 1942

As I arrived at the Canteen on Friday afternoon, the number of volunteers was larger than I'd expected. Apparently the little town of Stockville combined efforts with another small community to work the Canteen together.

"Oh, Margaret, this letter came for you." Rae handed me an envelope.

"Thank you, Rae." I took the letter and headed to the periodicals table, wishing for enough time to get the table organized before the next troop train arrived. I tied on my apron and slid the envelope into the pocket. Hopefully, today, the apron would keep the newsprint and dust of the periodicals off my dress.

We'd received some new donations, so I was pleased to be able to add to the small piles of *Time* and *Newsweek* magazines, as well as *Life*, *Look*, *Readers Digest*, *Good Housekeeping*, and *Popular Science*.

Once the magazines were in reasonable order and the guest book was open to the current page with a pen poised at the ready, I pulled the letter from my pocket. I hadn't heard the "coffee pot on" warning yet, so I probably had a few minutes before the next train appeared. When I read the front of the envelope and saw my own name, my breath hitched and my mouth went dry. Who would be writing to me? Especially in care of the Canteen?

To Margaret Parker
North Platte Librarian
Historian to the Servicemen's Canteen
North Platte, NE

January 1, 1942,
My dear Maggie,

Happy New Year! Let's hope 1942 is the year we see a speedy and successful end to this war.

I wish I could have seen your face when you received this letter. I'm sending it to the Canteen, but hope you'll send me your address by return post, so I can send my future letters to your home. I didn't have time to ask for your address when we met, so I hope you don't mind this letter arriving at the Canteen.

I told you I would think of you and I have been. After our train pulled out of North Platte, and the men were settled in again for our continuing trip west, I had time to eat the meal you so kindly provided for me. I will admit the pheasant sandwiches were much better than I expected. Of course, everything was more delicious because you took the time to bring it to me. My first concern is making sure my men are taken care of, so it was nice to have you worry about me. I truly appreciate your kindness.

The men were all much happier after our stop in North Platte, so thank everyone for their delicious food and the care they showed our troops by meeting our train and seeing us off.

The men don't know where we're headed, and they are spending a lot of time wondering and guessing, but I don't think any of them will be able to figure it out. Of course, I can't tell you, military secrets and all that, but I hope you will think of me and my troops, and keep us all in your prayers, as we head toward our destination. I will say, it will be unlike many of the places troops are heading when being shipped west.

So, tell me all about Maggie. What are your days like as town librarian? What do you do in your role as historian of the Canteen? What do you do for fun? Where did you get that beautiful auburn hair?

Have you seen any good movies lately? I'm sure you've read some good books, so what can you recommend? It's uncertain I can get a hold of anything good to read where we're heading, but I can always order some books from the Army if I know what to ask for.

I'm career Army, as you might have guessed by my somewhat advanced age, as compared to our new inductees. I joined up in WWI and decided to stay and make a career of the Army. Given that WWI was the "war to end all wars," I rather assumed I'd be working in peace-keeping and policing roles, training men, and helping to ensure world peace. I never thought the Germans and the Japs would drag us into another world war so soon. But I'm confident we have the man power, and after Pearl Harbor, the incentive, to give our all and win this thing.

Thanks again to you and the fine people of North Platte for your kindness at the train station. Your Canteen offered the only food, never mind the books, magazines, newspapers, cigarettes, and warm wishes, we saw as we crossed this great nation. The town of North Platte will never truly understand what a gift you gave us, and I don't mean the pheasant sandwiches or homemade cookies. To know folks on the home front, there in the middle of the country, would go out of their way to show us support, kindness, and love, well, it has made a big difference in the morale of my men. Please tell the volunteers of North Platte that we send our hearty thanks and blessings to you all.

Please write to me. I don't have a wife, a fiancée, or a girlfriend who is keeping the home fires burning for me. I'm hoping it's not only the young soldiers who earn the right to pen pals in this war – surely you won't deny me a few innocent letters?

I'm not sure when we'll reach our destination, but I know any letters you send to the address below will find their way to me eventually. Please...

All my best and warmest wishes –
Tom Carter

What was that man thinking, writing to me? We didn't know each other and had a conversation of a mere fifteen minutes. Was he crazy?

I certainly wouldn't answer his letter, despite the slight charge of electricity that raced up my spine and set my heart beating faster than normal. I didn't even know the man.

I quickly folded the letter, replaced it in the envelope, and slid it back into my pocket. Let the other volunteers assume it was a thank you letter to the Canteen. Well, actually it was, at least partly.

"Miss Parker, is everything okay?"

Rose was standing directly in front of me, unbuttoning her coat. Her pretty heart-shaped face showed signs of worry.

"Of course."

She pulled off her coat, hat and gloves, folding her coat lining-side out and sliding it onto a chair in the corner. "Your cheeks are a little pink, so I was hoping you didn't get bad news in your letter."

I stiffened and couldn't help myself from touching my cheeks. They did seem a bit warm. "No, nothing like that, just a thank you from the Army troops who went through the Canteen on New Year's Eve."

"Wow," Rose took her place at the table, smoothing the skirt of her red and blue shirtwaist dress. "Their letter got here quickly. Did they send it from the next stop down the line?"

It hadn't occurred to me, but Captain Carter must have done something like that in order for a letter he wrote yesterday to reach me today. "Probably." I shook my head. "They were very grateful to the Canteen and the volunteers and said ours was the only food they'd received as they crossed the entire country, other than the Army-issued C-rations."

"Are you going to write him back?" She was grinning like the child she was, oblivious to the invasive and inappropriate nature of her question.

Why would I write back to a stranger? Just because he wrote to me and had the clearest, beautiful blue eyes I'd ever seen, it didn't mean we were suddenly friends.

"As Canteen historian, I'm charged with finding out what I can about the servicemen who come through our Canteen. If I decide to write back to the captain, it'll be to ask him to let us know, if he can, what becomes of his men."

She stuck out her lower lip in some type of pout. "I was hoping you were going to say he is a great love and someday you'll be married because you met in the Canteen. Wouldn't that be romantic?"

I scoffed. Marriage? That was the last thing on my mind these days. "Don't be silly. The men are here for only ten or fifteen minutes. I don't imagine any romances will grow out of our Canteen service."

She crossed her arms. "It could happen though, couldn't it?"

I turned to look in her eyes. She seemed both determined and more than a little lost. "I think it's unlikely. But you'll meet a nice young man someday, although it might not be until the war is over."

"I have to find a great romance, Miss Parker, here at the Canteen. I want to be one of the platform girls, talking and flirting with the soldiers and handing out apples, cigarettes, and popcorn balls, giving out my name and address to soldiers. I want to find a pen pal, write to a soldier, fall in love, and get married. What other chance do I have to get out of North Platte?"

Her words reminded me of my own before the last war. How different my life would have turned out if only Fred had come home from France. I'd made my peace with spinsterhood years ago, but could well remember when I had dreamed like a young girl.

Rae walked through the lunchroom. "I put the coffee on."

The next troop train was almost here. I guess Rose could try to meet her great romance, but it would be hard to fall in love with a stranger in only fifteen minutes.

****

January 7, 1942

Those last two library patrons had trouble making up their minds, which left me a little late leaving work. There was a troop train in the station when I arrived at the Canteen, and Rose was chatting with some of the soldiers, doing a reasonable job of both being friendly and a little flirty, but letting them know what we could offer in terms of books, magazines, and newspapers. She caught on quickly. Whoever replaced her, when she inevitably deserted me for the excitement of being a platform girl, would have to work to be as bright as Rose.

I stashed my coat, hat, and pocketbook behind the table and quickly got to work directing young servicemen to reading material. Within moments, the call rang out and summoned them back to the train. Their hurried exodus, followed by a line of volunteers to wave them off, created an instant quiet in the depot. Waving these young boys off was a bittersweet experience every day, as we so needed them to succeed, but knew many would die in the effort. Sometimes their sweet young faces came back in my dreams and I knew it wasn't a good thing.

After we walked to the tracks to wave them good-bye, I returned to the table and Rose followed.

She gave me a lopsided smile as she took an envelope from her pocket. "Miss Wilson gave me this letter for you."

I took the envelope and, as I read the address, she slipped away.

The captain, again. Couldn't the man take a hint? The other women might start gossiping about me.

But I couldn't wait to see what he said this time.

January 4, 1942
Dear Maggie,
   I haven't received a reply from you to my first letter, but I'm going to assume it's the fault of the U.S. Mail or the Army and nothing more. Surely it's not that you didn't write. You're the kind of woman who understands how important it is to a soldier far from home and hearth to hear from the people back home. I am holding your warmth and support close to my heart, knowing soon, I'll be able to hold your written thoughts and wishes there as well.
   Any news from the home front? How's the Canteen? Are you getting enough volunteers? Supplies? Money? If this is going to continue for the length of the war, which I hope will be short, this could be a very expensive and exhaustive endeavor.
   I have to run now to get some sleep tonight before another day of drilling, training, and such for our troops. I hope you are thinking of me as you fall asleep tonight as I will definitely be thinking of you. Waiting for your letters, I'll be-
   Yours, Tom

****

January 13, 1942
"Miss Parker?"
   Rosemary Keeler was balancing several very tall and beautifully frosted angel food cakes in her arms as she walked through the Canteen doors. I rushed forward to help. "What lovely cakes, Mrs. Keeler. They look delicious."
   She chuckled. "Thank you. I guess I overestimated how many cakes I could carry at once."
   We walked into the depot kitchen to drop off her donations. "Do you have more you need to carry in?"
   She nodded. "Yes, actually. We're going to start giving a whole cake to any serviceman or woman coming through on their birthday." She smiled. "Or, at least, that's the plan."
   What a terrific idea. "The troops will love that. Most of them have never been away from home, or their mothers,

on their birthday before. I expect the extra effort on your part will mean the world to these young people."

We walked back outside, where a young boy stood at the side of a truck. The bed was filled with cakes, at least eight more, a blanket set up as a cover for the trip.

"These are really wonderful, Mrs. Keeler. You've surely been baking for days."

She blushed. "My Seth has been bringing me turkey eggs, and they're so much bigger than chicken ones, so I can bake more cakes." She nodded to the boy, who was carrying a basket and helping us with the cakes. "This is my son, Clifford."

He tipped his cap to me. "Ma'am."

"Nice to meet you, Clifford."

As we walked to the door, Rosemary turned to me and smiled. "Since I only use the egg whites for the cakes, I'm able to use the egg yolks to make mayonnaise for the sandwiches."

"Wonderful idea, Mrs. Keeler. Thanks for all your hard work." Women learned how to make food stretch during the years of the depression, but it was even more useful than ever now, with the increased list of rationed items.

When we brought the rest of the cakes in, the kitchen started to look like a bakery, except for the sandwich-making production line. After we unloaded everything, I walked back out to the periodicals table. Trudy walked over with a few letters and handed them to me.

"It looks like some of the soldiers who've come through the Canteen are already writing to thank us. I can't wait to see how you put together the history of the Canteen, Margaret. I think all of us will enjoy seeing the names of the boys, when they came through, their letters, and whatever else you learn about them. This was a good idea."

"Thank you, Trudy." Her sincere acknowledgement warmed my heart. I looked over the stack of letters, familiar handwriting showing on the last one. A shiver raced up my spine at the sight of his letter. Although nothing could come of it, I had to admit it was flattering to have such a handsome man show interest in me.

"There is one that seems addressed specifically to you, Margaret. Did you have a family member come through the Canteen?" She glanced at me out of the corner of her eye.

"No, but I have been making a point to introduce myself to the servicemen who sign our guest book, so one of them must have remembered my name." I put the letters in the pocket of my apron and pulled out the latest box of donated magazines, and started sorting them. "Thank you, Trudy."

As I stacked piles of *Look*, *Life*, and *Readers Digest*, she walked away. I had the lingering feeling of her eyes on me as I worked. That man was going to be the death of me.

January 10, 1942
Dear Maggie,

I realized in my last two letters I forgot to enclose a photo of me, so I'm sending it to you now. I'm sure it will help you to remember me fondly and encourage you to write lots of letters to this lonely captain. Of course, I'd be very grateful to receive a photo of you as well. I can well remember your soft chocolate eyes, sweet, sassy smile, and stunning auburn hair, but having a photo would allow me to boast to my fellow officers, which is an essential part of being an Army officer on deployment, as well as give me a way to wish you "sweet dreams" every night before I fall asleep.

We are well settled into our new "home" now, have the barracks set up, and camp is functioning as well as can be expected. As we discussed, these are not brand-new recruits, but even still, they are green, untested, and nervous. Only extensive training will allow them to react instinctively, without taking time to think about what to do, in order to save their lives, protect their brothers-in-arms, and achieve our objectives. My mission is to make them the most effective team possible. Some days it seems like I'm very far from succeeding.

I've been in "this man's Army" for twenty-five years now. I joined not long after my high school graduation, but when the U.S.

entered the Great War, I was still young and green. I try to remind myself they'll learn; it's the nature of the beast.

Tell me, what's happening in North Platte this week? What's playing at the local movie theatre? What's the hot gossip making its way around town? What are your plans for Saturday night? What's the war news? If it's not happening where we are right now, we're not getting a lot of information. I miss picking up the local papers on base, like I did in Georgia, and I'm not getting much news from the Stars and Stripes.

Well, I'll close now, as it's time for lights out, and I want to fall asleep thinking about you when you read my letters. Please, Maggie, write to me. I want to get to know you, and I doubt I'll be able to stop into the Canteen again anytime soon. Besides, I'll just keep writing to you anyway. Ha, ha.

Yours, Tom

CHAPTER THREE

November 3, 1973

I stopped my car on Front Street, but didn't get too close to the depot.

"Why are we stopping, Grandma?" Lisa was fidgeting in her seat. We had a Saturday morning tradition of breakfast at the diner followed by a fun outing. This week, given the weather was still sunny and unseasonably warm, we had plans to head to Buffalo Bill Ranch State Park, always one of Lisa's favorites. She was anxious for her chocolate chip pancakes and a fun day in the fall sun.

I was just anxious.

"I want to take a look for a minute, sweetie. We'll go to breakfast soon, I promise."

For two-and-half years, the good citizens of North Platte, myself included, had been working to get the Union Pacific to agree to turn over the old depot to the City of North Platte to use as the home of the Lincoln County Historical Museum.

After all the time I'd spent at the depot, the 55,000 volunteers who worked there over the fifty-one months the Canteen was in operation and the 6 million servicemen and women who had come through the North Platte Canteen, even if only for ten or fifteen minutes, it was wrong on so many levels that the only things left of that building were the scattered remains from yesterday's wrecking ball.

My heart was broken.

How could this have happened? After passenger trains stopped coming through North Platte two years ago, we knew we'd have to save the depot from destruction. Even the Nebraska State Historical Society had been called in to help, but nothing worked. I hadn't given up hope, at least, until I saw the destruction for myself.

Those of us who worked at the Canteen would never forget it. Clearly, based on the letters we still received from grateful servicemen and their families, thirty years after we closed the doors, the men and women who came through those doors would never forget it either. But, to me, as a librarian and preserver of history, never mind life-long North Platte resident, the destruction of this depot was shameful.

"Grandma? Why are you crying?"

****

April 1, 1996
"Grandma?"

The call reverberated through my house even before she got through the front door. I might be old, but I wasn't completely deaf. Sitting at my dressing table, I finished combing my hair and applied a little lipstick. She'd surely be rushing me out of my house soon enough.

"In here, Lisa."

She swept into the room, a bright smile on her pretty face, her blond hair in a pixie cut, and her blue eyes sparkling. "Are you ready?"

I sat for a moment, no longer than an instant, just taking in the energy of my granddaughter. I wanted to capture her image in my mind so as to remember her always as she looked today.

She wanted me to get moving.

"Let's go!" Her voice was a little too loud but very enthusiastic. She inherited her conquer-the-world personality from her mother. She walked to the back of my wheelchair and placed her hands on the handles.

"Give me a minute, there, girlie. I don't move quite as quickly as I used to, you know." I checked the mirror one last time and picked up my small pocketbook from the dressing table. "Please put this in the back pocket for me, will you, sugar?"

Now that my hair had gone completely white, I could carry off red in a way I'd never been able to as a younger woman with auburn hair.

"Do you want to put your blazer on, Gram?" She held it up for me.

"Let's wait and do that at the museum, okay? I don't want it to get too wrinkled before the ceremony."

When my late husband and I bought this little ranch house, I had no idea how useful it would be that it was handicap accessible. While I could still get around on my own, no one in my family liked to think of me walking, afraid they'd get a call that I'd "fallen and can't get up." Lisa wheeled me to the front door, where her eleven-year-old son Judson was waiting for us.

"Help Great-Grammy with her boxes," Lisa said.

He grabbed the box of scrapbooks I had assembled and pulled the door shut behind us as Lisa pushed me down the ramp to her car. She helped transfer me to the passenger seat, stashed my chair in the trunk, and then climbed in to drive us into town.

Jud slumped in the back seat.

"Are you excited about today, Gram?" Lisa turned her head briefly as she pulled out onto Buffalo Bill Avenue.

"Sure," I nodded.

"But…"

I smiled. "But, it's a little sad there are so few of us left to celebrate."

Fifty years ago, we had closed the doors on the North Platte Canteen for the final time. The war had ended nearly eight months earlier, and most of the troops had made their way home...or at least stateside. We had done what we set out to do and so much more.

"Do you think Trudy will be able to make it?" Lisa had met all of the women I worked with at the Canteen over the years and knew as well I did who was still alive and kicking.

"I honestly don't know, honey. She has had a hard time of it since her stroke at Thanksgiving. Trudy was integral to the Canteen, and kept working hard through to closing day. Even after she lost Walter on D-Day. I hope her daughter brings her, but...," I looked over at her and she turned to meet my gaze, "...not everyone is as lucky as I am."

She smiled and blew a kiss to me. "Well, I hope some of the men come, you know, the soldiers who passed through the Canteen. We invited enough of them; I hope some are able to make it."

I nodded, but the one soldier I'd most want to see wouldn't be there. He'd stopped in the Canteen so many years ago and changed my life.

We turned off the road into the parking lot of the Lincoln County Historical Museum. After the Union Pacific tore down the North Platte station in 1973, I was afraid the history of the Canteen that I had worked so hard to preserve would be lost. Luckily, this museum was built three years later and, over time, all of the Canteen materials, records, and displays were moved to the museum.

While Lisa parked and got my chair from the trunk, I checked my hair in the mirror. I didn't used to be so vain, but at ninety-six, I wanted to look as good as possible. After she helped me stand and slip into my blazer, I took a few steps to the wheelchair. My great-grandson pulled out the box of scrapbooks and handed them to me. I held them on my lap as Lisa rolled me up the walkway into the museum. I was starting to get some butterflies, wondering if I'd see any familiar faces.

As we neared the front door, someone held it open for us so Lisa could push my chair inside. As we entered the museum, my vision was temporarily impaired after the bright sunshine. But the first thing I heard was, "And here is our honored guest, longtime North Platte librarian and Canteen historian, Margaret..."

People were actually clapping. How silly. And even more embarrassing, my darned eyes seemed to be tearing up. Hopefully, no one else noticed.

"Here, Grams." Lisa slipped me a tissue. Always too observant, that girl.

I discreetly dabbed at my eyes, finally adjusted to the low light of the museum, and looked around at the crowd gathered there. A nice crowd, mostly antiques like me, but some young people as well. I saw a woman I knew to be a reporter at the *North Platte Telegraph*. She had a photographer with her and seemed to be deep in conversation with a couple of older gentlemen, whom I guessed to be former servicemen.

Milo Hoffman leaned down to take my hand in his, shaking it much too vigorously. Many of his shirt buttons were straining to contain his ever-widening waistline, but his smile was sincere.

"Miss Maggie. I'm so glad you were able to make it today. We couldn't celebrate the fiftieth anniversary of the closing of the Canteen without you."

I tugged my hand out of his, placing it on the side of the box in my lap. "Thank you, Mr. Mayor. I'm happy to be here."

He started to place his hands on the handles of the box on my lap. "Here, let me take those for you."

I put my hand on top. "No thank you, really. I want to deliver these to the Canteen exhibit myself. They've been a labor of love." And the last thing I'd be able to do for those troops.

He stopped mid-grab. "Are you sure..."

Lisa deftly moved me out of the mayor's reach, and I turned to smile up at her. "Good girl."

She winked at me and pushed me past many of the "town fathers," or at least, the men who considered themselves to be in charge of the goings-on in North Platte. I was sure they had a lot to say about this auspicious occasion, although none of them were old enough to have been to the Canteen, except maybe as young children, so I really didn't care to hear what they wanted to tell me. I waved vaguely in their direction and Lisa pushed on.

When I got back to the Canteen exhibit, I was thrilled by the large posters they had made out of some of the iconic pictures. Boys rushing into and out of the Canteen, women holding out cookies and pies, an African-American soldier getting an entire birthday cake, and the sign being taken down. How could it have been fifty years ago? It seemed like yesterday.

When I peeked around the corner of the display, there she was. While we talked and wrote regularly, I hadn't seen her since her son moved her to Florida to live with him. My eyes were definitely tearing up, but so were hers as she rushed into my arms.

"Rose."

CHAPTER FOUR

January 15, 1942

"Rose, are you all right?" The girl must have been lost in her own world. She was staring in my direction, but not at me, her lips bowed slightly down.

For a pretty young girl, she often seemed unhappy.

Finally, she snapped out it, her gaze meeting mine. Her eyes drooped, and her lips formed a sad little line. Not the chipper young girl she ought to be.

"Sorry, Miss Parker. Did you need something?"

She hadn't heard a thing I'd said. "I asked if you're working with me again today."

Rose had gotten to the Canteen before me, as I tried to keep the library open until 6:00 p.m. on Thursdays, despite having no money in the budget to pay for help. I didn't mind staying late because the library was important to the town and its people.

This meant I got to the Canteen a little later than usual on those nights after closing up alone, but there was always plenty to do when I got there.

"Yes, ma'am. I was alone at this table for the last troop train. It arrived after school, and I hardly had time to take off my coat, but all went well."

Her face said anything but, so I kept quiet and simply stared at her.

"There weren't any issues, really. It's that, well, I don't mean any offense, Miss Parker, but sometimes the magazine table is a little boring. When the boys rush in from the train, they run to the food, the sandwiches, cookies, deviled eggs, milk, and pies, but not many run to get magazines or books."

Many of these young men might not be readers, but those who took a book, magazine, or newspaper were always grateful.

"Did you remember to point them in the direction of the guest book?"

She nodded, "Yes, but Mrs. Bellows usually takes care of the guest book when you aren't here."

I straightened up some piles of magazines, fanning the few books we had to offer at the front of the table. Finally, I looked back at her. "Where would you like to be working?"

She blushed, looking down at the floor. "I'd rather be working the platform."

As I'd suspected. "You know you have to be sixteen to work as a platform girl, right?"

She nodded, looking forlorn. "I don't think I'll ever meet any soldiers working at this table. I want to find some men to write to, get to know, and maybe fall in love with me, but only the older girls get to put their names and addresses in the popcorn balls they hand out to the troops."

"Is that what you really want? For your name and address to be in some of the snacks given out to the servicemen?" It seemed simple enough to me.

She sighed. "Yes."

A tear escaped her left eyelid, although what could possibly cause her to cry eluded me.

"Just think of it. A soldier away from home, lonely and scared, unwraps the popcorn ball and finds my name and address. He writes first to thank us for the food, but when I write back, he keeps writing, longing to hear what's happening at home, to tell someone what he's going through and how he's feeling. Over time, those feelings grow into more; he's falling in love with me and can't wait to come home to marry me. I can boost his morale, send pictures and presents, tell him I love him too, and by the time the war is over, he'll come back to North Platte and whisk me off to the big city to be his wife."

I stared at the girl, watched the dreams fade from her eyes. Obviously, she'd been watching the same movies as Captain Carter.

"It could happen." She dropped her gaze to the table, shuffling magazines

"Yes, it could happen. But these boys are headed off to war. You know the odds are good many of them won't make it back alive. You understand that, don't you?"

She nodded, tears slipping down her cheeks again.

"Okay, then. As long as you understand the risks of planning your life around a soldier going off to war, I don't see why we can't put your name and address out there and see who writes to you."

She looked up at me, the barest smile on her lips. "But the platform girls won't let me. I'm not old enough, and the few months difference between my age and theirs makes them think they are in charge of everything."

The poor girl need a friend, even if was someone old enough to be her mother. I pulled a small notebook and pencil out of my pocket. "Write down your information on slips of paper, and I'll go put them in the popcorn balls. Those platform girls can't say no to me."

While tears filled her eyes, her face broke into the sweetest smile. "Oh, thank you, Miss Parker."

She was still crying, although more softly now, as I walked out onto the platform and stopped at the table where baskets of treats lay waiting for the next troop train. Two of the teenaged platform girls were talking at the table.

"I'm putting this address in some of the popcorn balls."

One girl raised an eyebrow at me (how did she do that?), but said nothing. She looked at her friend, and they both did a poor job of hiding their smiles. "Yes, ma'am," one of them said.

I opened the wax paper on six of the sticky treats and put in the slips of paper with her address before wrapping them tightly again. Who knew if any of the soldiers to receive her address would write to Rose? They could be married men, after all, but at least she wouldn't be so unhappy working at the periodicals table anymore.

As I walked away, the two teenagers started talking, something about "can you believe she…" and then they broke into gales of laughter. When I turned back to look at them, they stopped and turned their faces away from me. If they thought I was putting my own name in there, what did I care? I only wanted Rose to be happy.

When I walked back into the lunchroom, the familiar call of, "I put the coffee on," rang out, and we prepared for the next train.

"Dry your face." I looked at the girl. "I put your address in six popcorn balls. We can do another six tomorrow, and that should get you a pen pal or two. The rest is up to you."

Still smiling and crying, the child gave me a firm hug and skipped back to her end of the table. Started but pleased, I turned to face the servicemen coming through the doors.

I didn't see any harm in helping the girl find a soldier to write to, as long as she understood what might happen to him.

CHAPTER FIVE

May 11, 1995

The knock at the front door startled me awake. I had nodded off on the couch. I tried to jump up to rush to the door, but my jumping days were long gone. They'd just have to wait.

"Coming."

"It's Harold, Miss Maggie." My mailman's deep voice carried through the door. "No need to rush."

When I had propelled my walker as close to the door as I could, I pulled it open. "Good morning, Harold."

"Good morning." Harold was a heavyset African American man about fifty years old with a warm smile and kind eyes.

"Want to come in?" I started to push back a bit so he could come into the house. He often came in for a quick cup of coffee before finishing his route. Life was quiet these days, and it was nice to have some company.

"Thank you, kindly, but I have to be on my way. I wanted to make sure you got this package." Harold handed me a large yellow padded envelope. Luckily, it wasn't as heavy as it looked.

"My goodness." I pulled the label close enough so I could read the return address. "This is from the mayor's office? Why didn't they call us to come pick it up?" My daughter frequently picked up mail sent to the Canteen in care of city. If she was too busy, my granddaughter would do it. Seemed crazy to mail it to me.

"Well, now, I can't say. But, as long as you're good, I'll be on my way." Harold had a full sack of mail on his shoulder.

I raised my left hand to block the sun's glare. "I'm fine, Harold. You have a nice day and enjoy the sunshine."

He nodded, already backing across my front porch. "I will, Miss Maggie, and the same to you."

Once I closed the door and made my way to the kitchen table, I grabbed the scissors still on the table with all of the Canteen scrapbook materials. After running the blade through the edge of the envelope, I put the scissors down again and dumped the contents of the envelope onto the table.

While I'd anticipated the 50th anniversary of VE-Day this week would bring in a letter or two for the Canteen, I was surprised by the volume. More material for the scrapbook. I pulled out one at random, opened the envelope, and slid out the letter to read.

May 8, 1995
To the Town of North Platte, NE
 They had a big VE-Day celebration at the home today, being it's 50 years since the War in Europe ended, and it got me to thinking about how young and scared I was when I signed up and shipped out. I lived in Denver, Colorado and was drafted early in 1941, as part of FDR's peacetime draft. I went to basic training in Florida, but was sent back to Camp Carson in Colorado in early 1942 and got to stop at your Canteen for some delicious food. After a few months, I was shipped back to New Jersey and sent off to Northern Africa. We stopped in North Platte again, on my birthday, and couldn't believe it when some of those lovely ladies gave me my own birthday cake. Boy,

my buddies and I made quick work of that when we got back on the train.

I should have written long ago, but wanted you all to know your small kindnesses, good wishes, and delicious food meant the world to this scared soldier. Wherever I was, after North Africa and on through the march to Berlin, if somebody mentioned North Platte, we all cheered. What you did for a bunch of strangers made a lot of difference, and I thought, better late than never, you should know.

Dwight Stinson

CHAPTER SIX

January 22, 1942

"Really, you can go home, Miss Parker. We have plenty of volunteers today. We've got the periodicals table covered."

I nodded. "Yes, I see that, but I'd rather stand at the guest book to ensure some of the servicemen sign it." We hadn't been getting as many people signing the book on days the other towns worked the Canteen, not that it was necessarily their fault. Especially when the community was small, the volunteers had so much to do already, the guest book probably was the last thing they thought about.

Nonetheless, if we wanted to preserve the history of the Canteen and keep accurate records, we needed to encourage men from every troop train to sign it.

"Of course." The woman in charge hurried off to the pie table. Her name escaped me. She was from Big Springs, and they'd brought a lot of pies. The volunteers from Big Springs and Brule had combined their efforts and signed up to come the third Wednesday of every month, which was an impressive commitment, considering neither town had more than 600 residents.

When the next train stopped, I took my place by the guest book and asked every serviceman to sign it when he had time. There were no servicewomen or nurses on this train, nor did it appear any of the servicemen were traveling with their families.

"Can I help you tidy up before the next train arrives?" I asked the young girl, no older than fifteen, who was working the end of the table closest to the guest book, and she nodded. "How many troop trains have been through today?"

She looked to the ceiling, counting softly on her fingers. "I think about thirteen, so far."

"Wow," I said, shaking my head. "It's really picking up. I hope we don't run out of food."

"We brung a lot, ma'am. I'm from Brule, but between us and Big Springs, I know everybody's been cooking for days to get ready."

I nodded. "Did you help with the cooking and baking?"

She smiled. "I sure did. We don't get electric yet out at our farm, so we work off batteries and a generator. That's why we had to start last week, 'cause we only have so much power to a day. Most nights the radio cuts out in the middle of the war news. Working this table is great 'cause I can read the newspapers and magazines and tell my father what's going on in the war when I get home."

I smiled and straightened the silk North Platte Canteen volunteer ribbon pinned to her blouse. Every person at the Canteen, whether volunteer or serviceman, had a story.

One train after another came through North Platte that evening, but the volunteers from Big Springs and Brule never ran out of food. By the time I headed home, it was nearly 11:00 p.m.

"Thank you all for your hard work today," Trudy said as I walked out the back door of the depot. Exhaustion overwhelmed me, dulling my senses, and leaving me groggy. "Thanks, Trudy. See you soon."

Most likely, I still would be tired in the morning when I headed into the library. Perhaps I might not need to work at the Canteen every night. Surely, all the volunteer towns and groups could be instructed to keep a closer eye on the guest book.

When I got home, my mother had not only locked the back door, but turned out the light. She said she was worried about the "kind of people the Canteen attracted," but it was more likely she hoped I'd forget my key and need to sleep on the back porch. The "kind of people the Canteen attracted"—all of whom were kinder than my mother—weren't likely to break into our house.

I closed the door as quietly as possible and left my boots, hat, and heavy coat on the small back porch off the kitchen. I walked through the kitchen in my stocking feet, careful not to bump into the furniture or make too much noise. It was best if I didn't wake Mother when I came in at night. Her hateful words and acid tone didn't scare me, but I was unlikely to drift into a calm and relaxing sleep if I had a fight with her before bed.

Following the edge of the table with my left hand, the fingers of my right hand touched the envelope in my pocket. I had stuck it there earlier that evening, hoping for a private moment to read it. I carried it upstairs to my bedroom, but didn't turn on the light until I'd closed the door.

Even if he'd never sent me a picture, I'd have no trouble bringing his face to mind as I curled up on my bed to read his letter. Somehow, it seemed much more intimate this way, which both embarrassed and excited me.

****

January 18, 1942
Dear Maggie,

Thank you for your last letter-oh, that's right. It was my last letter and you've never answered it.

Don't you think it's your patriotic duty to write me back? I'm a poor, lonely soldier facing danger to protect your way of life. What would President Roosevelt say? What would Eleanor say? Come on, Maggie, write me back!

I'll go on writing as if you have, assuming you'll catch up someday.

While I can't tell you where we are, but I will say there isn't much happening here at the moment, which is both good and bad. We're not in much danger, but boredom is our main foe right now. The nights are quiet and dark, and we all get restless. Any diversion is welcome, and a letter from you would definitely be a wonderful diversion.

The men may be young, but they're riled up after Pearl Harbor and the attacks in the South Pacific. We haven't heard much about what's really happening there, but it doesn't sound good. Some of the men are frustrated by being stationed away from where so many other troops are fighting. I've been in the Army long enough to know there's a reason behind the decision to send us here, so we need to wait, be well trained, disciplined, ready, and do what we are being asked to do. If only I could communicate those concepts easily to the men.

How goes life in North Platte? What are your days like? Do you volunteer at the Canteen every day? You must be exhausted when you work a full-day in the library and then the evening in the Canteen. What about your family? Do they volunteer as well?

What made you decide to be a librarian? What do you enjoy about your job?

Tell me all about you. I can still see your face, your bright smile, even if you were a little annoyed with me, it makes me happy. I don't often come across a woman who intrigues me the way you do, so please write to me, tell me everything you do and think, and give me something to look forward to on these long, lonely nights.

Thinking of you —
Tom

I folded the letter and put it into my pocket. Silly, but it made me happy.

In my mind's eye, I saw him sitting at a desk with a seductive smile on his face, laughing as he chose just the right words to help in his attempt to woo me. While his

43

chances of being successful were low, I had to admit that I was intrigued, and my resolve might be weakening.

He didn't tell me a lot, other than he wanted to hear from me. For him, my letters could continue the hospitality that was the reason we started the Canteen in the first place. He was an incurable flirt, but I didn't have to flirt back. I could write to him out of politeness and, as he said, patriotic duty. That didn't mean a relationship was developing between us.

I could send him newspapers to keep him up to date on the news, as well as baked goods, like he got at the Canteen. There was nothing untoward about it.

I hadn't been pursued by a man for twenty-five years. The sparks of excitement rippling over my skin indicated I wasn't immune to the idea. But I wasn't a foolish woman.

However, I had to admit, at least to myself, that I enjoyed his questions, his letters, and his interest in me. If I couldn't be completely honest with myself, in my bed in the middle of the night, when would I be?

CHAPTER SEVEN

February 3, 1942
Dear Captain Carter,

Okay, I am giving you my home address, so please stop sending letters to me at the Canteen. I am writing you back in the spirit of patriotism and service to my country. I wouldn't want to disappoint Eleanor Roosevelt.

I'm happy to hear you are well and that your troops are getting trained and acclimated to your current location, wherever you may be. We, too, are getting little war news at this point, and what we are hearing isn't overwhelmingly good. I truly hope, now that the U.S. has joined the Allies, that it will make the difference in our success and bring a speedy end to this war. The alternative doesn't bear thinking about.

Life in North Platte is good. Winter is particularly hard this year, but perhaps it only feels so because we are trying to conserve heating fuel, so our houses are colder than usual. We have started conserving rubber and gasoline, so there are fewer people driving private cars. Walking in the snow and bitter wind is causing us to long for warmer weather.

The sense of community is growing as we're asked to alter our lifestyle to support the war. I think most people are happy to make the sacrifice for our troops, although there are always those few who grumble about it.

I live with my mother, definitely one of the grumblers, if I can be honest with you. I miss my father every day. He died when I was twelve and Mother never recovered. Don't imagine it was a tragic love story and she pines for him, but rather his death was a major inconvenience for her, and she is still angry about it.

Some people are decided upon having an unhappy life, regardless of the blessings that come their way. That's Mother to a T.

Compared to many people, my life is good, especially at the Library. I guess I wanted to work there because it was quiet, clean, dependable, and it gave me a chance to help others in a professional manner. I truly enjoy helping people find what they need and giving them someplace to find a little peace, especially now. Young mothers bring their children in to find books and, often, to burn off a little energy before going back home. High school students come in after school, often in need of some help with their studies. Fewer young men come in, obviously, but older men seem to need the library even more than before the war. They come for the chance to talk to someone with similar life experiences, as well as to read the newspapers we subscribe to from all over the country.

I have always believed it important to know what's going on not only in North Platte, Lincoln, and Omaha, but also in Denver, Los Angeles, Chicago, New York, and, of course, Washington, D.C. We may be in a remote part of the country, but we don't have to isolate ourselves and remain ignorant of what is happening elsewhere. I don't know how long we'll be able to afford to maintain all the subscriptions we have, but I think it's important, especially with the world at war.

For example, a woman I know from the Canteen came to the Library yesterday to look at our maps and information on the Philippines. Her son was sent there with the Army long before the Pearl Harbor attack, and she hasn't gotten any letters lately. She wanted to read about the islands and understand what the area looks like, so she could have a better picture in her mind of what it's like where he is, as she writes to him. We were able to find Fort Stotsenburg, where her son is stationed, and the nearby Clark Air Field. She was excited to look at the geography of the islands, just to think of him being there. I added him to the prayer list at church, just in case, as I could tell she was very worried.

I don't know what more to tell you about me. I read, do housework, work at the library, volunteer at the Canteen, and sometimes go to church. I haven't seen many movies lately, but I'm finally getting a chance to read The Grapes of Wrath by John Steinbeck. Have you read it? It is so popular, I couldn't keep it on the shelves. While not a happy, uplifting story, it is beautifully written and engrossing.

Best of luck to you and your troops. May God keep you and all of our American servicemen safe. All my best —

Margaret Parker

****

March 24, 1942

"Miss Parker, could you help this young woman?"

I arrived at the Canteen after leaving the library. Tuesday afternoons, I got off work at 2:00 p.m. and went directly to the Canteen. While Rae had been quite successful in getting many local communities to commit to a schedule of providing Canteen volunteers, for some reason, Tuesdays were often not well covered.

I put my coat and pocketbook behind the periodicals table and walked to where Trudy stood with a servicewoman.

"Of course, how may I be of assistance?"

Trudy motioned to the woman wearing an Army nurse's uniform. "This is Army Nurse Minnie Michaelson." Trudy nodded to the nurse, thanked me, and then hurried off to help another group of servicemen.

"I'm Margaret Parker, North Platte librarian and Canteen historian. How can I help you, Nurse Michaelson?" My heart always went out to the Army and Navy nurses who came through the Canteen. These women volunteered to serve and were sent all over the world, wherever our troops were, to serve. They earned our respect and admiration.

"Thank you, Miss Parker. I asked about the guest book and the instructions there regarding maintaining correspondence. Can you explain what that's about?"

I smiled. "Of course. As historian, I'm hoping to keep tabs on some of the servicemen and women," I nodded to her, "who come through our Canteen. We'd like to stay in touch and find out where you go, whether you come back through the Canteen, and when you come home. Obviously, we're not asking for strategic military information, but maybe a letter now and then telling us what it's like wherever you are, and once it is permissible to tell us where you've been, write and tell us where you were deployed and what you did there. We see a lot of service members for a very short time, and we'd like to hear how you are even after you leave North Platte."

She had been finishing her bottle of milk while I spoke, which I did not consider rude, given the small amount of time she had at the Canteen. After she finished, she smiled and said, "I think it's a lovely idea. I'm on my way to Oregon as I've been assigned to the 46th General Hospital. I'd be happy to let you know, as much as I'm allowed, what happens to us and where we go. I really appreciate what you all are doing for us here, so I'm happy to help you as well."

I gave her the address to write to me at the library, as mail was sure to find me there, took her empty milk bottle, and sent her on her way as soon as the conductor called everyone back to the train. I took a moment to send up a silent prayer for her continued safety and healing touch.

After we'd waived Nurse Michaelson and all the troops off on their journey west, I went back into the Canteen to prepare for more troop trains. We'd been getting more than twelve trains a day coming through lately, although we never knew exactly how many to expect.

At 4:00 p.m. Rose walked into the Canteen and joined me at the periodicals table. She didn't seem to have many friends among the other young volunteers, although she appeared friendly enough to me.

She rushed over to where I was standing, keeping her voice low. "Did you hear the news?"

"What? Has there been an attack?" These days, breaking news was not good, like no news is good news.

Rose shook her head. "Not that I know of." She looked around, turning back to me. "It's Miss Wilson. She's leaving the Canteen."

Gossip was a virus I had chosen to stay clear of in my life, especially something a teenage girl was worked up about, but Rae Wilson was the driving force behind the Canteen and the reason for its existence. If something had happened to her, I found I did want to know about it.

"I know she's been ill, but what are you talking about?" Rae had been spending less time at the Canteen due to her health, but she had a strong committee, so things had been running smoothly, nonetheless.

"My mother told me about it, although she said it's not yet been officially announced. Miss Wilson is too ill to continue on with her Canteen duties. She's moving to California."

I was not close to Rae, but she'd always been a friendly face at the drugstore, where she worked as a clerk. I admired what she was doing here at the Canteen. And, yes, it was a huge job, even with a good committee, to stay on top of fundraising, ordering milk, juice, and bread, which were delivered directly to the Canteen, in addition to the donations each community group brought with them. As a drug store clerk, she'd never had to organize so many volunteers before. While she had a lot of help, most of the big decisions and responsibilities landed on her shoulders; that couldn't be easy.

"I'm very sorry to hear that. She's done important work here." It was a good thing I kept such a complete history of the Canteen. Given the enormity of this endeavor, we might end up having a succession of women in charge.

She turned back to straighten magazines, looking over at the group of women working the food tables. "I wonder who will take her place."

Trying to be professional, although I was having the same thoughts, I shooed Rose down to her regular spot on the table. "That's none of our concern. Let's get ready for the next train. It's what we're here for, after all."

After the last train of the night pulled out and I had sent Rose home to get some sleep, I tidied up the table, gathered my coat and belongings, and headed out for the night. Walking out the back door, I was stopped by Helen Christ, a woman I knew from the committee.

"Before you leave, Margaret, I wanted to let you know I've taken over for Rae and will be the head of the committee now."

I nodded. Helen was a strong and organized person. She should be good at handling the responsibility of the job. "Thank you for letting me know and congratulations, Helen"

I buttoned my coat and pulled on my gloves, meeting her gaze once more before walking out. "I wish Rae well, and I'm sure you'll do a good job."

"Yes, of course, we all wish her well." She looked around, a look of mild bemusement on her face. "Good night, Margaret."

Perhaps she'd been expecting me to ask more personal questions about Rae's health, but again, gossip was not my style. Shaking my head, I stepped out in to the cold air. "Good night."

CHAPTER EIGHT

June 30, 1989

I pulled into the parking space, making sure the handicapped permit was facing out on my rearview mirror. As much as I hated that permit and the new cane that came with it, even I had to admit that a parking spot close to the front door was much more convenient.

I had just reached the glass front doors when a young man came rushing out. "Afternoon, Miss Maggie." He smiled at me.

"Good afternoon, Ned."

Ned held the door open, so I walked through into the cool air of City Hall. How much of my tax money went to pay for this air conditioning, anyway?

I walked to the front desk, where Bridget Kennedy seemed to be ready for me.

"Well, hello there, Miss Maggie. It's so nice to see you on this fine summer day. How's that little great-grandson of yours?" Bridget was in her early twenties, cute as a bug, and had always been a sweet child. It was nice to have such a friendly face working the front desk. Hopefully, all the disgruntled citizens who came to lodge a complaint against the city wouldn't dull the sparkle in her eyes.

"Thank you, Bridget. It's nice to see you, too. My little boy is getting big, I have to say. He'll be heading off to kindergarten next year."

She pulled out a stack of envelopes, tied up with a pretty string. "While time flies, doesn't it? Give my love to Lisa and her family." She handed me the envelopes. "I bet you're here for these."

I nodded. "I got a call regarding some Canteen mail, so here I am."

She smiled. "I can't believe people are still writing to the Canteen. It's been gone forever."

I chuckled, said my good-byes, and carried my stack of envelopes back to the car. Forever had a different meaning for the young.

I don't think any of us knew how many letters of thanks the Canteen would receive or that we'd still be getting them years after the war was over. But, I promised to keep track of the history. And so I did.

June 23, 1989
To the people of North Platte, NE
My wife and I recently had the pleasure of driving cross county in our new RV. Now that I have retired, we hope to see as much of this country as we can, while still taking time out from our travels to spend with our children and grandchildren.

As we left the Badlands National Park in South Dakota, on our way to Kansas City to see old friends, I noticed our route was going to take us very near North Platte. I decided to take the time to stop in and remind myself of the kindness I experienced there during the war.

I have to admit, I was sad to see the station was no longer there, but wanted to let you all know that, driving through the town, I was once again filled with the warmth and awe I felt stepping off the train onto your platform in February of 1942, on my way to the European Theatre of War. I could almost taste the sandwiches, cookies, and cold milk I had in the station, as well as the birthday cake my buddy Frank got that day – we all helped him devour it on the train. To think you people, to whom we all were strangers, would do all you did for us, showed us this was the real America, this is what we were fighting for and wanted to come back to. I wish I had written to thank you years ago, but wanted to let you all know your kindness has never been forgotten.

    George Mitchell, Boise, Idaho

CHAPTER NINE

April 22, 1942
Dear Captain Carter,

By now, you have probably heard the news of the Japanese capture of Bataan and Corregidor. I read about it this week and still am shocked to learn of the surrender of our troops and the escape of General MacArthur. I worry for the servicemen, and especially the nurses, who are left at the mercy of the Japanese.

Not knowing where you and your troops are in the Asian Theatre of Operations, I can only say I truly hope you are nowhere near the Philippines.

While morale at the Canteen remains strong and most volunteers are upbeat, many in town are struggling with the fear that the U.S. might not win this war. I have encouraged many more people to volunteer at the Canteen, as I find serving our troops and seeing the pleasure they get from a ham salad sandwich and a few cookies helps restore my faith in the men and women of our country. I know we're supposed to be helping the troops we serve, but I consider my Canteen work to be a blessing to help me keep my spirits high as the war continues.

I'm sorry if this letter is not as cheery as it should be. The government is constantly telling us here at home to write only happy and upbeat letters to soldiers and I shall endeavor to do so in the future.

This week, with the news such as it is, however, left me more anxious and worried than usual. Please stay safe, Captain. And be well.
  Sincerely, Margaret

****

April 25, 1942
"Miss Parker?"

"Yes, Rose," I turned to face her as I pulled on my coat.

"Do you mind if I walk with you? I was hoping we'd have a few moments to talk, but it was a busy night."

She was right. The Canteen was getting busier all the time. The War Department certainly had a lot of troops on the move.

"Of course, dear. Get your coat and we'll head out."

Once she collected her things and I said good night to the volunteers in the kitchen, we walked out of the Canteen and headed toward the boarding house her mother owned. I'd never given much thought to the fact that Rose lived only with her mother. I wasn't sure what had happened to Rose's father.

"What's on your mind?"

She looked straight ahead, although I had the impression she wasn't actually seeing the streets in front of us. "I wanted to thank you for being so kind to me, putting my name in the popcorn balls and everything."

I smiled. "You're welcome. It was no problem at all."

She looked at me, briefly, then turned her face away again. "I hope you don't think badly of me after saying how much I want to find a husband and get out of North Platte."

Shaking my head, I tried not to laugh in case it might hurt her feelings. "I don't think badly of you. It sounded very much like what I thought when I was your age."

A look of disbelief covered her face, although whether it was due to the idea of me wanting to leave North Platte or that I had ever been her age, I couldn't tell.

"You wanted to leave North Platte? Why didn't you?"

I sighed. "Things didn't work out as I had planned. There was another war on, remember."

"Oh," she said, tilting her head. "Did you lose someone in the war?"

I hadn't talked about Fred to anyone in a long time, mostly because no one asked. Sometimes, though, my heart still ached at the loss of him, but mostly his memory was a warm blanket on my soul, a memory of a happier time.

I didn't see the harm in sharing my story with her. "Yes. My fiancé went off to France, in the Army, and was killed. We had planned to get married when he got home and move away, but he never made it back."

She put her hand on my arm. "I'm sorry, Miss Parker. I had no idea. If you'd rather not talk about it…"

I smiled at her now. "No, it's fine, Rose. Fred was a good man, and I think we would have made a good life together, but it didn't work out. I've been very happy working at the library, and now at the Canteen, though."

In fact, I often thought Fred would have been proud of how I'd adapted to the change in my plans.

After a few minutes, her gaze met mine. "Why didn't you leave North Platte anyway? You could have gone to Lincoln or Omaha or some big city to work in a library there?"

My shoulders fell. There was the rub.

I was glad she couldn't see my expression very well, given the dark. "I had to stay and take care of my mother." That was a hard sentence to say in a neutral tone of voice. "Besides, where would I go, all alone?"

The life I had planned, the family that Fred and I were going to create together was gone in an instant. How could I explain to this child that my desire to find a new home, a new life, disappeared with it?

We walked on a bit, coming to the corner of her street. "Why are *you* in such a hurry to leave North Platte?"

She looked pointedly at the ground, not meeting my gaze. "I...I don't want to be stuck here my whole life and end up running my mother's boarding house. I want to find a man who will take me away to a big city and...stay."

That last word slipped out on her last breath, softer than the rest of her words, but it was clearly was of utmost importance.

She gave me a quick hug, as she'd taken to doing lately, and turned. "Good night, Miss Parker."

"Good night." I stood on the corner, watching her walk to her house and through the front door. Once she was safely inside, I turned to walk on to my own house.

Rose really was a sweet girl and did a great job at the Canteen. However, I needed to discover what happened to her father.

CHAPTER TEN

April 30, 1942

"Wow, is this all for us, ma'am?"

Several young recruits stood in the Canteen doorway, smiling and apparently amazed to see what was being offered to them.

Helen greeted them at the doorway. "Yes, soldiers, help yourselves."

"And if you have time, please sign our guest book, so we know who you are, where you're from, and can wish you well as you travel on to war." It was nice of Helen to add that last bit. We'd had a lot more signatures in the guest book lately, and I was receiving many letters each week, not just in thanks, but with tidbits of news.

One young man in an Army uniform walked up to the guest book. His posture was ramrod straight and his dark hair nearly nonexistent under his cap. But, goodness, he was young.

"Thank you for signing the book, soldier. We hope to hear more about where you go from here and wish you the best of luck."

He turned to me and smiled. "Thank you for all of this, ma'am. I'm Private Art Sampson from Denver, Colorado,

Army Air Corps. I'm on my way to gunnery school at Buckingham Air Force Base in Florida."

"It's nice to meet you, Private Sampson. Did you get enough to eat?"

"Yes, ma'am. I haven't been on the train as long as some of these guys, so I'm not starving as of yet. Besides, my family came to the station to see me off, since it's my birthday. They brought me some goodies for the trip."

"Happy birthday, Private." I smiled and touched his arm. "Would you please follow me over here?" I led him to the dessert table.

"Mrs. Keeler?"

"Yes, Miss Parker?"

I motioned to Private Sampson. "It's this young man's birthday today."

Mrs. Keeler squealed, even though she was a fifty-year-old mother of six. "Well, happy birthday, soldier."

When she turned around, Private Sampson started to leave, but I put my hand on his arm. "Just wait a moment."

Mrs. Wheeler turned back around with an angel food cake and handed it to Private Sampson.

"For me?" He looked from Mrs. Keeler to me and back again.

"Yes, dear," she nodded. "Any serviceman coming through North Platte on his birthday gets a cake. Enjoy and happy birthday."

He was obviously flustered, as he was blushing, but effusive in his thanks. His buddies seemed equally happy, probably anticipating sharing the cake with him once back on the train.

As he reached the door, he turned back to look at me. "Thanks, again."

I smiled. "You're welcome. Happy birthday and God bless you, Private Sampson."

****

May 10, 1942
Dear Maggie,

Well, hello, sunshine. Thank you for your letter and the newspapers. I really enjoyed the feeling of being back in Georgia, sitting on the back porch of my barracks there, going over the morning newspaper in the warm sunshine. I don't really have any of those things here, but taking my time to read every word of the newspaper made it feel like I wasn't so far away.

I think it's funny they are rationing sugar now. I can't answer your question of what military use it has, but my guess is the conflict in the Philippines has cut off a big part of the sugar we import. I'm sure it makes life difficult for those who bake for the Canteen, but I can tell you from experience, it's so worth it. The troops really appreciate your efforts.

I also appreciate you answering my many questions about your daily life. It helps me to picture in my mind what you are doing back in North Platte, whether it's working at the Library or the Canteen or even at home with your mother. It must be hard to have had the full responsibility for maintaining your home and lifestyle on your shoulders from such an early age. I admire your independence and strength, as long as you're not too independent to spend your time writing to a man.

What made you decide to be a librarian and when did you make that decision? I understand your father passed when you were twelve, but I might have guessed you would want to be a teacher, or wasn't that something you were interested in?

I started college and was enrolled in the Reserved Officer Training Corps, but I didn't want to waste four years on school, so I dropped out and enlisted. I would have joined as an officer through R.O.T.C., but was content to work my way up. My parents had both passed away, so I was independent and making my own way, like you.

Well, I am exhausted from some serious training today. I might not have as much time to write. Think of me often, as I remain
Yours, Tom

CHAPTER ELEVEN

April 25, 1980

"Hey, Mom, I'm here."

"I'm in the sunroom." I was enjoying a good book and some bright sunshine on my chaise lounge when my daughter walked into the room.

"What are you reading?"

"Oh, I finally got my hands on the large print edition of Kurt Vonnegut's *Jailbird*, which I've been waiting to read for weeks. I like it, although it seems like a dark editorial on our society as a whole."

She shook her head. "I don't know why you want to read that political kind of stuff, Mom. Life is too short to read depressing books." She plopped down in the arm chair and rested her feet on the ottoman. As always, she had her arms full of bags.

"Here's some more mail that came addressed to the Canteen in care of the library. When I stopped in to return my latest books, Marlene gave me this pile of mail for you."

"Amazing. The mail just keeps on coming." I took pulled some cards and letters from the bag.

She laughed. "I know, right? It's been more than thirty years since the war ended. Why do people keep writing to the Canteen?"

"It's taken some service members a long time to be able to talk or even think about what happened in the war. I think, once they let some of the memories in, they realize not everything was bad." I opened the first envelope. "I think they just want to acknowledge one of the good parts of it all."

April 10, 1980
To the Town of North Platte, NE, and the former Servicemen's Canteen
 I wanted to write, as I had promised to do all those years ago, and let you know what happened to me and my buddies in the war and to thank you all for your hospitality.
 I came through in April of 1942 on my way to Florida for training with the Army Air Corps. It was my birthday and was I ever surprised when one of you ladies gave me a whole cake. My buddies were happy, though, when we got back on the train and gobbled down the whole thing. It sure was delicious.
 You all saved my neck, too. While I was at the Canteen, I lost a button. One of your fine ladies snapped it up and sewed it back on, lickety-split. I would have been in trouble if I didn't get it fixed before inspection, so thanks for that, too..
 I was trained as a bombardier and sent to England to join the 8th Air Force. We flew bombing raids over the enemy as far away as Berlin. Flying those missions, it was like everything was in slow motion up there, it was like we had no feeling of movement. The only noise you would hear would be the engines. It was like I was the only man in the world until it was time for me to drop the bomb. My kids often asked me if I have nightmares after bombing all those people, but it was us or them back then. They were killing Americans all over the world, and we had to stop them. I never had nightmares about doing my job over there, although I still have bad dreams about some of the stuff I saw up close and personal on the ground. But not from up there.
 Anyway, no matter where we were or what other Americans we ran into along the way, if somebody mentioned North Platte, everybody smiled. And when I got to tell them I got a whole cake for my birthday, I'd hear a lot of laughs, followed by "lucky dog" and "man, that's the

life." What you people did for us will never be forgotten, not as long as a single serviceman who went through North Platte is still alive. Thank you from the bottom of my heart.

Art Sampson, Army Air Corps, retired

CHAPTER TWELVE

June 14, 1942
Dear Tom,

I am concerned by what we are hearing about the loss of life in the battles in the Pacific, at Coral Sea and Midway, and the possible invasion of the Aleutian Islands in Alaska. I don't know where you are but none of the news coming from the Pacific sounds very promising at the moment. Please be careful and stay safe.

You always ask what I'm up to, but I have to admit I'm rather dull. When I'm not working at the library, I'm volunteering at the Canteen or home sleeping. I don't listen to many radio programs. Mother is always caught up in some radio drama, so I stay away. As I mentioned, I usually get my news via the national newspapers we get at the library. If I have time for entertainment, I read.

The Canteen continues to run well, and we have more communities signing up for volunteer shifts all the time. This is particularly helpful as it gets harder to find rationed ingredients. We're only allowed one-half cup of sugar per person per week. That makes it difficult for our volunteer bakers, but most people are using their sugar rations for Canteen baking and using alternatives, such as molasses and honey, for their families. The popcorn balls we give out on the platform are being made with molasses. I actually think they taste better this way.

Just this week I received a letter from a grateful father. It seems the gentleman's son came through the Canteen in February and promptly wrote home to tell his parents about the wonderful treatment he received in North Platte (his words). His father is a coffee importer, so he sent us a shipment of coffee and promised to do so regularly. That will be a huge help. We've had a few traveling salesmen bring us back donations as they share news of the Canteen on their trips.

While our kitchen at home is now much emptier due to rationing and the scrap metal, aluminum, and even cooking fat drives, the Canteen kitchen is exempt. We need our coffee urns and other cooking equipment to keep morale up.

It seems silly to worry about coffee urns as compared to having enough ships, planes, and tanks for our troops overseas. Which brings me back to you. Please stay safe and write when you can. I'll be praying for you and your men.

All my best, Margaret

****

June 20, 1942

"Good morning, Margaret."

Rose and her mother, Trixie Nelson, were walking down Front Street toward the Canteen and me. The girl always seemed more subdued when her mother was around, although I'd never seen any cause for concern.

"Good morning, Trixie. And to you, Rose."

Rose smiled. "Good morning, Miss Parker."

As we turned into the station, loud, fast music was blaring from the Canteen.

"It sounds like we have a party going already, doesn't it?" Trixie was a little taller than her daughter, but neither were much over 5 feet 2 inches.

Rose was already bouncing to the beat of the music coming out of the Canteen doorway. "Must be one of the soldiers at the piano."

"Sounds like much more than simply a piano to me." Often, a piano-playing soldier or a local volunteer would pound out a dance number to the delight of the servicemen and platform girls. While I had to admit some of the pianists had real talent, the music coming out of the Canteen on Saturday morning sounded more professional than I'd heard before.

Maybe someone had donated a new radio, and they had the volume up as high as it would go.

When we walked onto the platform and turned into the Canteen door, we stopped in our tracks. Trixie had been right; there was a real party, or maybe even a carnival, going on.

The crowd was divided into a large circle, of which five couples were dancing and swinging at the center. Everyone in the circle was bouncing and swaying to the music, which was a lively swing tune.

In addition to a master at the piano, there was a drummer, someone playing a clarinet, and someone else with a trumpet. Where had all those instruments come from?

One of the couples caught my eye because the man was a phenomenal dancer. Each of the Canteen volunteers was getting a turn to partner with a man who looked and danced remarkably like Fred Astaire. In fact, it had to be Fred Astaire, not only because he was so fleet of foot, but also a reporter and photographer were circling around the dancers.

"Can you believe it, Miss Parker? Fred Astaire is here in North Platte!" Rose was leaning in, practically shouting in my ear in order to be heard over the music.

I nodded and turned to drop my pocketbook and coat behind the periodicals table, which had been pushed back to make room for dancing.

We'd had some celebrities come through the Canteen on their way to entertaining the troops, but Mr. Astaire was definitely one of the most famous. It was thrilling to see him dance in person.

The servicemen in the circle were clapping or hooting as they gobbled down their sandwiches and coffee. The other couples on the dance floor were made up of servicemen and other Hollywood movie stars.

I walked to the doorway of the Canteen and glanced out at the tracks, noting the special services train heading east, as well as a regular troop train heading west. As I turned around to watch the festivities, Fred Astaire grabbed my hand and started swinging me around the room. I hadn't danced in years, not since my own Fred had left for France in WWI, but it came back quickly enough. I was laughing and smiling at Mr. Astaire when the music stopped, and everyone broke into applause.

"Thank you so much, Mr. Astaire. What a pleasure." I may have been blushing, but certainly anyone who noticed would simply think I was winded from the dance.

He bowed slightly, a twinkle in his gaze as he winked at me. "The pleasure was all mine, ma'am. Keep up the good work you're all doing here at the Canteen."

With that, he turned and ushered the other movie stars, all women, out to their train. Although I hadn't seen a lot of movies, I couldn't hide my surprise when I recognized Ginger Rogers and Carole Lombard. The young soldiers who got to dance with them were more than a little starstruck, as well.

The musicians packed up their instruments and hurried out. Helen, Trudy, and Lucy came running out of the Canteen with cookies, sandwiches, milk, and coffee. Hopefully, the special services train would stop at the next station, as the regular troop trains did, so they could send their coffee cups back on the next west-bound train.

I returned to my table, put on my apron, and with Rose's help pulled the table away from the wall and began straightening piles.

"What was it like?" she asked with much excitement.

"What?" I briefly turned to look at her, while working my way down the table.

"Dancing with Fred Astaire, of course." She giggled.

I stopped, stood up straight, and met her gaze. "He's a wonderful dancer." I'd forgotten how much I liked to dance.

Laughing out loud, she shook her head. "Everyone knows that. Did you two talk while you were dancing? Is he a nice man?"

"We did not talk while we were dancing, but afterward, he thanked me and said to keep up the good work here at the Canteen. He seems like a nice man, but we only exchanged about a dozen words, so I can't say more than that."

More importantly, he, the movie stars, and musicians with him had boosted the morale of everyone at the Canteen, whether service member or volunteer.

"You're impossible!" She giggled again and returned to her own end of the table.

I had no idea exactly why I was impossible, but another troop train was arriving, so we both went back to work. I had to admit, though, I had an unusually big smile on my face all day.

Sometime later that afternoon, during a lull between trains, Rose walked over to me, her head down. "Miss Parker?"

"Yes. What's on your mind?"

She looked around the room, but turned back to face me. "Can you put my name in some more popcorn balls?"

"What's the matter? Didn't enough servicemen write to you?"

"Shh," she hissed. "I don't want my mother to hear." She looked around the room again, but as neither of us could see Trixie, so she continued. "I've only had letters from three soldiers after you put my name in those popcorn balls. When one of them asked my age, I didn't think I could lie, but I haven't heard from him since. The other two wrote me a couple of letters, but not lately. I kept writing to them, but my last letters to both of them were returned."

I sighed. That was not a good sign. When a soldier was killed or captured, his mail was returned.

"Aren't you sixteen yet?" We'd been working in the Canteen for months now; surely the child was old enough to be a platform girl now, although I would miss her help.

She looked down at the floor again. "I turned sixteen last month, but the other platform girls told me there are too many girls who want to work the platform, so I should stay inside with you."

Well, who did those girls think they were? "Did you speak to Mrs. Christ?" I doubted the teenaged platform girls were in charge of who got to work the platform, and Helen would probably be none too pleased that they were turning away volunteers on behalf of the Canteen.

She shook her head. "I don't want to get anyone in trouble." She looked up at me out of the corner of her eyes. "Besides, I don't want to work the platform with them if they're going to be like that. I like being in here with you, I just want my name and address in some of the popcorn balls."

I smiled. I liked having her working here with me, too. "Have you made any popcorn balls yourself? If you donate some, you can put your name and address in them yourself."

Rose shook her head. "No, are they easy to make?"

"Yes," I said. "Why don't you come to my house tomorrow after church, if it's all right with your mother? We'll make some popcorn balls, put your name in them, and I'll bring them with me when I come in to work in the evening."

She smiled, nearly jumping up and down on the spot. "Thank you so much, Miss Parker. That would be wonderful. You are so kind to me." She gave me a quick hug and ran back to her end of the table.

Hopefully, this simple act wasn't going to cause the girl too much pain in the long run.

CHAPTER THIRTEEN

June 30, 1942

"Would you please sign our guest book, soldier?"

A young man, who didn't seem old enough to even be in uniform, quickly swallowed what appeared to be a mouthful of oatmeal cookie and nodded.

"Excuse me, ma'am," he finally said after chewing, "the food is delicious, and we were told this will be the best stop all the way to California."

It warmed my heart that North Platte was getting a good reputation among the servicemen.

As he leaned over the guest book, he signed two names. When he looked up, he noticed me watching. "My brother is here, too." He pointed to the coffee table. "That's him right there." He waved to his brother. "Roland!"

Roland walked over to us, a coffee cup in one hand, a sandwich, piece of pie, and three cookies in the other.

The younger brother put his coffee cup down and shook my hand. "I'm Walt, and this is my brother, Roland Rogers. Thank you, ma'am, for all this wonderful stuff."

Roland nodded, but again, had his hands full. "Yes, ma'am. We haven't been on the train too long yet; we signed up in Kansas City, and then they put us on a train to Omaha before we transferred to this one headed to training in California. But the other boys we met on the train told us not to miss out on getting some great food in North Platte, and man, they weren't kidding." He smiled and the two brothers looked so similar it made my soul ache for the mother who had to wave them good-bye back in Kansas.

"I'm glad you are enjoying it, boys, and it's nice to meet you. Thank you, Walt, for signing our guest book. If you think of it sometime in your travels, drop us a letter, addressed to the Servicemen's Canteen in North Platte, Nebraska, and let us know how you're doing."

Walt paused in drinking his coffee to swallow. "Yes, ma'am. We sure will. I don't know where the Third Infantry Division will take us, but when we can, I'll send you a note letting you know we're okay."

The conductor called for them to board the train, so they handed me their empty coffee cups, gave me their thanks, once again, and rushed off.

As we waved the train out of the station, I wasn't the only one saying prayers for the safe return of these young men.

****

July 3, 1942

"Miss Parker?" Rose stuck her head in the doorway to my office.

I motioned her to one of my wooden guest chairs. "Rose, how nice to see you. What brings you to the library today?" Since the girl rarely came into the library for a book, her visit took me by surprise.

She had on a pretty summer dress, although it was wearing through, and she'd had to mend it many times. More than six months into this war and we were all having to make do with what we had, repairing, repurposing, and reusing everything until it was beyond repair. She took a seat

71

without looking at me, her eyes on her hands, which were folded in her lap.

"Rose," I leaned forward in my chair. "What's wrong?"

When she looked up at me, there were tears in her eyes. I quickly pulled a handkerchief from my desk drawer and handed it to her.

"Thank you." She dabbed at her eyes and then looked into mine. "I don't know what I was thinking, writing to all of these soldiers. I got back two more of my letters this week with *Return* stamped on them and *Deceased* written beneath it."

Tears were streaming down her face now. She was worrying my handkerchief between her hands, but seemed unaware of the tears dripping off her chin.

I rose and walked around the desk, sitting in the second guest chair. "I'm so sorry," I began, patting her left shoulder. She dissolved into tears and buried her head on my right shoulder, throwing her arms around me. Holding her, I rocked back and forth and patted her back. "Let it all out, honey."

After a few minutes, the tears subsided. She released me, straightened up, and wiped her face. "I'm sorry, Miss Parker." She blew her nose and took a deep breath. "I know you warned me about this when you agreed to put my address in the popcorn balls. I guess I never really believed those boys might be killed."

I nodded, taking her hand in mine. "I understand. Unfortunately, it's a fact of war. Young men die, and there's nothing we can do to change it."

"I'm sorry. I didn't mean to remind you of, well, your fiancé. That must have been so hard for you."

"It was." Sometimes I still felt the sharp sting of pain. "Fred and I had planned to move to Lincoln after the war." I always thought I'd work in a library at the university while he went to college. "It was difficult to adjust to the idea of him never returning, but I did what I had to do." And died a little myself.

It all happened so long ago, it was almost like a recurring dream, at least when I remembered the happy times. And a nightmare, when the loss flooded my system again in the deep of the night.

She nodded. "That's just it. Once I start writing to some of these boys and begin to develop a friendship, it's hard to hear that they died. The plans and dreams I'm making in my head die with them, and I'm so sad."

I patted her hand. Not a new story, to be sure.

"Rose, you're young and have plenty of time to meet a man, fall in love, and get married. I know, right now, it's hard for you to think about anything else, but you need to be writing to these soldiers because *they're* lonely, not because *you* are. Because they're far away and want to think about home, family, and friends when they're scared, not because you're afraid you'll never find a man to take you away from North Platte. Writing to servicemen is the patriotic thing to do; it keeps their spirits up and lets them know all of us on the home front remember them and are wishing them well."

"But I didn't have time to make a boyfriend before nearly all the boys I know went into the service, like you did, so I don't have a special fella to call my own." Her lips had turned down, and I was afraid she'd start to cry again. "Is it so wrong to want to fall in love with one of the men, to worry about him, write him letters, and to have someone to bake for and send packages to?"

My mind turned not to Fred, but to Tom. I hadn't received a letter from him in several weeks, even though I kept writing and even sent him two packages. He couldn't tell me where he was, but I had a feeling he was in Alaska, which scared me because we were hearing bad news about the battles in the Aleutian Islands every week.

When he started writing to me, I was amused, but determined not to care about a man who'd gone off to war. For once, my will and determination seemed to desert me.

Despite myself, I was worried about him and looked forward to his letters.

"No, there's nothing wrong about caring for one of these men, if you care about him because of him, not because of what he might do for you after the war. I want you to be careful with your feelings and the feelings of the servicemen. They are the ones who are vulnerable; they're far from home, frightened, and in danger, and we are the ones who have to help and support them."

She nodded but then bowed her head. "Are you angry with me, Miss Parker?" Her voice sounded like she was six instead of sixteen.

I put my hand on her arm again. "No, of course not. I see what a sweet girl you are, and what a wonderful woman you will be, and I want you to see the best in yourself. It's okay for you to write letters to a number of servicemen, but you also need to know that some of them will die, and most will not be the man you fall in love with—but maybe, just maybe, one of them will. Don't rush yourself. Take your time getting to know these men through your letters, and then see what happens. But understand, we are in a war, and many of our young men will not come home."

When I was her age, I didn't understand the inevitability of it all either. Sadly, Rose was learning the truth of war.

"Miss Parker, would it be all right with you if I call you Miss Maggie? I feel like we've become friends, with all our hours working together at the Canteen, even though I'm only sixteen, and it feels so formal to call you Miss Parker all the time."

I looked at her earnest young face. Her eyes were puffy and red from crying; her expression was serious but kind. Maybe we were becoming friends, although who would have thought it possible? I was old enough to be her mother, but I gathered she and her mother didn't get along. I could definitely understand that.

Taking her hand and pulling her to her feet, she was probably surprised when I drew her into a hug. "I think that'd be nice. I'm glad we've become friends, but I really need to get back to work now. I'll see you at the Canteen tomorrow. All right?"

Squealing, she hugged me back. "Thank you so much, Miss Maggie." She released me. "I'm sorry to have taken up so much of your time, but I knew I needed to talk to you."

With her smile back firmly in place, she glided out of my office and practically ran to the front door of the library. I moved back to my desk to tidy my files and walked back to the circulation desk.

****

July 15, 1942
Dear Maggie,

I know it's been a while since you heard from me, and I don't have much time to write, but I wanted to reassure you I'm alive and well and very grateful you are worried about me.

Of course, I can't tell you where we are, other than "somewhere in the Pacific theatre of war," but you are not wrong in thinking we've been seeing a lot of action. I hope it won't be too long before we've won the day, and I can tell you more.

Luckily, my unit has suffered no casualties, although a few men were injured. I hope we can maintain such a clean record going forward, but am unsure of what to expect from the Japanese.

Thank you for continuing to write, even when you didn't hear from me, and for the packages. I appreciate the newspapers and magazines, in addition to the cookies and Rose's popcorn balls, of course. If they were the results of lessons, she must be a fairly accomplished baker by now. It's great you're teaching her.

While it might help you to determine what her home situation is like, it certainly helps her to have you spend time with her and teach her things either her mother never did or that Rose was unwilling to learn from her. You're being a good friend and mentor to her.

You never talk about spending time with friends other than Rose, but you're such a caring person, I'm sure you must have many friends. What do you do when you get together?

I got quite a kick out of the story of young Gene Slattery auctioning the shirt off his back to raise money for the Canteen. He's a smart nine year old and an enterprising young man. I'm impressed that he seems to be able to raise so much money selling the same shirt over and over.

I have to cut this short, so I can get my letter in the mail. We aren't getting our mail on a regular basis at the moment, but please keep writing. I feel like a kid again when I see your handwriting on an envelope or package. Thanks for keeping me tethered to North Platte and to you.

Yours, Tom

CHAPTER FOURTEEN

July 24, 1942

"May I help you?"

The young woman, a nurse by the look of her uniform, seemed to be searching for something specific on the Canteen's periodicals table. She looked up at me and smiled. "I was looking to see if you had any novels or interesting books to read. Something more than a magazine. Reading makes the time pass so much more quickly, and I have a lot of travel ahead of me."

I could definitely understand that sentiment.

"Let's see what we can find." I walked down to the center of the table, pulling out a box of recent donations. I put the box on the table and started sorting through it for books. As the demand increased, we'd begun putting out requests to the community for more books.

As we sorted the books, I asked her name and hometown.

"Oh, I'm sorry." She put down the book she was holding and offered her right hand to me. "I'm Ellen Cogsworth from Door County, Wisconsin. I finished basic training and am heading east. I'm assuming we'll be deployed to England or North Africa, but I don't know anything for sure yet."

I nodded and motioned to the guest book. "Nice to meet you, Nurse Cogsworth. Be sure to sign our guest book, as we hope to keep track of some of the many service members who come through our Canteen."

After the last of the books from under the table were spread out, she started rifling through them. "These are great. If you don't mind, I'll look through these to see if there's something to spark my interest."

"Of course. Help yourself, dear." I put the empty boxes under the table and walked back to the guest book to help a couple of sailors.

When the young men had signed their names, units, and hometowns, Nurse Cogsworth was at my elbow. "Yes, dear?"

She smiled. "I want to sign the guest book, too. I like the idea of writing to letting you know where we go and what is happening to us over there."

She filled out the information, noting she was assigned to the 56th Evac. Hospital.

"I look forward to hearing from you and wish you the best of luck."

She picked up her books and the food she'd retrieved from the other tables and waved good-bye.

Such a brave young woman. I'd had no money for nursing school and didn't have the calling to be a nurse when I was young, so these nurses amazed me with their sense of duty and spark of life. I only hoped they would be safe until they returned home after the war.

When the train left the station, and we'd all waved the troops away, Rose and I walked back to the table. "We're going to need more books, aren't we, Miss Maggie?"

I nodded. "We certainly are." I walked from one end to the other, checking our supply of extra materials. "We have plenty of magazines and quite a few newspapers, and while they are always popular, what we really need are books."

Helen Christ was standing near the dessert table, so I asked her to put the word out, especially with other communities working the Canteen. We had over 100 towns in both Nebraska and Colorado that had signed up for regular shifts.

Hopefully, some of the libraries in those towns had books to spare for our troops.

When I got back to our table, Rose had tidied it up and was ready for the next troop train. When the men started pouring through the open doors, two came straight to our table, their faces familiar.

"It Roland and Walt, right?" I smiled at the soldiers.

"Yes, ma'am," said Walt, nodding his head. "I can't believe you remember us with all the uniforms coming through here every day."

"Of course we remember you."

Roland smiled. "We finished basic training, so we're headed east now. I'm guessing that from there we'll be on a ship to Europe at some point."

"Well, good luck and God bless." Placing a hand on the arm of each brother, I looked first at Walt and then Roland. "I hope I'm working here when you come home from war. Until then, we'll all be thinking of you."

The Rogers brothers signed the guest book again and then hurried to the food table to stock up.

By the end of the night, more than sixteen troop trains had stopped in North Platte, our magazine selection was seriously depleted, my feet hurt, and I was tired. Anxious to get home and to bed, I tried to keep a smile on my face when Helen stopped me on the way out to give me a letter addressed to the Canteen.

July 12, 1942
Dear North Platte Canteen,

I am writing to express my thanks to you, mother to mother, for the kindness you showed my son, Seaman Arthur Hoffman, who went through North Platte on a troop train from Fort Pierce, Florida to Coronado, California.

Arthur told me what a wonderful thing you are all doing for the servicemen in North Platte. May God bless you all for looking after every mother's son who is leaving home, and their country, for the first time.

I am trying to organize a large enough group of volunteers from our little town of Petersburg, NE, to donate food and supplies, and work at the Canteen soon. I think what you're doing is important work and thank you on behalf of my son and his shipmates.

All my best to you, Esther Hoffman

Letters like this one made me feel better. Knowing how much our simple work comforted a young sailor and his mother gave me the boost I need. My feet didn't even hurt all the way home.

****

September 19, 1942

When Rose walked into the Canteen, I met her on the platform. "I have a little surprise for you today."

I handed her a basket of apples, popcorn balls, and candy, and pointed her toward the platform. "How'd you like to be a platform girl today?"

Her eyebrows shot up and her mouth broke into a smile. "Really? How did that happen?"

I smiled. "I saw Mrs. Keeler this morning, and she was trying to find more platform girls as the Adams twins are sick today. I suggested you." I nudged her toward the platform while stepping back toward the door to the Canteen. "Have fun."

She set her basket on the ground and ran to give me a hug.

"Thank you, Miss Maggie. Thank you so much." She ran back to get her basket, her smile a mile wide, and found a place to stand on the platform just as someone called out the train was approaching.

Simple pleasures.

The Canteen was busy that day, with a lot of servicemen and women signing the guest book. Rose stopped by the table each time she came in to get more supplies for her basket, and she was beaming. About time.

"Excuse me, ma'am?"

An earnest Army private stood in front of me, biting his lip and worrying his hat in his hands. He couldn't be much over sixteen.

"Yes, Private. How can I help you?"

"I got a call this morning telling me my unit is shipping out soon, and I'm trying to make it back to Florida as soon as I can."

I nodded. "You're still a long way from Florida, son."

"Yes, ma'am," he nodded. "Is there a way for me to send a telegram to my sergeant at Camp Blanding, ma'am?"

I smiled. "Of course." I pulled out the pad and pencil that I kept under the table for exactly this type of situation. "Write down what you want to say, who it's going to, and where, and I'll get it sent right away."

He wrote everything down and handed me the pad. I read it over to be sure. "I'll send it right now."

His shoulders expanded as he straightened. "I can't thank you enough, ma'am. I came out to see my girl in Denver and asked her to marry me. Now, I'm going to be AWOL if I don't make it back before my unit ships out."

"Did she say yes?"

His worried face broke into a shining grin. "Yes, ma'am, she did." His eyes were sparkling, and his whole body seemed to ignite.

His happiness was contagious. "Do you want me to send a telegram home to your family with the news, in case you don't get time to send one yourself before shipping out?"

He pulled me into a hug, but then quickly stepped back. "I'm sorry, but you're so kind. My parents would be grateful for the news." He scribbled their information on the paper as well.

"Congratulations, private. Be sure to sign the guest book and let us know where you're from. If you get a chance in the future to write to the North Platte Canteen and tell us how you're doing, we'd love to hear from you." I pointed to the food table. "Now get yourself something to eat before your train pulls out. It's a long way to Florida."

He nodded. "Yes, ma'am." He scribbled down his name, John Lee, and hometown of Bedford, Virginia. After he got some food, I saw him sprinting back to the train as I walked to the Western Union desk in the depot. Many servicemen asked us to send a telegram for them when they stopped in the station, and we set aside some of our funds to pay for it. Usually, the telegrams went to men's families or girlfriends, but if this one could keep the private out of Dutch with his sergeant, all the better.

When I walked back to the periodicals table, Rose was waiting for me. "Are you enjoying yourself?"

She didn't meet my gaze, but seemed to be unfocused, although smiling. "Oh yes."

I waited a few moments, finally touching her arm to get her to look at me. "Is everything all right?"

She softly chuckled. "Better than all right. I met the most wonderful man."

I nodded. "Did you now?"

She turned, her eyes lit with excitement, grabbing my hand. "His name is Harry. He couldn't get off the train—it was a hospital train, you know—but I was able to talk to him and pass him things through the open doorway."

"He was among the injured?"

She smiled. "He broke his foot in basic training, so he is going to an Army camp on the East Coast to await deployment, after he's better. His unit already shipped out."

"Oh, I'm glad it wasn't anything more serious." If he was headed east, that meant the European theater of operations.

"He's wonderful, Miss Maggie. So kind, and sweet, and really handsome. He has dark hair, and of course, it's short like everyone else, but his eyes are a beautiful shade of green. Just dreamy."

She was glowing. "I'm glad. Did you give him your address?"

Nodding, she looked around us and then turned back to me. "I even asked him for his. I may have spent the whole time talking to him, but he passed my basket around among the other soldiers on his train car."

"Good." I pointed to her empty basket. "You should probably stock up again."

She nodded and rushed off to the kitchen. Even knowing that her heart could be broken, I couldn't deny the air of jubilation looked good on her.

At the end of the day, Rose caught up to me as I headed out the door. "Can I work the table with you again, tomorrow?"

So I hadn't lost her to the excitement of being a platform girl… "Are you sure that's what you want?"

She shook her head. "I didn't really like being out there too much, other than meeting Harry. I didn't get to talk to you very much, and that's half the fun of working at the Canteen." She leaned her head on my shoulder and wrapped her arm around my back. "Plus, my feet hurt."

I couldn't hold back my laugh.

CHAPTER FIFTEEN

May 28, 1979
As Lisa walked across the stage and accepted her diploma, tears covered my face. I didn't even try to pretend I wasn't crying on this wonderful occasion.

I thought my daughter might poke my ribs, as she often did when I got emotional. But when I turned to look at her, sitting next to me, watching her own daughter's graduation, she wasn't laughing at me. She was crying, too. I felt my husband squeeze my left hand, which he held in both of his.

"That's our girl," he whispered.

I turned to him, smiling. "I'm so proud my heart feels like it could burst."

He wrapped one arm around my shoulders. "We can't have that, my love. We have too much life left to live."

He was right. We were some of the lucky ones, and we had to make the most of it.

****

May 17, 1979
To the ladies of the North Platte Canteen,

I wanted to write to thank you for your kindness toward my husband, Wren Brower, when he came through North Platte in October of 1942. Wren was already a family man, married with a two year old and a four year old when he enlisted in the Army in August 1942. Almost a year of training followed his induction a few months later into the Army Air Corps. Wren arrived in Italy as the pilot of a B-24 bomber in the spring of 1944.

He survived the war, although he was injured on a mission, and the injury finally claimed his life, just this spring. Near the end, his memories of the war were utmost in his mind, and he said many times he wished he'd stopped in North Platte after the war to tell you all how much your smiles, sandwiches, prayers, and good wishes warmed him and his buddies over the years. You reminded Wren of why he was fighting and who he was fighting for. He said he saw me, his mother, his sisters, and his children when he looked at the people of North Platte, and he wanted you to know. He has gone to a better place, where he will no longer suffer any pain, and I wanted to tell you all that some of his final thoughts were of you.

God bless you — Grace Brower

CHAPTER SIXTEEN

October 10, 1942
Dear Maggie,

I was so happy to receive your latest letter and must thank you for your gifts. I can't tell you how wonderful it is to have someone thinking of me back in the States and sending me care packages.

I'm amazed the package got through to me, but the cookies, socks, muffler, newspapers, and magazines are much appreciated. I confess I devoured the cookies, sharing few with my fellow officers. I did share, however, the newspapers and magazines, after I finished reading them. It's interesting to know what the government is saying about what is happening with, and near, us.

I'm glad to hear the Canteen is going well and smile when I think of you helping Rose to meet her young man. She's lucky to have you watching out for her. You said her father served in WWI. If he's no longer living with Rose and her mother, do you know what happened to him? He must have come home, as she is too young to have been born before the war.

Your father sounds like was a great guy. I can picture you, as a little girl, sitting on his desk at the bank, "working" steadily beside him. What a daddy's girl you must have been. Was your mother already having trouble with the drink back then? It must have crushed you when he passed away. I remember the influenza outbreak of

1911—a lot of people died that year. I'm so sorry you lost him when he was so special to you.

My parents were fine people, hard-working and kind. But, they didn't think they would have any children, so I was a bit of a surprise, especially as they were both in their 40's. They died within months of each other when I was 26 and stationed in Florida.

Well, I have to get this out in the mail before I miss my chance. We never know when tides may change the access we have to the rest of the world out here. Know I think of you every day and look forward to the day I can climb off a train in North Platte and see your beautiful face again. You have my heart, so treat it kindly.

Forever yours, Tom

****

December 24, 1942

When I rushed into the station, I saw Rose's mother, Trixie Nelson, talking to Helen Christ. Several other volunteers were milling about, although the Grand Island volunteers were running the Canteen. After Helen's emergency phone call summoning me to the Canteen, it had been a challenge getting across town due to the howling winds and heavy snow.

Trudy and her hospitality committee had done a lovely job with the holiday decorations. Fresh green garland was draped around the doorway into the Canteen, fastened in places by bright red bows. The grade school children had even provided snowflakes, which were dangling from the ceiling. Bing Crosby's "Silent Night" was softly setting the mood.

Helen motioned for me to join her, so I walked over to the group of women.

"There's been an accident, Margaret. The storm caused a B-17 out of Rapid City to make an emergency landing in a field just east of town."

"Is everyone all right? Are we needed for hospital duty?" While I could roll bandages with the best of them, I wasn't going to be a great deal of help if actual nursing duties were required.

"Oh, no. Thankfully, the crew survived unharmed." Helen's smile was shaky and hesitant.

"It was a miracle," said Trixie.

Relief shot through me, although it was mixed with curiosity about what the emergency might be.

Helen nodded. "Yes, yes, it certainly was. But there are nine crew members who need places to stay, perhaps for a week or more, until another plane is ready and can come pick them up."

I nodded, but said nothing. She wanted me to house a stranger for a week or more? Could I subject a stranger to the uncertainty of Mother's behavior?

Helen seemed to sense my reluctance. "We've called all of the volunteers who could get here. Trixie is taking three of the men home with her."

"Trixie owns a boarding house. I do not."

Helen twisted her fingers together, her gaze darting around the room. When she finally turned back to me, she seemed apologetic. "We need one more volunteer to house a member of the crew. Eight have been handled, Margaret. Can't you take one airman into your home?"

I took a deep breath and nodded. "Of course I will, Helen." As I started to turn away, I mumbled. "I hope he doesn't mind being alone with Mother much of the time."

Helen nearly gushed. "I'm sure that will be wonderful, Margaret. Thank you so much."

She walked to the station telephone and placed a call. Before I had time to change my mind, Helen informed me Sergeant Douglas Christensen of the Army Air Corp would be our guest for the next week or so.

When the crew arrived at the depot, they quickly made introductions and sent us on our way. Sergeant Christensen and I walked the eight blocks back to our house with little conversation due to the freezing temperatures and howling winds.

Once at home, I ushered Sergeant Christensen into the kitchen to warm himself by the stove. "Please make yourself at home. I'll pop out front to let my mother know we're here and then warm us up some dinner."

I left him in the kitchen and found Mother sleeping in her room. Although she would be very unpleasant when woken now, it would be worse if she awoke in the morning and found a strange man in our home.

"Mother?" I shook her gently. She smelled strongly of sherry and did not wake easily. I shook her harder.

"What?" Her eyes opened merely a fraction of an inch, raging slits of anger. "Leave me alone!"

"Mother, there was an airplane crash tonight. While the crew survived, they needed housing, so we will have an airman staying here for a while."

She opened her eyes a little more, but her brow crinkled and her upper lip snarled. "What? You brought a man to stay here? You floozy! What will people think of us?"

Other than that the poor man would have to ignore her ire? "Please keep your voice down. As you well know, Mother, I am no floozy, but I am a concerned human being trying to help someone in trouble. Be kind to him."

She rolled away from me, apparently no longer interested in this conversation. "Go away."

It was always my pleasure to leave her to her own devices, but I was hoping Sergeant Christensen hadn't heard her.

As I walked back into the kitchen, he stood. "Please, keep your seat, Sergeant. You've had a trying evening, and I'm sure you're tired and hungry." I walked to the stove. "Would you like coffee or tea?"

"Coffee would be wonderful, ma'am, if it's not too much trouble." He was young, maybe twenty-two, and thin. "You're very kind, you and your mother, to let me stay here."

I smiled. Let him think Mother kind. I could only hope she didn't prove how wrong he was. "I haven't eaten dinner yet, so I thought I would heat up some soup, if that sounds good to you. We have some bread and cheese to go with it."

He nodded. "It sounds wonderful, ma'am."

I chuckled. "As long as we're going to be sharing this house for the foreseeable future, Sergeant, why don't you call me Margaret or even Maggie?"

He laughed softly. "I don't think my captain would approve, ma'am."

I nodded. "Okay. I understand." I got the soup into a saucepan on the stove and poured us each a cup of coffee when it was ready. "So, tell me, Sergeant, where are you from?"

His eyes lit up. "Los Angeles, California, ma'am, although it's been some time since I was last there."

"It's definitely a long way from North Platte, Sergeant. How long have you been in the Air Corps?"

I dished up the soup as he told me about his enlistment, training, and work in the B-17.

"They're called a flying fortress. We usually have a ten-person crew, although we're missing one of our gunners. We'll pick him up at camp before we're shipped off to our POE next month."

"POE?"

He smiled. "Sorry, the point of embarkation. That's where we'll go to be sent to Europe. We know we're going east, so that means the European theater of operations, although we don't know anything more at this point."

"What's your position?"

He watched as I dunked the bread in the soup and then smiled and followed suit. We couldn't get much butter or sugar, and what we got, I used for Canteen donations, so the bread needed the added taste of soup.

"I'm the radio operator. That means I monitor our position, keep a log, work closely with the navigator, and when necessary, I'm an additional gunner."

"You have a lot of responsibility, Sergeant, especially for one so young. Do you enjoy what you're doing?" I finished my soup and sat back to watch him devour his.

"I love it, ma'am. The B-17 is the best plane in the air and will help us win this war." He talked on about the rest of his crew, how the weather caused their emergency landing tonight, and what he hoped they could do once they got to Europe.

Eventually, we both realized it was late, and we were tired. "Let me show you the spare room, Sergeant."

He followed me up the stairs, carrying his gear. At the door to the spare room, I wished him good night and Merry Christmas, headed to the bathroom to complete my nightly ablutions, and then shut myself in my room to write Tom and pray for Sergeant Christensen, both once he was facing the enemy and as long as he was in our home.

CHAPTER SEVENTEEN

December 31, 1942
Dear Tom,

Happy New Year! I hope 1943 is the last year of the war and we see you and all of servicemen come home safe and sound.

It's been a year since your train stopped at the Canteen and I can't help but think of how much has changed since then. I'll admit, I thought you silly and outrageous when you spent the short time you had in North Platte talking to me instead of stocking up on food for the rest of your journey, but I am glad you did. Despite my reservations, I find myself thinking about you, worrying about you, and wishing I could talk to you often. You have become a regular part of my life, if only by letter, and I do care about you. You wore down my defenses, showed me what a nice and honorable man you are, and made me miss you. Knowing, as you do, how I lost my fiancé, Fred, in WW1, you can understand my reluctance to develop feelings for another soldier away at war, but you broke through my wall and my heart is, cautiously and fearfully, yours. Please keep your heart beating and stay out of danger as much as you can, as I don't think I could bear it if anything happened to you.

As I mentioned in my last letter, several of us Canteen volunteers have been hosting the stranded crew of a downed B-17 Flying Fortress, but they climbed aboard their repaired plane today and flew back to Rapid City. They had to make an emergency landing on Christmas Eve, due to weather. One fellow's wife was expecting a baby any minute, and he was a nervous wreck all week. They are heading east to their POE and then on to the front, so I wish them God speed and good luck.

Rose is good; thanks for asking about her. She is a wonderful young woman, if only she'd believe it. Living with her father, and the shell shock he suffered before she was even born, left her lacking in self-confidence, confused, and angry at her mother. I fear something bad happened to make Trixie kick Rose's father out of the house, but I haven't wanted to push the girl to talk about it. Without a many friends her own age, I believe she needs some time away from her problems, whatever they are. She seems to enjoy working with me and comes to the house after I get out of work when we aren't at the Canteen.

I want to get this letter in the mail, or rather sent with Victory Mail. I hope the V-mail letters get to you quickly. Please be safe and know I'm praying for you.

Your Maggie

****

January 15, 1943

"I'm told you're the woman in charge." I said, smiling.

The buxom woman in a navy-blue dress and pink-and-white flowered apron turned to me, also smiling. "I guess I am. Can I help you?"

"I'm Margaret Parker, Canteen historian. I can see the ladies of Maxwell have everything well in hand, but I wanted to offer my help, if you have need of it."

She glanced around the room and then turned back to me, shaking her head. "That's very kind, but I think we've got it all covered."

I nodded. "Do you mind, then, if I talk to a couple of your volunteers, when they're not too busy, to gather information for the Canteen records? Just how much food you brought, number of servicemen served, whether they're traveling with family members, those types of things."

"Sure, go ahead. But, it will be a challenge to catch them when they're not busy. We've had eighteen troop trains come through already today, and we're not even close to done yet."

"Thank you." I took a step and then turned back. "If you change your mind about help, even if it's making calls for more food, flag me down."

She nodded and rushed off toward the kitchen.

The troops came rushing out of the Canteen and back onto the train. Even on a run, most tipped their hats to me or tossed a "ma'am" or "thanks" in my direction as they ran past. This train was a long one, carrying Army, Navy, and even some nurses.

Once the train pulled out, I hurried inside to talk to some of the volunteers. I found a woman at the end of the food table, restocking the cookies trays. She introduced herself as Muriel Allen.

"Do you mind if I ask you a few questions for the Canteen records?"

"Not at all, as long as you don't mind me working while we talk."

I pulled out a small notebook and pencil. "Certainly, and if a troop train pulls in before you're finished, I'm happy to help."

She smiled at me. "What do you want to know?"

"Well, do you volunteer at the Canteen often?"

She nodded. "The Women's Club of Maxwell starting coming the third Friday of the month early last year, so I try to make sure I'm here each time it's our day."

I nodded. "That's wonderful. What all do you ladies bring with you?"

She chuckled. "Well, the usual, of course, in terms of cookies, birthday cakes, pies, and the like. My daughter and I started on the chickens for the chicken salad sandwiches last night. My husband, too, since he builds a big wood fire in the yard, hangs my largest iron kettle over it on a tripod, and gets the water rolling."

I nodded, writing as quickly as I could. "So your husband's also a volunteer, even though he doesn't come to the Canteen."

She pulled out another tray of cookies, nodding. "Sure, and it's his corn cobs we use to start the fire. Like I said, my daughter and me dress the birds and drop them in, just for a couple of minutes. Then we clean them with baking soda and water and soak those chickens in salt water until 2:30 in the morning. We line a bushel basket with oilcloth, fill with the chickens, and put one of my cooking lids on top. We left the farm at 5:30 this morning, with the chickens and everything we baked, and here we are."

"I bet those chicken sandwiches are a big hit with the boys."

She looked up at me smiled. "I haven't gotten any complaints."

I nodded, thanked her, and moved on. So many of the Maxwell women had similar stories. One woman brought thirteen birthday cakes, as well as four hams for ham sandwiches. I made sure to note in the history that all of the women talked about saving their sugar and coffee rations for the Canteen. Now that meat, lard, and even cooking oils were being rationed, women had to be more creative when cooking for their families, because they wanted to save their precious supplies for their donations to the Canteen.

****

February 14, 1943
My dearest Maggie,

Happy Valentine's Day! I wish I were there, so I could spend the day with you, instead of stuck here where it sometimes starts to feel like "no-man's land." The news you're getting there might not be entirely a reflection of what's happening here, but know I am okay and most of the men are holding up well, although I have lost some men and the battle here continues.

I couldn't help but smile when you said "Betty Crocker" visited the Canteen. I wonder if she'll start advertising some of the recipes volunteers use to create Canteen favorites, including those pheasant sandwiches. I hope FDR doesn't try to push his meatless Mondays idea with the Army. Our food is unpleasant enough most of the time, but the boys have to have meat to keep them going.

I was sorry to hear the airman who stayed with you at Christmas has been killed, and so soon after joining the fighting in North Africa. It was good of the Air Corps to notify you all that their plane had been shot down, given the relationship you and the volunteers developed with them. You're right, he was much too young; they all were.

Yes, I heard about the deaths of the Sullivan brothers. I know many people argued against the Navy's policy of allowing brothers to sign onto the same ship, and I'm sure there are many in Congress now moving quickly to change that policy. Can you imagine the pain of those parents, and I believe they have one daughter, upon learning all five of their sons were killed in the destruction of the USS Juneau? Regardless of the preferences of the brothers when they enlisted, the Navy was reckless in putting them all on one ship for that very reason. I believe they are taking steps to separate brothers going forward, even in Army units.

There's no way to avoid the fact that men die in wars. I don't say this to scare you, as I am doing my best to stay safe and sound, but the American people cannot be so surprised when the general concept becomes a reality, no matter how tragic. We must put everything we can into defeating the armies of Germany, Italy, and Japan, if we hope to return to our well-known and loved life of peace and democracy.

Okay, that's more than enough of my soap box for this romantic day. Keep sending me letters, packages, and, of course, photos. Some of my officers were teasing me for having a fiery redhead writing to me. Even though you and I know your hair is a beautiful shade of auburn, I let them think what they like. If they think you're a strong-willed woman simply because of your hair color, they're half-way right. Ha, ha.

By the way, the V-mail does get to me quite quickly, so keep them coming. Give my regards to Rose and your mother, but save my best for yourself.

All my love, Tom

CHAPTER EIGHTEEN

April 1, 1943
Dear Tom,

You'll never believe who came through the Canteen last week—Genevieve Sullivan, sister to the famous five Sullivan brothers. She joined the WAVES, as the Navy's Women Accepted for Volunteer Service is called. As you know, the family is from Iowa and she was headed to San Francisco to be sworn into the Navy.

I couldn't decide if she was being brave or a little reckless by joining the Navy after her parents lost all five of her brothers. I understand that the WAVES mostly stay here in the U.S. and don't see front-line action, but there have been casualties among the women in service, even those in the Red Cross. I don't know if I could stand for her to join up, if I were her mother, and risk losing my last child too.

We actually get a lot of servicewomen coming through the Canteen these days, not only nurses, including the women of the Army Women's Army Corp (WACs), the WAVES, and even the Coast Guard SPARs. I have no idea what it stands for, but they look quite smart in their uniforms. President and Mrs. Roosevelt encourage us all to step up and do our parts in this war, so many young women feel compelled to sign up and serve in some way. I'm not ready to desert the library to don any of those smart uniforms, so I'm glad the Canteen is such a success. I know I'm doing a service to the troops here.

While we still operate solely on donated funds, we are able to feed all the servicemen and women each day, and have been getting up to twenty troop trains some days. Luckily, some of the traveling salesmen in the area bring us donations, particularly coffee and sugar. A local bakery donates ten loaves of bread per day, and the dairy donates a portion of the milk.

We have expanded our list of volunteer communities to cover much of central and western Nebraska and even into Colorado. It's amazing to hear the stories of the small communities who coordinate their efforts to volunteer, some coming as far as 200 miles by train or car.

I've been talking to volunteers about their experiences, including a woman named Rosalie. She travels whenever she can from her small town of Shelton, NE, which is over 120 miles away. The volunteers get a pass from the Union Pacific Railroad to get a free ride on the 3:40 a.m. train to North Platte on their scheduled days. She normally spends three hours making egg salad sandwiches, including peeling the eggs, using homemade mayonnaise, and stacking sandwiches in baskets on a clean white dish towel. She gets back on the train to Shelton at 11:00 p.m. arriving home at 1:00 a.m. after a long day serving eighteen to twenty troop trains.

She makes me feel proud to be a part of the Canteen. With the efforts of women like her behind our troops, how can we fail?

I know you can't confirm for me where you are, but I am still operating under the impression you are in Alaska, so I keep constant watch on the news across the country for updates on the fighting there. If I read the various releases and articles correctly, it seems like the Aleutian Islands, clearly property of the United States, have in fact been invaded by the Japanese.

Why is there so little outcry in the nation about this? When the Japs attacked Pearl Harbor, also an American territory, the nation stopped and lashed out in a collective scream of outrage. It shocks me that we seem to have no idea the Japs have invaded and taken our territories by force, leaving American troops to fight to regain our land.

I know little about Alaska and would likely be equally ignorant of the military action there if I didn't think you were stationed there, but I am consistently appalled our government is not giving us more information about this invasion of a U.S. territory.

Meanwhile, back in North Platte, life goes on. Rose is really blossoming with Harry's letters and is well and truly in love. I've gotten to know her mother, Trixie, better and she seems like a good woman to me, so I'm still stumped as to why Rose is so hard on her.

Please take care, know a goodie package is on its way to you, and keep yourself out of the line of fire as best you can.

Love, Maggie

****

August 17, 1943

Rose was leaning against the back door of the depot when I walked up after work. She seemed to be oblivious to my presence, wrapped in a shroud of melancholy, and crying.

When I asked what was wrong, her head hung a little lower. "I haven't heard from Harry in weeks. I know he's busy, but he always writes to me. I'm scared. What if he's been killed? How would I even know?"

I pulled her into my arms, but instead of harsh crying, she was filled with wounded silence. How would we know what happened to the men who filled our hearts and minds when they were so far away? I had to admit, that my thoughts were the same when Tom's letters were slow to arrive. Sadly, this was a woman's lot in war: waiting.

"Were any of your letters to him returned, like those before?"

She shook her head. "No."

I patted her back. "Don't you think they would be if anything had happened to him?"

She nodded against my shoulder. "I guess so, but it takes so long to know anything for sure, and it's killing me not to hear from him."

I hugged her tight and then pushed her from me, lifting her chin so I could look in her eyes. "I know how hard it is to wait and how frightening it is to think of a man you care about in danger."

She nodded, her eyes swimming in tears again. "It stinks." She wiped her tears and pulled away. "I'm sorry to go on about this. I know you've been through it, too."

I wasn't sure if she was thinking of Tom or Fred, but I was as worried for Tom as I had been for Fred all those years ago. When had that happened? When did I truly fall in love with the man?

"You have to keep yourself busy, refuse to give in to sad feelings and scary thoughts. The Canteen is the best place for you to be to keep your morale up."

She nodded.

"Remember when we got the news Herbert Swanson had been killed in action? His mother was here at the Canteen when the telegram came."

Rose's lips thinned but she nodded. "She fainted when they handed her the telegram."

The woman's face had gone chalky white, and her lips were nearly blue. It had taken a few minutes for her friends to revive her. "Remember how surprised everyone was when she showed up for her Canteen shift two days later?"

She inhaled and tilted her head. "I couldn't understand why she didn't stay home. No one would have minded covering her shifts for her."

"She said Herbert would want her to go on helping others, even though she couldn't do for him anymore. I know how it feels."

She looked into my eyes again. "From the last war?"

I nodded. "Yes, when I got the news Fred had been killed in France, I cried for three days straight. Then, I got up on the fourth day and walked over to the library, asking if they had a job for me. Some people thought it was disrespectful to Fred, but it was the best way for me to move on with my life. Fred would have understood I had to support myself and my mother, because he wasn't going to be there to do it for me."

"Weren't you too sad to work?"

I smiled. "Not really. I mean, when I got home and the house was quiet and I was trying to fall asleep at night, I couldn't keep the tears from coming. But when I was busy helping people at the library every day and learning how to be a librarian, I hardly had time to grieve. It worked for me and for Mrs. Swanson, and I think it will work for you. If you simply keep working and helping others, you will have less time to worry about Harry."

Rose pulled me into another hug. "Thank you. You always know what to say to make me feel better, but even more important, you listen to me. I don't feel like you think I'm whining about some foolish thing. You treat me like I matter."

"Oh Rose, you do matter, and what you feel matters. I'm sorry if you are made to feel foolish. You're a smart young woman."

****

September 30, 1943
Dearest Tom,

Although I know you still can't tell me where you are, I was happy to hear President Roosevelt announce the Japanese have fled the Aleutian Islands, and we are no longer occupied by the enemy. If you are truly there, you must be celebrating. I thank God you have survived this unscathed, although I understand the same cannot be said of all the men in your troops.

As we draw close to the second anniversary the attack on Pearl Harbor, I can't help but think about how life has changed since that fateful Sunday. I never asked where you were when you got the news. I know you and your troops were already in the Army, and I seem to remember you saying you were in Georgia before coming through North Platte, but is that where you heard about Pearl Harbor?

As it was early on a Sunday afternoon in Nebraska, I was finishing the dishes after our Sunday dinner. Mother was listening to one of her radio programs, but I was heading up to my bedroom to relax and read. When she yelled from the parlor, I thought she was talking back to her shows, as she does from time to time. Instead, she was yelling at me to come listen. I couldn't believe what I heard.

Everything changed in one moment; one news report on the radio.

Now, I keep busy working the library with fewer employees, as Ralph finally joined up, and volunteering at the Canteen whenever possible. When I'm not working at the Canteen, Rose often comes here to help me bake cookies, cupcakes, or popcorn balls. I still try to get a lot of reading done, but find my late-night reading time is taken up with writing you letters.

You have become very important to me, Tom, and I finally had to admit I am in love with you. I know you've been professing your love for months now, but I was determined not to risk my heart to another man away at war. I was satisfied that, this time, the war couldn't steal my love away from me. Please don't let it happen again, even if that's an unfair thing for me to ask of you. Now that I've admitted I love you, please keep yourself safe and come home to me.

I keep you in my prayers, along with Rose's Harry, our North Platte young men, your troops, and well, every mother's son. I know it's unrealistic, but when I see the fresh, young faces of the servicemen, and women, coming through the Canteen, I hate to think of any of them being killed or even injured. So, I smile, bake, and pray.

All my love, Maggie

CHAPTER NINETEEN

November 25, 1943

Rose had promised to stay home and help her mother serve Thanksgiving dinner at the boarding house. Nonetheless, she walked into the Canteen early on Thanksgiving morning and immediately came over to assist me with unloading a delivery. She didn't seem unhappy, although I certainly wasn't expecting her.

"What happened to helping your mother with dinner?"

She shrugged. "There's not really much to do. We got the turkey in the oven this morning, and I peeled the potatoes, but she's handling everything else by herself. We don't have too many guests, what with the holiday and all."

Rose and her mother were often at odds, so I wouldn't have been surprised to learn there was more to the story than she was letting on.

"Where did all this food come from?" She held up a can of cranberry relish.

Trudy Bellows leaned over, joining our conversation. "Isn't it wonderful? Father McDaid brought it over from St. Patrick's first thing this morning. He donated twelve turkeys, twelve cans of cranberry relish, and 100 candy bars.

Our soldiers will get a taste of Thanksgiving when they come through the Canteen today."

"St. Patrick's must have been roasting turkeys for the past several days to get these all ready for us." I smiled at her and she nodded.

The volunteers in the kitchen quickly got to work making turkey sandwiches—heavy on the lettuce and tomato to spread the turkey over as many sandwiches as possible without grinding it into turkey salad.

Most of our sandwiches were some type of ground meat, stretched with the homemade mayonnaise. Not the most exciting sandwiches ever, but with meat rationed and so hard to come by, it was the best we could do. I'm sure they helped fill the stomachs of these hungry servicemen just the same.

By the end of the evening, Trudy came running out of the kitchen. "We're almost out of turkey. I don't know what to do. I don't want to disappoint anyone who comes in on a train later tonight."

Helen Christ stepped out from behind the table, and the women talked it over. Soon, Helen was walking out to the depot platform.

Within twenty minutes, Father McDaid himself came hurrying into the Canteen with a roaster pan filled with a turkey and all the trimmings.

"Can't let these boys do without Thanksgiving, now, can we, ladies?" The good Father smiled at us all as he rushed into the kitchen.

I looked over at Trudy, who followed the priest into the kitchen. By the time the next troop train arrived, not only did we have Father McDaid's Thanksgiving dinner served up for the soldiers, but Father McDaid himself stepped up to the serving line to help hand out the sandwiches himself.

"Wow," She moved in close to my elbow. "That's so nice of Father McDaid to give up his Thanksgiving dinner for the Canteen."

I smiled. "It certainly is. And I think the boys are enjoying getting served by a priest tonight."

Giggling, she winked at me. "It looks sort of like communion."

****

December 1, 1943
Dear Maggie,

I can admit to you finally, yes, I am in Alaska. The Battle of the Aleutian Islands ended in late August, as President Roosevelt announced. I can heartily thank you again for all the socks, hats, mufflers, and gloves you've sent me, as I have treasured and relied on them over the past two years. It's dang cold up here.

I can't say where we will be deployed to going forward, but troops will remain here in the Aleutian Islands to protect this land from future invasions. Thank God we didn't lose more men.

Our Thanksgiving was quiet, but I really appreciated the banana bread you sent, as well as the cookies. Food is always a big hit here.

Yes, I am friends with some of my fellow officers, but it is a bit of a tightrope. We aren't a big enough outfit to have many other officers near my own rank. I can't really be buddies with my superior officers or with the enlisted men, so I am usually alone or sometimes go out for a drink with some of the junior officers. I have to be careful not to make them uncomfortable as well. That's why I keep all of your letters to reread when no new ones have arrived; they make me feel like you're here with me.

Although I know the end to the fighting here in the Aleutians is not the same thing as the end of the war, but, along with the successes at Midway and the Solomon Islands, it does get me thinking about what I will do when the war is over. Have you given it much thought?

You'll probably say you'll go back to only having one job—working only at the library with no more Canteen duties. Of course, from what you've told me about the tutoring work you do with the high school students, it's more than just a library job, isn't it?

But I'm talking about you and me. I want there to be a "you and me" after the war, Maggie. I realize your home is in North Platte; your mother is there, your job, and your friends. There's no reason my home can't be in North Platte, too. I want to be where you are, to get to spend time with you, every day, and hopefully make my home with you.

I admit this seems fast, but really I started falling in love with you the day I first saw you, nearly two years ago. You're probably saying I'm rushing you, since you were so stubborn about admitting how much you cared about me in the beginning, but we both know it's true. Ha, Ha.

Seriously, please start giving it some thought. I'd like to leave the Army; it's well past time for me to retire. I could take my final troop train to North Platte, step onto the platform, and stay there for the rest of my life. How does it sound to you?

While I don't need your answer now, please give it some serious thought. I'd like to make my forever home, really the first one I've had since my parents passed away, with you, my dear Maggie.

*Until then, you remain in my heart and thoughts and I remain,
Yours forever, Tom*

****

December 19, 1943

"Isn't this exciting?" Rose rushed up as soon as she arrived at the Canteen, her coat already hanging off one shoulder and her hand smoothing her hair.

"Remember, just because NBC radio is broadcasting from here today, no one outside of the Canteen will be able to see you." I smiled at her, raising my eyebrows.

She laughed. "Don't be silly; I know how radio works. I want to look nice for the award ceremony." She folded her coat and slid it under our table. "Besides, this broadcast is going coast-to-coast, Miss Maggie. I can't believe people all over the country are going to hear about our Canteen here in North Platte."

The mayor, board members, all the big shots, and even some of the little shots in town were in the Canteen tonight because the War Department was awarding the North Platte Canteen the Meritorious Wartime Service Award.

It was all well and good, and I was proud to be part of this effort, but we still had troop trains coming in and servicemen to feed. Everyone knew things were heating up in Europe. Whatever the War Department had planned, more and more troop trains were coming through the depot, mostly heading east, every day. Some days we served more than twenty trains, which stretched even the best-prepared volunteers and their food contributions to near the breaking point.

Just as a west-bound train pulled out and another east-bound one pulled in, I told Rose to go watch the ceremony, while I listened from inside the Canteen. A young Army private approached my table, looking confused.

"May I help you, Private?"

He smiled, but still turned his head side-to-side, scanning the tables. "I'm looking for a young lady, ma'am— Rose Nelson?" He swallowed and finally fixed his gaze on mine. "I was told I'd probably find her at the magazine table."

"Miss Nelson is in the main part of the depot right now, watching the award ceremony going on. Come with me and we'll find her."

I started toward the door, checking to ensure he was following me. He looked longingly at the food tables, but he turned and continued to hunt for Rose.

I called her name. She looked up and seemed surprised to see me, but walked over to join me.

"This soldier is looking for you." I motioned her over to where the private was waiting and then hurried back into the Canteen to grab some food for the young man. When I came back out with a couple of sandwiches, an apple, and some cookies, I nearly ran into him returning to the Canteen.

"Oh," I said, trying not to drop his food.

"I'm sorry, ma'am." He held out his hands to keep me and my armful of food from falling.

"These are for you, private. I didn't want you to run out of time to get something to eat." I looked around him. "Where's Rose?"

He took the food from me, smiling. "Thank you, kindly. I gave Miss Nelson the message there was soldier in the hospital car asking for her, and she rushed off to the train."

"Oh, very good, Private. Why don't you get some milk or coffee, quick before you have to get back on the train?"

He smiled. "Yes, ma'am. I'll do that. Thank you, again, for thinking of me."

I put my hand on his arm. "Thank you and God bless, Private."

I hurried to the train, praying Rose was all right. I was hoping it wasn't Harry on the hospital car, as that would mean his injury was so severe as to get him sent back to the States. Never a good sign.

She was talking to a soldier who was leaning out a window from inside a hospital car. He looked nothing like the picture of Harry she'd shown me, so I was completely lost as to what this was about. But, as she wasn't crying and didn't seem upset, I went back to the table to offer help to additional service members.

After that train pulled out and the ceremony was over, she finally returned.

Since she didn't look upset, I took a deep breath, relaxing my shoulders. "Is everything all right? Was there someone you know on the hospital train?"

She smiled and nodded. "Well, sort of. When Harry started writing to me, his buddy Pete did, too. When they both realized they were writing the same girl, and Harry and I had started to realize we really liked each other, Pete told me he wasn't going to write to me anymore. I mean, I wrote to him a couple of times and sent him a small package, but just as friends, you know?"

I nodded, but kept working.

She sat on the stool we kept behind the table. A dream-like expression came over her face. "That was Pete on the train. He was injured in Italy and sent home because he won't be able to march long distances and carry heavy equipment anymore, so the Army sent him home for rehabilitation. He says he might get office work, if the war isn't over once he's recovered."

I shook my head. "He must have been badly injured."

"He didn't tell me exactly what happened, and I didn't want to pry, but he said it was serious but not life-threatening, so he guessed he was one of the lucky ones." Shrugging her shoulders, she started to help me sort magazines.

I smiled. "It was very nice of him to look you up when the train stopped here."

"Harry asked him to."

"What?"

Pausing her work to look up at me, she smiled. "Harry asked him to send someone to find me if he stopped in North Platte, to bring me these." From beneath our work table, she pulled out a stack of letters and a wrapped gift. "Pete was going to mail them once he got to the rehab hospital if he didn't get a chance to see me."

"That was really sweet, both of Pete for doing it, but also for Harry to send you a gift."

Her eyes fill with tears. "Harry is so sweet. He's the nicest man I ever met." She wiped her tears and then looked into my eyes. "I'm in love with him."

I put my arm around her shoulders. "I know, my dear."

She tilted her head. "How do you know? I only now realized how much I care about him." She looked totally confused.

I chuckled. "You may just have realized, but I'm the one who has been watching you talk about him and pour over his letters for months. I could tell Harry wasn't like any of the other boys you'd written to before."

She smiled and leaned her head on my shoulder. "You're so right. I pray every day he will come home safely to me when this war is over. I love him so much."

I patted her back, but couldn't shake the thought of Tom's words about coming home to North Platte, and to me, when the war was over. Was 1944 going to be the year our troops came home? Would the war be over soon?

But, did I want Tom to come home to me? Should he retire from the Army and move to North Platte permanently? Did I see us together in my mind's eye? I wasn't sure I could see him living in the house with me and my mother, nor could I see us leaving Mother alone.

He asked me to give it some serious thought, so that's what I was doing. I would not rush to answer him, because it was too important to make a mistake.

CHAPTER TWENTY

February 14, 1944
Dear Tom,

Happy Valentine's Day, sweetheart. I hope you are safe and warm (but not too warm) wherever you are these days. It's not warm at all in North Platte, but I am sending you my love, strength, and prayers.

You'll never guess what happened today. I was interviewed for a radio program, live on the air. Last month, KODY radio started broadcasting from the Canteen a couple times a day. Since they can't really talk to the servicemen and women who come through, troop movements, military secrets, and all that, they mostly end up interviewing us volunteers. Today was my turn. Although I didn't have much to say,. I did put in a nice plug for the library.

It's useful to have the radio station broadcasting from here when we're running low of specific food items at the end of the day. As soon as the announcer mentions on air how we need more bread or ham or whatever, someone runs into the Canteen with supplies.

I went to watch "The Fighting Sullivans" movie with Rose over the weekend. It felt like the right thing to do, given what the Sullivan family has been through, especially after we met the men's sister, Genevieve. She was such a nice girl and so patriotic to join the Navy after all five of her brothers were killed. It was a very good movie, although, of course, very sad.

I opened a letter to the Canteen this week from the mother of a young man who came through North Platte almost two years ago. He was trained as a bombardier on a B-17. He and his crew survived many bombing runs and were quite successful until recently. They were shot down somewhere over Germany, and she received a telegram informing her he is now in a German POW camp. She wrote to thank us for our kindness to her son, and I wrote back to her because I believe she can use all the prayers and good wishes possible. I'm sure she is worrying herself sick over her son.

It made me think about you and the questions you asked me about after the war. I've been studiously avoiding answering you because I didn't want to say more than I honestly believe.

Yes, I want you to come home to North Platte after the war. Yes, I want us to be together, or at least for us to give it our very best try. I'm in love with you and want to spend my life with you, so please, stay safe, stay healthy, and come home to me.

There were so many questions racing through my mind while I was thinking this over, as I did give it serious thought. But, with perspective, I can admit those details don't really matter. We'll work them out once you're home. So, please, come home.

Rose got a letter from Harry this week. He's in a hospital in England and wrote to let her know he's injured but not seriously. You may remember he broke his foot in basic training and apparently he broke it again in the same spot. He had to have surgery and is out of commission for a while. Maybe the Army will move him to an administrative position.

Well, I want to get this letter sent off, so it's not too long after Valentine's Day when you receive it. I mailed a package a couple of weeks ago, so please let me know what condition everything is in when you receive it. Not having an idea of where you are makes it harder to know what to send, but I'm going with the principle that the rest of the Pacific is more tropical than Alaska was. Seems like a safe bet.

Enjoy the goodies when they arrive and think of me when you're reading this. I love you and am sending you all my best.

Yours always, Maggie

****

June 6, 1944

"Can you believe it?"

Trudy Bellows was rushing around the Canteen, not seeming to know what to do with herself. I reached out a hand, laying it gently on her arm, and she stopped fluttering, looking me in the eye. "Did you hear?"

I nodded. "Yes. Everyone's talking about the Allied troops' invasion on the coast of France." I moved my hand to pat her back. "You haven't heard anything about Walter's location have you?"

Trudy's son, Walter, was in the Army, but she only knew he was "somewhere in England."

"No." Her color wasn't good, and she seemed to be trembling.

"I'm sure it will be a few days before Walter has time to contact you and let you know he's all right."

She nodded, but still couldn't seem to focus. Instead, she grabbed tightly onto my arm.

"Maybe it'd be better if you went home today." I looked over to catch Rosemary Keeler's eye and motioned for her to join us.

"Trudy, why don't we get you home? I bet your mother-in-law is in a frenzy." Rosemary knew that while Trudy and her husband's mother weren't particularly close, she wouldn't want the older woman to make herself sick with worry.

"Oh, yes." Trudy nodded. "I should be with Hazel."

As I started to ease my arm out of Trudy's grasp, I looked into her eyes, seeing recognition return. "I'll be praying for Walter and his unit."

She shook my hand, squeezing once more. "Thank you, Maggie. Thank you so much." She pulled me into a hug and then turned to leave. Trudy had never called me Maggie or hugged me before. The war turned those of us left behind into a close community of ladies-in-waiting. Rosemary led her out of the Canteen.

I sent up a silent prayer for Walter Bellows and all the young men on those beaches in Normandy.

None of the other committee members or Canteen volunteers ever called me Maggie. I'd never told them they could. Despite living in North Platte all of my life, I hadn't been close to anyone after Fred died. Because I was so focused on paying the bills and keeping my mother away from others, I'd closed myself off to the rest of the town— at least on a personal level.

I'd been working closely with the Canteen ladies for more than two-and-a-half years now, never mind the fact many of us had lived in North Platte all of our lives. Why had I not made the effort to become friends with these women?

When I was younger, the thought of bringing friends to my home, with Mother's anger and unpredictability, was too embarrassing. But it was long past time she should have any control over me or my life.

"Did you hear they rang the Liberty Bell in Philadelphia?" Rose came rushing to my side when she arrived that afternoon. "I heard it from some of the women behind me at church."

I nodded. "I stopped at church before I came in today, too, but I didn't know about Philadelphia. I did hear the New York Stock Exchange observed two minutes of silence. I think the entire nation is praying for those troops."

"It's so hard to know that something is happening, but not *how* it's going."

Wrapping my arm around her shoulders, I gave her a quick hug. "The news has been full of speculation for months, so it was hard to ignore the fact that something big was coming. Just think of all the troops that have been moving east in the past year."

She bit her bottom lip, her telltale sign of worry.

"Are you worried about Harry?" I asked, keeping my voice low.

She nodded, her eyes filling with moisture. "I don't know where he is. If he got out of the hospital, he could be in the thick of it and not really at his best. I guess it's wrong to hope he's still too injured to have been released from the hospital yet."

I patted her on the back. "It's not wrong to hope the man you love is safe. While I know Tom is somewhere in the Pacific, I have no idea what he's facing or what battles his unit is a part of. Sadly, that's a woman's lot in war. We wait for news: good news, bad news, any news. We just wait and pray. We pray a lot."

CHAPTER TWENTY-ONE

July 4, 1944

"Good morning, Mrs. Tenney." Ann Tenney was standing at one of the food tables, setting out deviled eggs decorated with red-and-blue sugar crystals in honor of Independence Day.

She knelt down to straighten the bunting on the tables. "Good morning, Miss Parker."

Mrs. Tenney had been an avid patron of the library for years, always bringing her four children in for books as they grew up. Even with only the youngest girl at home, they were still regulars.

"Please, Mrs. Tenney," I said smiling back, offering a hand to help her back to her feet. "After all the years we've known each other, call me Maggie."

Her eyebrows shot up, but then her expression opened into a warm smile. "Well, thank you, Maggie. And please call me Ann." She placed a hand on my arm. "We have known each other for many years, haven't we? It's silly we're still so formal with each other."

I nodded. "Those deviled eggs are very patriotic, Ann. I'm sure the servicemen will love them."

She beamed. "My daughter, Lorma, and I have been boiling and peeling them for two days, trying to get enough deviled eggs for today. The boys sure do love them."

I saw several familiar faces around the food tables that morning because the ladies of North Platte had taken Independence Day as our own volunteer day. While there were other towns willing to volunteer, we'd given them the day off for celebration and catching up on work at home.

Ann called to a woman at the pie table, "Good morning, Sue."

Mrs. Barber walked to where I was standing with Ann. Where Ann was tall and blond, Mrs. Barber was tiny and dark. The women hugged in greeting.

"Good morning, Ann. I see you and Lorma finished in time. The eggs look great."

"We did." Ann gestured toward me. "Maggie was complimenting me on them, but when I saw the pies you were setting out, I realized they are truly deserving of praise."

Again, Mrs. Barber looked somewhat surprised, but smiled. "Good morning, Miss Parker."

"Good morning, and please call me Maggie." I smiled.

She nodded. "Only if you'll call me Sue."

"Ann is right. Your pies are also wonderful. I love the way you made fireworks and flag shapes on your top crust. What delicate work. It will almost be a shame to cut them and watch the boys devour them in one bite." I smiled, hoping she realized I was teasing.

Sue smiled. "So, true, Maggie. But, I bring them for eating, so it's rewarding enough to see them enjoyed."

While the encounter was slightly awkward, I was hoping going forward, I would be able to become friends with Ann and Sue, as well as some of the other women at the Canteen. I hadn't tried making friends since grammar school and was very rusty at it, but there was no time like the present.

I'd been able to thin out the shelves at the library and donate many older, uncirculated books to the Canteen. When I saw Rose arriving, her head down and eyes averted, I walked out to meet her.

I slid my arm through hers. "Can you help me bring in some boxes of books?"

She looked up in surprise. "Oh, I'm sorry. I didn't see you." She didn't meet my gaze but nodded. "I'd be happy to help."

We walked out to the back of the depot, where I parked my car. I didn't usually drive to work, to the Canteen, or anywhere these days. When I'd left the library last night, however, I had too many boxes full of heavy books to carry them home myself.

After we took the first load into the Canteen and returned to my car, I tried to snap her out of her mood. "I think the servicemen will be happy to see all these books to choose from, don't you?"

She made a vague sound of agreement, but didn't actually speak.

She started to turn, barely able to see over the boxes, but I grabbed two boxes off the stack, and she finally looked up.

"What?" She sounded like someone coming out of a deep sleep.

"That's what I'd like to know. What's going on? What's the matter?"

She started to walk back into the Canteen, but I tugged on her arm.

I lowered my voice. "Rose? What's going on?"

Her face reddened. "I had a hard day yesterday, that's all. It's nothing important."

She shrugged off my hand and headed into the Canteen, so I followed. When we got back to the car for the last trip, I stood in front of her, blocking her way. "Come on. Is everything okay at home? Did you get bad news from Harry? What's going on?"

She leaned against the side of my car, her arms laced around her own waist. "I got a letter from Harry a couple of days ago—good news, really. He was still in the hospital on D-Day, so he's safe and not ready for active duty yet. The Army has assigned him office work until he's deemed fit again. I was relieved and happy and made the mistake of reading his letter again during lunch."

I nodded. "And what happened then?"

She stared down at the ground. "Mary Beth Morris grabbed the letter out of my hand and, before I could get it back, she'd read most of it and started…well, she was taunting me about Harry."

I sat on the lip of the trunk, looking up at her. "What do you mean 'taunting'?"

Rose's gaze met mine; her eyes narrowed. "She was joking with some of the other girls because I've never…well, I've never had a date. Some of the boys have asked over the years, but I never said yes. I didn't want to. So, Mary Beth was teasing me, saying I had a soldier man convinced of my love, but when he comes home, won't he be disappointed? I'll turn him down like I do all the boys."

"What does she care if you go out on dates or not?"

She shrugged. "One of the boys who asked me was her older brother, Bob. Mary Beth found out last week he was killed on D-Day."

"I'm so sorry to hear that." I said as I took one of her hands in mine. "I'm sure Mary Beth and her family are in pain, and that's why she lashed out at you. She probably doesn't even realize how much pain she's in."

She nodded, but her eyes filled with tears again. "I understand. I feel so bad for her, you know, about Bob, and sad for him, too."

I stood. "But then why is this bothering you so much?"

She swallowed and whispered. "What if it's true?"

I put my arm around her shoulder. "Why do you think it could be true? You weren't in love with any of the other boys who asked you out, but you're in love with Harry, right?"

"Sure." She nodded. "But I'm scared. What will I do when Harry wants to touch me? I mean, if we're going to be married, he's going to want to hold my hand, kiss me, even more, right?"

I tilted my head. "Have you talked to your mother about this?"

She shook her head vigorously and started to pull away. "Forget it!"

I held tightly to the girl. "How's this? We'll take the last of these boxes inside. Once we've displayed some of the books, I'll let Mrs. Bellows know we have an errand to run, and you and I will take a walk, so we're less likely to be overheard. How's that?"

She nodded and followed me silently into the Canteen.

Once we squared things away inside, I grabbed my hat and we headed back outside. If Trudy thought we were going for more books, let her.

"Why don't we drive my car back to my house and then we can walk back to the Canteen? I won't need the car later." I got into my car and she climbed in the passenger door. It might be easier to start this conversation if we weren't looking at each other, anyway.

I asked her, "What do you know about marriage? About when husband and wife are alone and when they want to have children?"

She was staring so hard at the floor of the car, it looked as if she was wishing it would open and swallow her whole. "I know some."

"Let's start this way, what questions do you have?" While I was certainly no expert, I knew enough to relieve Rose's fears. The kids might call me an old maid or the spinster librarian, but libraries are full of books, and books are full of knowledge.

She mumbled her way through some basic questions about kissing and dating, but clearly had no clue what would be expected of her once she got to the wedding night.

"Honey, I'd be happier if your mother talked to you about this, or at least knew I was answering your questions, but…"

"I already told you, forget it!" Luckily, the car was still moving, so she couldn't jump out.

"Let me finish." She nodded, but her arms were crossed over her chest, and she had a look on her face that could scare a bear. "As I was saying, this is the kind of thing a mother and daughter usually discuss, but you can be sure I never learned anything about this from my mother either. Even though I haven't been married, I can answer your basic questions."

I pulled into the driveway, parked the car behind the house, and we both climbed out. I tried to get close to her as we started walking back to the Canteen, but she seemed to need some distance.

As I explained the basic mechanics of lovemaking, I tried to gauge the girl's reaction. She stayed fairly straight-faced and silent, so I covered as much as I thought she needed. She was only eighteen, and the man she hoped to marry was at war, several thousand miles away.

"Does it make sense to you, honey? Do you have any questions?"

She walked in silence for a while, but then drifted closer to me. "These feelings; this is something a man feels for a woman, for his wife, right?"

I nodded. "Well, he can feel those feelings for a woman who isn't his wife, but hopefully, they get married before they act on them. Sometimes it doesn't work that way, though."

She held her head low. "Why would a father have those feelings, try to do those things, to his child?" She was whispering again, but the soft sounds nearly broke my heart.

I wanted to wrap my arm around her, but didn't want to scare her off. "Oh, Rose. No man should try to do those things, to have sex with, a child, whether it's his own daughter or some other child. That's wrong, sweetheart."

She nodded, but said nothing.

I tentatively put my hand out, patting her back. When she didn't pull away, I wrapped my arm around her and pulled her in tight. "Is that what happened with your father?"

She nodded, the tears flowing silently down her face. "He came to my room one night, tried to climb into my bed. When I started crying, my mother came in and found him." She took a deep breath and then let it out. "He was taking down his pants."

"Oh, sweetie." I tried to send my strength and love to her through the arm I had around her.

"She started hollering at him, so he quick pulled his pants up, and they went out into the hall. There was lots of yelling, and when I got up in the morning, she said he was gone and was never coming back. I didn't really understand why my daddy was gone, but I was scared."

I nodded. "Of course you were." I took a cleansing breath of my own, trying to reign in my anger at a man I'd never met. If I'd been Trixie, I might have killed him. "Your mother protected you and saved you from him, as any good mother would."

She nodded. "I understand that now." She was silent for a moment. "But she's never talked about it at all, only saying she needed me to work more at the boarding house because it was only the two of us now. I thought she was angry at me because I made him leave somehow. That it was my fault he left."

I stopped and pulled Rose into my embrace. After a good long hug, I looked her straight in the eye. "None of this was ever your fault. Your father was to blame. I promise, your mother isn't angry at you for any of it."

She pulled me in for a hug again and then, after a few moments, let me go.

"Do you think…"

I pulled her hand into mine, not wanting to let her go. "What, sweetie?

She swallowed hard and then looked into my eyes. "Do you think I'll be okay, you know, when Harry wants to touch me that way?"

There was the real question, wasn't it? I would pray for them both.

"Of course you will. You're in love with Harry; he's a good man; and you're going to marry him. The love between you and Harry—the intimacy, touching, and sex—will be a normal, happy part of your marriage. You don't have anything to worry about." Please, God…

She seemed relieved.

When we were nearly back to the Canteen, she stopped and looked me in the eye. "You haven't been married, Miss Maggie. Right?"

I smiled. "No. I've told you about this. Fred and I were engaged, not married, before World War 1. While Tom and I may be talking about marriage, we've only been in the same room for about fifteen minutes."

Her cheeks turned a warm shade of pink again. "So…how do you know all this stuff, about marriage and all?"

I smiled. "I read, Rose. I read."

****

August 26, 1944

After the news was announced last night that Paris had been liberated from the Nazis, everyone who walked into the Canteen early on Saturday morning was smiling. All the troops coming through the station all day, even though boys headed to the Pacific, seemed to have a spring in their step. We were making progress against the Germans to the east and the Japanese to the west. The tides had finally turned. We were going to win this war.

The only cloud on my personal horizon was I hadn't gotten a letter from Tom in weeks. While none of my letters or packages were returned, thank God, I needed to hear from him to be reassured he was safe and well.

"Good morning, Maggie," Sue called, as I passed her table. "Isn't it a beautiful day?"

I waved in her direction. "Yes, Sue, it is. You heard about Paris, right?"

She nodded. "I think every American is a Parisian today."

When Trudy came into the Canteen a few minutes later wearing a beret, I caught Sue's eye, and we both smiled.

Rose and her mother walked in about five minutes later. Trixie didn't often have time to work the Canteen, but as this was a regular North Platte volunteer day, it was nice she came.

"Good morning, Trixie. How nice to see you."

Trixie smiled at me. "Thanks, Maggie. Nice to see you, too. What a wonderful day." She waved as she walked into the kitchen.

I turned to Rose. "How are you this morning?"

She shrugged. "Good."

I tilted my head. "Did you hear the Allies liberated Paris yesterday? That the Nazis fled the city?"

She nodded. "Yeah, that's great."

Her enthusiasm was decidedly underwhelming.

"What's the matter?"

She looked toward the kitchen door, but then turned back. "I had a big fight with my mother last night."

Oh, no. Maybe she took my advice about talking to Trixie about what happened with her father didn't go well. "What happened?"

She shook her head. "She's been on my case all summer, ever since graduation. She keeps harping about what I'm going to do with my life. That I should get a job, go to school, something. She says I can't simply volunteer at the Canteen and wait for Harry to come home."

I nodded, but she was getting wound up, so I let her say her piece.

"Like there are so many great jobs out there anyway. I enjoy volunteering at the Canteen, and I can't wait for Harry to come home so we can get married and move away from her…uh, here."

Interesting. Clearly she hadn't worked out her issues with her mother yet.

I patted her back. "Have you thought about what kind of job might appeal to you?"

"Not really." She shrugged. "I did okay in school, but I don't want to be a teacher. It's too much work, between working all day in the school and all the work they have to take home at night."

"Teaching is a demanding job, that's for sure."

"The best thing about working here is getting to make all the servicemen and women smile simply by helping them."

I smiled. "I know what you mean. It makes me feel good to help them."

"What kind of job might give me that feeling?"

"Maybe something where you get to serve the public."

"Like what? Working in a diner?" She turned her nose up at that.

I laughed. "I was thinking you should volunteer at the library for a while to see if you like helping people find what they need there."

She turned to me, meeting my gaze. "You help people in the library?"

I laughed out loud, but felt bad when I saw I'd hurt her feelings. "Sorry, but what exactly did you think I did all day?"

The girl blushed. "I don't know. I've never really thought about it. I figured you put books away, moved them around, and dusted them. I thought it was more about books than people."

"The books are there for people to use, right?"

She nodded.

"Certainly, people come to the library for books, so I help them find ones they will enjoy reading. People come to the library to find out information on many different topics, and I help them with their research. They come to read newspapers and magazines, so I decide which ones we should order and keep updated. Students come for help with homework, so I spend a lot of time in the afternoons either working with the kids myself or finding someone who can. Sometimes, people come to be around others for company, so I set up presentations and groups, particularly for our older patrons. My work at the library is mostly about helping people."

"Nice."

"Come to the library tomorrow, and I'll show you around."

She shook her head. "I've been there plenty of times."

I chuckled softly. "You haven't been there plenty of times, and you definitely haven't seen everything there is to the library. A good library is like the center of a community, where everyone is welcome for many different reasons."

"Okay, I'll come, but I'm not sure I'll want to work there. I don't know if I could stand to work somewhere so quiet all the time."

I smiled. "Fair enough. Come take a look around with me. If nothing else, there is a community bulletin board where businesses advertise if they want to hire employees. And the newspapers have a 'help wanted' section, so you can check those out and see what other types of jobs are available."

Just then, the call that the coffee was on came echoing through the station and the first train arrived. Time to go.

CHAPTER TWENTY-TWO

March 31, 1962

"For she's a jolly good fellow, and nobody can deny! Yay!"

The library workers weren't the best singers, but I had tears in my eyes. They were very sweet, and Rose's face glowed. She'd even brought me a cake.

"Thank you all so much. I didn't expect such a fuss." Even though I put in for my official retirement as of April 1, I was going to continue working at the library as a volunteer. Also, I planned to join the library board, so I wasn't completely leaving. It was sweet of everyone to throw me a retirement party, nonetheless.

"Well, we couldn't let you sneak out without a celebration, Miss Maggie. You practically *are* the North Platte Library. None of us can imagine what it will be like tomorrow, to come in and not have you here." Bill Regan was the new head librarian, as of tomorrow. He had worked for me since he got home from the war in 1945, and it was long past time for him to step up. Even if some of the people in town didn't believe a man could be a librarian, he had earned the job.

"That's very sweet, Bill, but I imagine in a week's time, you'll forget to miss me."

All of the part-time workers and volunteers gathered around, clapping and claiming they couldn't get by without me, but mostly they wanted cake.

Rose dished out the cake, but had to rush out early to get her children. "I'll talk to you later." She kissed my cheek.

"Thanks for the delicious cake, sweetie."

After everyone went home, only Bill and I were left in the office. I was cleaning out my desk, filling boxes with a lifetime of memories.

"When did you start working at the library, Maggie?" When there were no other employees around, he dispensed with the "Miss Maggie" bit.

I smiled. "My first day of work, for which I was not paid a cent, was in 1913. I was fourteen years old and begged to be allowed to work here as a volunteer."

"Fourteen? I can't believe they let you work so young." Bill shook his head.

"Well, times were different. I really wanted to get a paying job at the library, and heaven knows, we needed the money, but I knew I had a lot to learn, so I started as a volunteer."

"Well, thank you to the library gods that someone had the sense to hire you eventually."

I laughed. "And here we are, fifty-one years later, and I'm still not done."

He nodded. "Having you on the board will be a great help to the library, never mind how you are graciously volunteering your time on the weekends. I can't afford to hire weekend staff, so if we didn't have the volunteers, we'd have to close our doors."

I nodded. "Don't I know it, Bill. The budget will be the hardest part of this job, but I think you're the man to handle it. And I think it's so important to the people of this community, especially the students, to be able to come to the library on the weekends, when they aren't busy with school or work. It's a valuable service to the community, so I'm happy to help."

As I finished emptying out my drawers, Bill picked up my boxes and started carrying them to the back door. I had my car parked in the back lot, like all the employees were supposed to do. With fifty years of accumulation in this office, I was not too proud to accept Bill's help getting these boxes to my car.

The last thing he loaded into the car was the leftover cake. I had told Bill my family would be celebrating my retirement tonight as well, so he suggested I take the leftovers home, as we might as well not let the cake go to waste. Of course, when the library employees showed up tomorrow, I could image they would have been all too happy to eat the rest of the cake.

When everything was packed into the back of my station wagon, Bill gave me a hug, which embarrassed him more than it did me, and then said he'd see me next week at my first board meeting. I was going to be back at the library on Saturday, but would have most of the weekend hours to myself.

I drove home, something I still rarely did, except on those bitter cold winter mornings which made my arthritis act up. As I pulled into the driveway, my granddaughter, Lisa, was running around in the back yard, being chased by her father, and squealing with delight. At six, she was already tall and blonde, like her mother, and the apple of her grandpa's eye. Well, mine too, if I was honest with myself.

My handsome husband bounded down the back door to help me with my boxes. How was it possible he still bounded anywhere, at our age?

He planted a kiss on my lips and made quick work of carrying the boxes into the garage. I'd pour over them in time and decide what to do with everything in there. As I walked to the backyard to grab a quick hug and kiss from Lisa, my daughter stopped me, bending to pick up an envelope off the ground.

She leaned in and gave me a kiss, before handing me the envelope. "Looks like this fell out of one of the boxes, Mom."

"Oh, thanks, honey."

"Grandma!" Lisa came running for me and I stooped to hold out my arms for her.

"There's my girl." I scooped her up and stood, smothering her face with kisses and she squealed.

"Careful, Mom." My daughter stood at my elbow, apparently sure I would fall apart now I was no longer gainfully employed.

"We're good," I said, hitching Lisa up onto my hip. "What are you up to, young lady?"

She told me about her day, her friends' days, and her plans for tomorrow, but finally stopped to look me in the eye. "We're having a party."

I smiled. "Well, yes, we are."

She poked my nose with her finger. "Your tired-est party."

I laughed, and my husband chuckled beside me. "My retirement party, you mean."

"Yup!" Lisa wiggled until I put her down and then started running again, looking back now and then to make sure someone was chasing her.

She might have liked chasing in the snow-covered yard, but I was getting cold. "Let's go inside. The wind is picking up."

My husband took my bags in his left hand and my hand in his right one. My daughter held open the door as we climbed the back stairs. Once we were inside, I took off my coat and hung it in the closet, dropping my boots by the back door.

My son-in-law scooped up Lisa and was bringing the squiggling girl into the house, muttering something about cake. As soon as her boots and coat came off, she took off running through the house, squealing about cake. Luckily, my daughter had already hidden it away in the kitchen.

"Did you have a good last day?" My guy pulled me into his arms, making a quiet moment for us. He'd always been good at that.

"I did. It was nice and not too many tears. Of course, I'm working again on Saturday, so this could explain why."

He laughed. "How is the cake, by the way?"

I smiled. "You'll like it. It's a little too sweet for me, but it was very kind of Rose to take time out of her busy day to make it and bring it by."

"Did she cry?" He knew her so well.

I nodded. "Of course she did. That's our Rose."

"Why don't you have a seat and relax, and I'll help get dinner on the table?"

I laughed. "You don't have to ask me twice. I'm beat."

****

June 6, 1964
To the Volunteers of the North Platte Canteen

I remember well the lovely women and delicious food I had both the first and second times my brother Roland and I stopped in North Platte. Our buddies told us about how great you all were and they sure were right. Yours was the best food I ate during the whole war.

I wanted to write and thank you, for both Roland and me, but it's been hard coming home knowing he will be in Normandy forever. Roland was killed on D-Day, twenty years ago today.

Even though we were both on those beaches, I didn't know he had been killed for a month, and our dear mother didn't get the news until the end of July. It was very hard for our family to lose Roland, and I apologize for taking so long to write to you with our thanks.

We all lost a lot of wonderful men—brothers, fathers, sons, husbands, and friends—during World War II, but especially on that bloody day twenty years ago. Thank you for showing us your love and appreciation while Roland was still alive to receive it.

Sincerely and gratefully yours, Walt Rogers

CHAPTER TWENTY-THREE

September 15, 1944

Rose and I walked from the library to the Canteen together to see if any volunteers were needed. It turned out the towns of Julesburg and Ovid, Colorado were working the Canteen and had plenty of people to help.

While the Canteen was buzzing with activity, all the stations were covered, so we weren't necessary, and we didn't want to step in on their volunteer day.

As we left the Canteen and stepped back out on the sidewalk, we started walking toward my house.

"I guess we have our Friday night free." I turned to her. "Why don't you call Jewel or some of the other girls from school and see if they have plans for tonight?"

She looked down at the ground. "I really don't see any of those girls very much anymore, now school is over."

"Why do you think that is?"

She shrugged. "I don't know. I guess I didn't really have too much in common with them, except for school, and now we don't even have that. I don't have much to talk to those girls about."

"So, what do you do with your spare time these days?"

She glanced at me, apparently surprised. "How can you even ask? I'm at the Canteen, at the boarding house, or volunteering at the library. I don't have a lot of free time."

The Canteen had been accumulating more and more volunteers, so even I wasn't working there as many hours as I had at the beginning. "With all the towns and volunteers that have signed up to work, there aren't many 'North Platte' days at the Canteen each month, so you can't spend too many hours there."

"Sure, but sometimes those other towns still need help. They don't always have as many volunteers as tonight."

Often, the smaller communities needed help with both volunteers and fund-raising. Each community raised money of their own, and the town of North Platte maintained a budget fueled by donations, fundraising efforts, and penny drives. With everyone saving up to buy war bonds as well, the people of North Platte were strapped.

When we got to my house, I poured us each some iced tea, left the glasses on the table, and then left her in the kitchen. After peaking in at Mother in the parlor, I eased the door shut, gathered my box of Canteen mail and scrapbooks, and brought them to the kitchen table. "You can help me sort through some of this…" gesturing to the box, "…if you don't mind."

She smiled. "Sure, I'd be happy to help."

We pulled out the photo taken of the list of volunteer cities. "Amazing how far some of the volunteers come to help out, isn't it?"

I took out the current scrapbook and started adding in letters, newspaper articles, and photos as Rose handed them to me.

"What's this?" She held up a slip of paper with some handwriting.

I took it. "This is one day's donations. I asked the women to track for me last week. The towns of Merna and Anselmo were there. They came seventy miles in twenty-two cars and three pick-up trucks. Their volunteers brought fifty-three birthday cakes, 127 fried chickens, fifty-eight dozen cookies, thirty-two dozen cupcakes, seventy-three pounds of coffee, 163 dozen eggs, sixty-eight dozen doughnuts, forty-one quarts of pickles, three crates of oranges, nine pounds of ham, 160 loaves of bread, forty popcorn balls, fifty pounds of sandwich meat, four carts of cigarettes, four decks of cards, and $600 in cash."

She whistled. "Wow, that's incredible. And those are small towns, too."

I nodded. "I think between them, they don't have more than 500 people in total. They prepared to meet 5,000 servicemen and woman in one day, and I believe it may have even been more."

She smiled. "The troops were probably pretty happy when they saw all the glorious food."

She flipped through the pages I'd already completed. "Incredible. I didn't realize we'd had people come through from so many of our Allied countries."

I nodded. "Yes, we've had servicemen from England, China, Russia, France, Brazil, and Norway. I wish I could have met them all."

She looked through those pages again. "Me, too." She poured over the cards and letters with a dreamy look in her eyes. "Can you imagine what it must be like for them, coming from so many exotic places and ending up in boring old North Platte?"

Sighing, I shook my head. "I doubt any of those Allied soldiers thought of North Platte as boring when they stepped off the train to free food, drinks, reading material, and moral support."

Chuckling, Rose said, "I suppose your right. I just can't help but think how exciting it would be to visit some of these places, maybe even move there." She looked me in the eyes. "After the war, of course."

"Once our men get home, they might not be that anxious to leave the good old U.S.A. again, at least not any time soon."

She turned to the next page of the scrapbook, looking a little forlorn. "True. But at least you kept the envelopes with their thank-you letters. The stamps, the paper, and the handwriting are beautiful."

"I was so excited when their letters arrived."

Rose pulled out another sheet of paper. "Holy cow! This is from the White House." She handed it to me.

Smiling, I added it to the scrapbook. "President Roosevelt heard about what we're doing here in North Platte and sent us a $5 bill. It's the only money we've taken from the federal government."

She laughed. "Not like the money Gene Slattery has been raising."

Gene Slattery was nine years old when the war broke out, but he'd done more than his share for the Canteen. While at a cattle auction one day, he jumped up and said he'd auction the shirt off his back and donate the money to the Canteen. After the first time was so successful, he'd done it over and over again, raising thousands of dollars.

"I'm glad a lot of people gave him back his shirt." She smoothed the photo down on the page of the scrapbook.

"Gene's been doing great work, but I'm glad O'Connor's Department Store has been donating shirts for Gene to auction off, so his family doesn't have to bear the burden of that cost, as well."

She leafed through more of the letters, helping me get them in chronological and alphabetical order. "What do you think of the women who come through the Canteen?"

She was looking down at the letters, so I couldn't see her expression well.

"What do you mean? The volunteers?"

She shook her head. "No, the servicewomen, you know, the nurses, the Army and Navy women in uniform, even the Red Cross volunteers. Why do you think they joined up?"

"President Roosevelt charged all of us to find a way to contribute to the war effort. Some women serve their local communities as volunteers, like with plane spotters in coastal areas or at the local Canteens. Some women serve by keeping their family farms running or taking over businesses for men who have gone to war. Lots of women have taken jobs in factories making tanks, airplanes, guns, and other war machinery. I think the women who join one of the armed forces, whether as a nurse or in some other role, want to take a more active role, doing essential war work, whether it's somewhere in the United States or abroad."

Her gaze met mine. "Do you think I should have done something like that? I'm young and healthy. I could be doing more for the war."

"Think of the faces of those servicemen, and the women, too, who come through the Canteen and eat the eggs you peeled, the sandwiches you made, or even the popcorn balls we make at my house. Do you think they wish you were in the Navy instead?"

She chuckled softly. "No."

I nodded. "That's right. What we're doing at the Canteen is important. All the war work is, even though it's all different. Just think of all of these people writing to us to give us thanks for helping them."

I motioned to the piles of mail we'd just sorted. "We're getting so many thank you notes, I don't know where we're going to store them all. Look at this one." I passed a card to her.

September 1, 1944

To the fine ladies of North Platte, NE

Never once did this country boy from Maine expect to ever be in Nebraska. I couldn't believe my eyes when I got off the train at your Canteen. In all the 50 states, in fact the whole world, there is no equal to the beautiful people of your fine city.

I hope I come through North Platte again on my way back home so I can give you my thanks personally, but if it doesn't happen, for one reason or another, know I have thought of you all often.

Eternally grateful, Robert Lewis, Camden, Maine

After Rose and I organized all of the letters and photos, I carried all of my Canteen boxes up into my bedroom. When I came back downstairs, my mother was in the kitchen yelling at Rose. "What are you doing in my house? This is my house, not yours. You get out now, girl. You tramp. You're probably trying to steal all the good silver and all my jewelry. I'll call the police if you don't get out of here. Go on home." Mother was unsteady on her feet, leaning on the back of a kitchen chair, but waving her index finger in Rose's face.

Rose was edging off her chair, her face pale and her eyes wide. She started to stand, was probably planning to run, when I walked in and put my hand on her shoulder.

"Just sit, Rose." I turned to my mother. "Go on. Get out of here. Go back to your radio program and leave us alone."

She drifted near me, her ire focused on me now. "Don't get so bossy with me, girl. I'm still your mother and, as long as you're in my house, you'll do as I say."

I walked close to my mother, staring her down. She smelled of whiskey and her eyes were glazed, but she could tell I was in no mood for her temper. She backed up a step.

"As you well know, this is *my* house. You haven't paid a dime or done a lick of work around here in more years than either of us can remember. You don't have to live here, but if you're going to, just go to your room, and leave us alone."

My mother crumpled, her bravado gone, although she tried to hide it. "You ungrateful child," she mumbled as she turned and plodded back to the parlor. "No way to treat your mother."

"Ha! Don't even try your guilt on me. I'm passed that. Just go away and don't bother my friend again."

Once she retreated to the parlor and closed the door, I turned back to face Rose. "I'm sorry. I wish you didn't have to see that, or her, but sometimes she drinks too much and forgets how pitiful she really is."

She nodded, but stayed silent. I pulled my handkerchief from my pocket, dabbing at the tears trying to leak from my eyes.

"Mother has always had a drinking problem. After my father died, it just got worse. Day to day, I wasn't sure if I was going to have anything to eat or if she might have burned the house down while I was at school. She was completely erratic, and I don't believe it was due to grief. That's why I started volunteering at the library when I was fourteen.

I knew I'd need a job to be able to take care of myself. Dad had always cautioned me about financial responsibility. He used to take me to the bank with him, and we'd talk about why the bank approved or denied loans to different people. He instilled in me a sense of independence that allowed me to pay off the back taxes on this house and end up buying it outright. Once she couldn't threaten to kick me out of it, I stopped falling for her pathetic whining. We rarely talk."

Rose looked up. "You live in the same house and don't talk to her?"

I shook my head. "All she does is complain about how hard her life is, and I don't want to hear it anymore. She stays in the parlor and her bedroom, which is off the parlor at the front of the house. We share the kitchen and the bathroom, but never see each other deliberately."

She reached out her left hand, resting it on my right one. "I'm sorry, that your mother is...well, the way she is." She pressed her lips together before continuing. "I fight with my mother from time to time, but nothing like this."

I nodded. "Good. I hope not. You should work things out with your mother. It'll be worth it."

She shook her head but didn't answer.

"Want to go to the movie show?" We still had a lot of Saturday left.

She perked up. "What's playing?"

I smiled. "When I walked by the Paramount this morning, I saw they are showing *Since You Went Away* with Claudette Colbert. I've been hoping to see it."

She stood, clapping her hands. "Me, too. Let's go!"

By the time the movie was over, the bad mood which started after my run-in with Mother had turned into full-blown melancholy. While the movie was good, and I was a big fan of Claudette Colbert and Shirley Temple, the story had made me sad.

"It was so sad when Bill was killed." Even Rose seemed more subdued then when the movie started.

I nodded. "I agree. It was all a little too close for comfort these days."

She turned to meet my gaze. "You're right. They should only make happy movies in the middle of the war. No pictures about soldiers dying at the front. What are they thinking?" Her voice got louder as we walked away from the theatre.

"The newsreels are enough to deal with. I don't want to see my favorite actors dealing with the war. What about some escapism, like *The Wizard of Oz*?"

She nodded. "You're right. That would be so much better. Or musicals, where everyone is dancing and singing. Fred Astaire and Ginger Rogers always make me smile."

I laughed. "Especially after I got to dance with him."

We walked on in quiet, headed for her house.

After a few minutes, she leaned her head on my shoulder. "Are you worried about Tom, you know, after the newsreel about the battle of the Philippine Sea?"

I couldn't deny it, but wouldn't really admit it either. I nodded and laid my head on the top of hers and held onto her hand as we walked.

I hadn't heard from Tom in weeks now and, late at night, when I wrote him my daily letter, even I had to admit I was frightened he might not come home. He couldn't control his time and might not be able to write, but when so much time passed between letters, my worry mounted.

Eventually, she stood up and put her arm around my shoulders. "I'm sure he's coming home. There's nothing to worry about."

I smiled. "What makes you so sure? Do you have some secret information the rest of us don't?"

She chuckled, as I hoped she would. "I have faith in Tom and in the Lord. I don't think God would have brought you this man to fall in love with if he wasn't going to come back to you when the war is over."

We said our good-byes at the corner of her street. When I got back to my own house, it was quiet. Mother had surely retreated into her parlor and her whiskey bottle, and I probably wouldn't be bothered by her again. I fixed myself some dinner, ate quickly at the table, and headed up to my bedroom. I found the day's mail waiting on my bed. My mother never came upstairs, but she must have felt bad about causing a scene with Rose.

Either way, I was grateful to pick up the stack of mail and, in addition to a letter from a nurse I was becoming quite friendly with, at the bottom of the stack, I saw three envelopes written in Tom's handwriting, numbered one through three on the outside.

August 31, 1944
My dear Maggie,

I'm sorry you haven't gotten a letter from me in a while, but you can (hopefully) see I have been writing anyway. I numbered them so you'd know which one to read first, even though the others were written earlier.

I know the news has released some of the facts of what has been going on over here in the Philippine Sea on Guam, Saipan, Tinian, and the rest. We have been involved in a great deal of fighting, and I'm sorry if the lack of mail worried you.

Rest assured, I was always thinking of you.

We weren't allowed to send or receive any letters for weeks. My men made it through fairly successfully, although we did suffer some losses, which is always hard.

Even before sending your letters, I had to send several to parents of young men who will not come home. That is the hardest part of my duties and one I will not miss once I leave the Army, for even in peacetime, men die in the military. Before I started imagining a life at home with you, I was better able to detach from the emotions of this kind of letter and give the family members more details of their husband's or son's military record and acts of valor.

Now, imagining how you would react at receiving such a letter about me, I find it harder to leave my own emotions out of the letters. I imagine the future each young man might have had upon returning home, and it's hard to come up with the right words.

This war needs to end before there are no young men left.

Enough of this. I'll get emotional all over again, and the only emotion I want in this letter is my love and happiness at having you to write to and come home to. Marry me, Maggie. Don't just wait for me, meet me at the station, or see me when I'm home.

Marry me. Be my wife. Let's make a home together.

Please say yes, even though it's crazy, and I'm crazy, because I'm crazy in love with you. If we've learned nothing else from our two world wars, we know life is short and precious. Let's not waste a moment of it.

The letters numbered 2 and 3 are regular letters, with the news of what's been going on; asking you questions about what's new with you, the library, the Canteen, and your friends. That's why I numbered this letter first. I wanted you to know I'm committed to you. I want to know everything about you and spend the rest of my life making you happy. Please make me the happiest man in the world by saying yes.

All my love, now and forever, Tom

CHAPTER TWENTY-FOUR

September 20, 1944

Before I could even knock on Sue's front door, she pulled it open.

"Oh, Maggie, right on time." She leaned in and gave me a hug. Although I'd never been much of a hugger, Sue was big on hugs. I was learning.

She grasped my hand and led me into the house, taking my coat and hat. "I'm so glad you could join us today. It's so much more fun to do together."

Sue had stopped me at the Canteen on Monday and invited me to join her regular knitting group as they made socks, mufflers, and hats for the Red Cross. I was used to knitting alone in my room at night, so I was looking forward to spending time with Sue and her friends.

When I walked into the parlor, I saw Ann Tenney already working on a project with a beautiful blue yarn. "Hi, Ann."

She looked up from her stitching. "Hi, Maggie. I'm so glad you could join us today."

Sue came back into the parlor with a cup of tea for me. "I don't know who else will be joining us tonight. But, I'm glad you could make it."

Over the past few months at the Canteen, my burgeoning friendship with both of these women had become a joy to me. I was comfortable around them, and we were of a similar age. Both women were married with children; in fact, Ann often brought hers into the library, but neither made me feel uncomfortable because I'd never married.

Married.

I hadn't been able to think about much else since I got Tom's letter proposing to me. This was the longest I'd gone in a couple of years without writing to him, but I couldn't answer him until I knew what to say.

"Is everything all right, Maggie?"

I looked at Ann and saw she and Sue were both looking at me with concern, their knitting momentarily forgotten.

I let out a breath and looked down. It was only the three of us, and I trusted that I could talk to Ann and Sue confidentially. I wasn't ready for my news to be common knowledge I knew what I wanted to say about it.

I dropped my knitting into my lap, took a deep breath, and looked back up at them.

"As I've mentioned, I have been writing to an Army captain…"

Sue nodded. "Tom, right?"

I smiled. "Yes, Tom Carter. We met at the Canteen when he came through with his troops in December of 1941." It seemed, simultaneously, like yesterday and many years ago.

Ann started knitting again, but her eyes stayed mostly focused on me. She had to be a good knitter to look so rarely at her stitches. "So, soon after we started the Canteen, right?"

I nodded. "Yes. He started writing to me the next day and kept after me to write back, being very charming, but I really wasn't interested in a war-time romance."

Sue nodded. "I understand. It's hard to love someone who is far away, and in danger." Sue's husband was somewhere in France and Ann's was in the Pacific theater. They both seemed to hold up well under the pressure, but in private moments, the strain, undoubtedly, got to them, too.

"Right." I took a few stitches on my knitting, then abandoned it again. "Well, I finally gave in and started writing him. He's been career Army since WW1 and has been in the Aleutian Islands and is now in Guam. We've gotten to know each other very well, and slowly…well, I've fallen in love with him."

Sue smiled. "That's wonderful."

Ann looked up from her knitting, catching my gaze. "What's wrong, Maggie? Has something happened?"

I nodded, glancing down at my hands and trying to find the right words. "I believe he's in love with me, too. He certainly says he loves me in nearly every letter, and we've talked about a future after the war. He wants to retire from the Army and move to North Platte."

Sue clapped her hands. "Congratulations! It sounds like we're going to be hearing wedding bells."

I felt the tears in my eyes, although I couldn't explain why they were there. Ann took one of my hands. "What is it?"

Looking up, I met her gaze. "In his last letter, he proposed."

Ann waited, not reacting, although Sue inhaled. After dropping her knitting onto her lap, she crossed her hand over her heart. "Are you happy?"

"Have you answered him yet?" Ann asked.

I shook my head. "No, he wrote four days ago, and I usually write every day. I need to write to him, or he'll be terribly worried." I looked to Sue. "I don't know what to do."

Sue walked over to me, crouching down at my feet and placing her hands on knees. "Do you want to marry him when he comes home? You said you're in love with him. Do you want to be his wife?"

I took in a deep breath and slowly released it. "I think so. I picture us living at my house, without my mother," I chuckled. "I like the way it feels to think about being his wife, Mrs. Carter, but then I start to panic." My voice was getting higher.

Sue moved into the chair on my left and Ann sat to my right. They formed a circle of strength—an instant support system.

Ann nodded. "I can only imagine how frightening this is for you. I'm scared every day of this war, not only that Joe will be injured or worse, but also he won't be the man I married by the time he comes home to me."

Sue nodded. "I understand what you mean. Martin has always been a quiet, gentle man. I don't know how it's possible for a man like that to fight a war and stay true to who he is. I'm afraid he'll come home changed somehow, and the man he becomes will change our marriage and how our life together has always been."

"That makes sense." I thought of Rose. "Some men have such a bad time with shell shock, or battle fatigue, or whatever they call it, they have a hard time getting over it."

Ann put her arm around my shoulders. "Exactly. Even if they come back unharmed, with all their arms and legs and everything, who knows what they've been through?"

"I didn't know Tom before the war, so I don't have to worry as much about how he's changed. But, I do worry I don't know him very well and have only spent about fifteen minutes with him. How can I possibly think of marrying him?"

Sue chuckled. "Many couples fall in love in those first fifteen minutes, even without a war going on." She smiled. "I know it was that way for us. Martin walked into my ninth-grade homeroom, sat down in the empty chair next to mine, and that was it. As soon as our eyes met, we knew we were meant to be together."

I put my hand on Sue's arm. "That's wonderful. You are so lucky."

She nodded. "Yes, we are. And that's why I'm so afraid he won't be that man when he comes home." She stood up and retrieved her knitting. "But, I try very hard to choose to believe we will go on being lucky. That he will escape this war intact, mentally and physically, and come home to me and the girls, and our life will be as rich as it ever was."

Ann smiled. "And that's the secret to loving a man at war. You have to believe he will come home to you and everything will be okay. I tell that to my kids every night."

I bowed my head again. "So you think I'm foolish to be worried about saying yes to Tom?"

They both laughed.

"Not at all," said Ann. "You'd be a fool not to be worried."

"True," Sue continued. "Marriage is a risk, and a lot of work, even when you're both in the same place and safe from the danger of battle. War makes it ridiculous." She sighed. "But, I wouldn't change a thing. Martin is the love of my life and worth every moment of worry and fear. I love him and that's it for me."

I took another deep breath, letting a picture of Tom's smiling face fill my mind. "I love Tom." I nodded. "I think I have to say yes. I can't imagine a future where he doesn't come home to me, so why would I say no?"

Again, my friends chuckled, a warm and supportive sound.

"Why, indeed?" Ann said.

I'd have to write to Tom as soon as I got home.

CHAPTER TWENTY-FIVE

October 28, 1944

I headed out the door early, walking to the Canteen for another North Platte volunteer day. I was hoping to catch up on the mail there, as well as unpack a load of donated books Helen said had been delivered on Thursday. We easily had 1,000 requests for reading material every day now, so keeping up with the demand was much of what I did with my off-hours.

Bert, our long-time mailman caught me as I rounded the corner. He handed me the days mail, which I slipped into my pocketbook, but then also dug through his sack for a small box wrapped in brown package. Tom's familiar scrawl covered the top, along with the traditional Army postal markings.

I'd been sending packages to Tom for nearly two-and-a-half years now, but this was the first time I'd gotten one from him.

I thanked Bert, but continued my walk to the Canteen. I didn't necessarily want him telling everyone on his route what "Captain Carter sent Margaret from the Pacific." Bert had always been a gossip.

On my walk, I only made it as far as the front doorway of the Pawnee Hotel before the package was burning a hole in my coat pocket. I stepped off the sidewalk, hiding slightly under the hotel awning, and ripped into the wrapping. The box was white and, when I opened it, I found a small note and a smaller box.

I unfolded the note. "I love you! Please send me a new picture of you wearing the enclosed. Love, Tom."

I opened the small black box and found a stunning diamond engagement ring. Tears filled my eyes. I had no idea he would send me a ring. Where did he even find it?

In my mind, once I sent the letter to Tom saying yes, I would marry him, I always pictured him buying a nice wedding ring, maybe set with some small diamonds, to give me when we actually got married. It never occurred to me he would have a ring, or be able to buy one, anywhere near where he was stationed.

I pulled the ring out of the box, checking to make sure I was alone. I wasn't ashamed of Tom, the ring, or our impending marriage, but if I couldn't share this moment with him, I didn't want to share it with anyone else.

I slid the ring onto my finger, and it was a perfect fit. It sparkled and shone, and I couldn't take my eyes off of it. As I walked the rest of the way to the Canteen, a smile permanently affixed to my face, I couldn't stop pulling my left hand out and staring at the ring.

It felt so heavy on my hand. Would I ever get used to it being there?

My eyes teared up. He really was the best man. How had I ever been so lucky?

I put the ring box back in the outer box with Tom's note and put both into the deep pocket on my coat.

When I walked into the Canteen, I decided to send him a telegram. I never sent them for myself, although I'd sent many for servicemen stopping at the Canteen over the years. It seemed extravagant, but how often does a woman get engaged?

Apparently, for me anyway, twice. I didn't feel guilty about falling in love with Tom. Fred would be happy for me. Heavens knows, I mourned him and the life we had planned together for years. Whenever I thought of him now, I smiled at some silly thing we said or did together or at the love I'd felt for that boy. He was nothing like Tom, but I loved both of them more than life itself. This was a nice feeling.

When I walked into the Canteen, I waved to Ann and Sue, stopping at the periodicals table first, to store my coat, hat, and pocketbook under the table. While we were getting as many as twenty-five trains a day sometimes now, it didn't appear one had arrived yet. I was tempted to show off my ring to my friends, but I wanted to savor my secret joy for a few more moments, before someone noticed.

Within ten minutes, Rose showed up at the table. "Good morning, Miss Maggie."

I looked up. "Oh, hello, Rose dear. How are you this morning?"

She had started to walk past me to her traditional end of the table, but suddenly stopped in her tracks. She stood directly in front of me, uncomfortably close, and looked me up and down, but didn't seem to notice the ring.

"Yes?"

"Something's different this morning." She stared into my eyes. "What's going on?"

The girl would be hurt if I didn't tell her my news. I hadn't mentioned Tom's proposal earlier because Rose was currently in a long-distance disagreement with Harry. While they seemed to be as in love as ever, Harry, apparently, wasn't on the get-out-of-North-Platte-as-quickly-as-possible bandwagon Rose was leading. He liked the idea of living in a small town and thought North Platte, as a small city, was a compromise. She was adamant she wanted to move to a big city, so they were arguing via the U.S. Postal Service.

I asked her to follow me out the Canteen door. I stopped in the entry way of the depot, where fewer Canteen workers would overhear us. I wasn't ready to share my news with everyone.

She looked worried, but then confused when I smiled.

"Okay, I don't want to make a big deal of this in front of the Canteen volunteers, so please keep it to yourself, at least for now."

Her brows came together and small lines bracketed her eyes in a way she'd come to rue in her forties. "Why? What's wrong?"

"Nothing. Tom, well…Tom asked me to marry him, and I said yes." I held up my left hand for her to see, while stealing another glance at it myself.

She started to scream, but I clamped my right hand down on her arm. She immediately stopped, covered her mouth with her other hand, and silently mouthed her scream instead. Finally, once she seemed to have collected herself, she pulled me into a hug.

"Oh my gosh—that's wonderful news. Best wishes to the bride!"

She pulled back, looked into my eyes, gave me another quick hug, and then released me.

I held my right index finger against my lips. "Please don't broadcast it. I got the ring today, and I want to savor it on my own before everyone knows about it."

She smiled. "Of course." She reached for my left hand, bringing it up to her face and turning it side to side. "It's a beautiful ring. Wherever do you think he got it?"

I laughed. "I wondered the same thing. He's a long way from anywhere, as far as I know."

She put her arm through mine, and we walked back into the Canteen. We had just made it back to the periodicals table when Helen announced the arrival of the first troop train. Rose and I started unloading a box of books, but when the servicemen and women came into the Canteen, we had to stop, as we had so many requests for specific items.

Many of the troops coming through that day were replacement troops. The long-running battles in France, and as the Allies made their way toward Germany, were taking their toll on troops in the European theater. Between the wounded soldiers, those killed in action, and the men who had earned enough service points, entitling them to come home, replacement troops were moving out at an alarming rate.

Even though the replacement troops were as young as the soldiers they replaced had been when they'd headed out, these boys seemed cockier and a little less scared than their predecessors. I tried to caution them to be careful, but they joked about now that the Allies had the Axis troops on the run, it was simply a matter of mopping everything up. The war would be over soon, and they'd come home again, only this time as heroes.

Young men can be so foolish. I prayed they would have as easy a time of it as they hoped and that they and all the men would be home safe and soon, despite the reality of war.

****

November 1, 1944

"I'm the worst girlfriend ever." Rose plopped down in the visitor chair in my library office.

The last of the patrons had just left; I'd locked the front doors and was going through the paperwork on my desk. I was hoping to get out early to go meet Ann, Sue, and several other ladies at the knitting circle. We were meeting at Ann's house this time, and I wanted to stop at home and pick up a loaf of zucchini bread I'd made for us to share.

"I find it hard to believe." I looked up. She was sprawled across the chair, her head hanging low, and her legs splayed. "Are you and Harry still fighting?"

She sighed and nodded, without looking up.

"Well, that happens in relationships. You'll work it out."

Her gaze met mine, despondency showing in her beautiful young face. "How am I supposed to know what we'll work out and what we won't? I've never been in a relationship before." She crossed her arms over her chest. "Why does it have to be so hard?"

Suppressing a chuckle that would probably have come across as patronizing, I pasted a sympathetic smile on my face. "Maybe because you chose to have your first relationship—a serious, marriage-oriented one—during a war via letters from thousands of miles away."

Her chin dropped down to her chest again. "I can't believe I was arguing with him by mail, when all the ladies magazines and radio serials talk about keeping the boys happy and not bothering them with domestic details." She leaned forward, placing her forearms on her thighs. "What could be more of a domestic detail than where our domicile will be?"

I smiled at her distress, although I couldn't really mock her. It was hard to avoid writing anything substantive when you write every day and want to plan a future with a man. There were bound to be occasional disagreements.

"I'm sure Harry isn't angry with you. You'll see." She snorted. "You could consider a compromise, you know."

She looked up. "What do you mean?"

I packed my pocketbook with the last minute things I wanted to take home. "You want to live in a big city, and he wants to live in a smaller city or small town. Right?"

She nodded, although her expression fell again. "Right."

"Maybe you could consider living in a small city that isn't North Platte."

If her silence indicated she was thinking about it, her sigh might mean she rejected the idea. "I want him to be happy, but he seems to think he'd only be happy in North Platte. That's what we keep fighting about."

"I understand. But, maybe you could think about an alternative, so you don't have to keep fighting with him via mail."

"That's the thing. I may have sent him into battle angry."

I tilted my head. "Into battle?" Last I knew Harry was slowly recovering from his twice-broken foot with a desk job in London.

She pulled the chair up close and shoved a V-mail letter across the desk to me. "Read it for yourself. I'm the worst girl in the world."

I shook my head, picking up the letter. "I seriously doubt it."

October 10, 1944
To my sweet Rose,

Let's not argue about our home after the war any more—it's not too important right now. What's important is I love you, you love me, we want to be married, and we'll go from there.

My foot has finally been declared full healed, so I am being reinstated to my unit and I'm heading off to "somewhere in France," as they tell us to say. I don't really know what will happen from this point, or how often I'll be able to get or send mail, but please keep those letters and packages coming.

The boys on the front have been making great strides, but I'm anxious about joining my unit again, as they are much more seasoned soldiers than me now. I've been sitting on my backside in an office for months and haven't done more than clean my rifle.

Please pray for me, Rosie. I don't mind saying I'm scared. We may have beaten the Nazis back from the beaches of France and liberated Paris, but there's still a lot more ground to cover.

Please know I love you with all my heart and don't care where I live with you as long as I get to lay down beside you each night and wake up next to you each morning. Nothing else matters.

I kiss your picture good night, but wish I were able to kiss you in person. Please keep me and my buddies in your prayers, and listen for good news from the front lines.

All my love forever and ever – Harry

I could understand why Rose was upset and worried, as Harry had spent a lot of time away from the front lines, and he might not be able to slide back into his unit easily. He was afraid, and so was she. I got up and walked around the desk, kneeling down at her side.

"Now you see what I mean. I've been fighting with him, writing terrible, selfish letters to a man who is thousands of miles away, who loves me and wants to be with, as he prepares to go fight the Nazis and maybe get killed." Her voice got higher, her face redder, and her breaths started coming more quickly. "Then it won't matter where we agree to live after the war because there won't be any life together at all."

Tears poured down her face, even as she rested it in her hands. Her shoulders shook.

I put my arms around her, patting her gently on the back.

"You are not a mean person, and you're not selfish. You're young and very far away from the man you love. It's okay to be focused on life after the war sometimes. Harry isn't going to be angry with you for making those plans. It lets him know you love him and want him to come home. Right?"

She kept crying, but didn't disagree.

"He wants you to pray for him and his buddies, so let's do what he asks, okay? It's the best thing we can do for these soldiers, along with sending them our love in letters and packages. So, we'll bake, knit, write, and pray, okay?"

She nodded. "Do you really think both Harry and Tom can make it home safely after the war? Can we possibly both be so lucky?

I took a deep breath. "I don't see any other outcome in my mind. I worry and I pray, but I also completely believe they will both come home to us."

"But North Platte has already lost five men to this war. Why should we be luckier than Mrs. Bellows or any of the families who have suffered a loss?"

I shrugged. "I don't know. Anything is possible. But in the depths of my heart and soul, I truly believe Tom and Harry will come home safe and sound. And I have to keep going, day to day, as if what I feel to be true really is true. I have Tom's ring on my finger, and he's in my heart. I can't even imagine what it would feel like to lose him like I did Fred. It feels different this time."

Rose wiped her face on her handkerchief. I stood and pulled her to her feet.

"Go on home, now. Write to Harry; tell him how much you love him and you'll live anywhere he wants to live."

She started to speak, but I put my index finger against her lips.

"Does it matter *where* you live with Harry or *that* you live with Harry after the war? What's more important?"

She nodded. "What's important is that he comes home to me, wherever home is."

I smiled. "Exactly, so tell him that. Then, come over to my house tomorrow night after work, and we'll bake something to send to our men. Okay?"

She smiled, her eyes still puffy and rimmed in red. "Okay. Who knows when either of them will get our packages, but it would make me feel better."

"Good."

She walked out of my office and I sat again at my desk. If I finished this paperwork quickly, I could still get to the knitting circle. It would be good to have a productive evening with friends. Tomorrow, I'd make up a package to send Tom and that would ease my jitters as well.

While what I told Rose was true, I did believe both men would make it home safely after the war, I felt unsettled about something. My feelings about Tom were different than the cold fear I'd felt while Fred was at the front lines. I couldn't explain why I'd never believed Fred would come home, but I absolutely believed Tom would. Still, something nagged at me.

I clung to the euphoria of the engagement and everyone's excitement at seeing my ring, but it didn't dull the underlying buzz I felt that something bad was going to happen.

Obviously, Tom was on the front lines of a war, so bad things were happening all around him. But, this felt different. I'd never been one to believe in premonitions, and I wanted to continue believing there was no such thing, but I vowed to spend extra time in prayer this week. For both men.

CHAPTER TWENTY-SIX

November 13, 1956
To the ladies of the North Platte Canteen

My name is Julie Munemoni, and my father, Grant, was one of the 2,500 Japanese American soldiers to come through the North Platte Canteen in August 1943. Dad was in the 100th Infantry Battalion and distinguished himself with honor on the field of battle in Africa and Italy. As you may know, the Congressional Medal of Honor was awarded to many soldiers of this Battalion of loyal Americans of Japanese descent.

My father recently passed away, but I wanted to convey his thanks to you because he remembered the kindness of the people of North Platte until his death. He always said you treated his unit with decency, respect, and affection. They did not experience this elsewhere, which made the town of North Platte special to him always.

With my heartfelt thanks and appreciation – Julie Munemoni

****

August 13, 1958
My husband walked into the library and I knew. One look at him and I felt a ripple of excitement racing up my spine. The hair on my arms was standing on end. It was time.

I raced to him. "Is she at the hospital?"

He smiled and nodded. "Yep. Get your pocketbook and I'll drive us over there."

I couldn't stop the tears already filling my eyes, despite the smile so wide it hurt my cheeks.

"Is it time?" Rose asked as she saw me race passed the circulation desk.

"Sounds like it," I whispered.

While I retrieved my pocketbook out of my office, I saw Rose walk to my husband and throw her arms around him. They had become so close over the years, as she was like a daughter to us. I'd been so excited each time Rose and Harry had a baby as well, but this was my turn to be called "Grandma," and I felt almost faint.

"I'm ready," I said, as I walked up to them.

She wrapped me in her arms before letting me walk out the door. "Good luck, Grandma," she whispered into my ear.

I hugged her back. "We'll call when we have news."

After we made it to the hospital, we joined the many people sitting in the waiting room. My husband leaned back with a paperback novel he always kept in his back pocket for just such occasions, but I couldn't relax. I pestered the woman at the reception desk, checking for updates I knew she didn't have. I walked the length of the halls framing the waiting area and got coffee from the machine which neither of us could drink.

Our girl was in there and they wouldn't let me in. She needed me and I was stuck out here. What a ridiculous system!

Hours later, although it felt like days, our son-in-law, Michael, came rushing out. "She's gotten to the pushing point, so they kicked me out." His normally calm and happy eyes were tight with worry, and his mouth, always wide in smile, was compressed into a thin line. "She's my wife, and it's my baby, too. Why can't I be in there with her?"

I tried to wrap my right arm around him, but he pulled away and started pacing along my paths in the hallways. At least we knew she had to be getting close, if she was at the pushing point.

I'd never gone through childbirth myself. I'd certainly read enough about it over the past seven months, and I'd been there for Rose when her kids were born. She, in fact, had been able to answer some of our girl's questions, things I couldn't learn in books and hadn't experienced.

It made me a little sad, especially when she'd first announced her pregnancy, that this wasn't an experience we could share. We couldn't compare notes. But when it came right down to it, I had a daughter who was about to give us a grandson or granddaughter, and this fact was all that mattered in the world.

After I lost Fred in the Great War, I'd never expected to have a family. It had nearly broken me to think I'd never be a mother. Never thought I'd experience a day like today. I prayed everyone was healthy. How we came into the world was not nearly as important as how we chose to live it, together.

A nurse in a crisp white uniform came through the maternity ward doors and walked up to Michael where he paced the hallways. As she spoke to him, he pulled her into a crushing embrace and then let out the loudest whoop. Michael came rushing to us. Pulling me into a hug that pulled me off the floor, he shouted in my ear. "It's a girl!"

When he dropped me back to the floor and shook hands, and then hugged, my husband, Michael ran off with the nurse to see his wife and daughter. I turned to the man I'd loved all these years, my heart overflowing with wonder and delight, unable and unwilling to stem the flow of tears rushing down my face.

He gave me his devil smile, the gaze filled with bits of mischief which I'd so come to cherish over the years. While pulling me into a warm, enveloping embrace, he placed a kiss on my cheek. I laid my head on his shoulder, our world complete.

"Congratulations, Grandma. It's a girl!"

CHAPTER TWENTY-SEVEN

November 23, 1944

"I'm glad Mrs. Christ decided Thanksgiving Day would be a North Platte volunteer day. I can't think of a better way to spend the holiday." Rose had taken special care with her hair and dress for the holiday, as had all of the volunteers.

We had turkey sandwiches and some of the trimmings, all donated by local families, along with many desserts, candy, and reading material. We had decorated the Canteen with turkeys and pilgrims made by local schoolchildren and a local boy played the piano. Several of the young girls—too young to work the platform, but old enough to dance—had been dancing their shoes off with any servicemen who took the time for a spin around the floor. It all made for a very festive atmosphere.

"I agree. I'd rather be here on a holiday like this than anywhere else. I like making a difference." And it helped to distract me from my wish that Tom were here for Thanksgiving, from my worry about what he was facing today instead.

The piano was spilling out a tune that sounded like "Don't Sit Under the Apple Tree with Anyone Else But Me," and I couldn't stop my toes from tapping.

With the addition of the public address system at the Canteen, servicemen didn't have to worry so much about missing the train. So when the announcer called out the "All Aboard" message, the men went running. As always, we followed them out to the platform to wave good-bye, but it was nice they could also hear the announcer call out, "Come back; we'll be waiting for you."

My eyes were damp all morning. Emotion always made a weeper out of me, and I couldn't stop feeling like and hoping this might be the last Thanksgiving of the war, the last time the Canteen would host so many young men for their holiday meal. At least, I prayed that was true.

More and more trains were coming through the Canteen. It seemed like we didn't have but a moment between waving them good-bye and hearing the announcement of the next train's arrival. At one point, the music coming from the piano was amazing, but I didn't even have a chance to go see who was playing. Rose and I exchanged glances.

"That's not Tommy Kennedy. I wonder who's playing now."

I shook my head. "Whoever it is, it's fantastic."

But as soon as the next train moved out, the music changed again. When the fourth train in a row pulled out, Helen Christ walked over to speak to me.

"Write this one in the books, Miss Parker."

I looked up, smiling. "What's that, Mrs. Christ?"

"We served 2,000 soldiers from four troop trains in thirty minutes. I think it's a new Canteen record."

I chuckled. "No wonder we all look exhausted." I got out my notebook and wrote it down. "Happy Thanksgiving, Helen."

She smiled. "Happy Thanksgiving, Maggie.

The next train coming through was filled with German POWs, so we were able to spend some time restocking the tables. By order of the War Department we did not serve the POW. trains. Given what little the Army gave our soldiers to eat on troop trains, the POWs certainly couldn't be getting much food on their trip. It seemed a shame we weren't allowed to offer at least some platform baskets of fruit or popcorn balls. Almost un-American, really. And, besides, I'd hate to think our men were being starved in Axis POW camps.

After we'd unpacked all the boxes and bags of books and magazines, Rose walked to my end of the table. "Did you hear the latest?"

I shook my head. "Seems unlikely," I said, smiling.

She laughed. "Jewel told me one of those MPs, you know the military police who hang out in the back room? Well, it seems like he got friendly with Beatrice Long, since she was working on the platform, and they ran off and got married."

"I hope they didn't really run off." I smiled. "Who would the military send to arrest an MP who is absent without leave?"

She shook her head, although she was still smiling. "Very funny, Maggie."

I nodded. "I'm very happy for Beatrice and her MP."

Her lower lip stuck a little ways out. "Me, too." She sounded wistful. "I wish Harry had a safer job like an MP here in North Platte."

I put my hand on her arm and met her gaze. "Just be happy for them and any good that comes out of this war. There's nothing we can do about what Harry or Tom are going through, except love them and pray."

She nodded. "I know."

I gave her a quick hug and then told her I'd be right back. I walked out of the Canteen and on to the platform, checking to ask if anyone knew who had been playing the piano earlier.

"Hello, Elmer," I said.

Elmer Koch had worked the ticket counter at the depot for at least the past forty years. He was as much a fixture of North Platte as was the Canteen. He tipped his hat to me inside the booth.

"Afternoon, Miss Margaret. Busy day today."

I nodded. "That it is, Elmer. If fact, it's been so busy, I didn't get to see who was playing the piano earlier. Do you happen to know who it was?"

Elmer scratched his chin and then got a twinkle in his eye. "Oh, you mean that fancy stuff?"

I nodded, and Elmer's face broke into a wide grin. "That was some musician fellow from Hollywood. He's traveling with a USO group, performing for the troops. The lady with him said he'd played in a lot of clubs in New York City, too."

"Do you remember his name?"

Elmer looked at his schedule. "I wrote it down right here. Anybody who plays like he did will be really famous someday. The USO lady said his name was Liberace. Never heard of him, but he sure can play a piano."

I smiled. "You're right, Elmer. He sure can."

I had never heard of Liberace either, but anyone with his talent would be a great entertainer for the troops.

The announcement came over the P.A. that the coffee pot was on, so I hurried back to my post at the table. No sooner was I at the guest book than a young man was there to sign in.

"Happy Thanksgiving, Staff Sergeant."

He slipped off his hat. "Happy Thanksgiving, ma'am."

I tilted my head. "You look familiar, son. Have you been through the Canteen before?"

He laughed. "I should say so. This is my seventh time through North Platte and I've enjoyed your hospitality each and every time. In fact, the train car I was on included a lot of young replacement troops and I told 'em, I said, you don't want to miss this next stop, fellas. The food and friendliness of North Platte can't be beat. I told 'em you can even read about the North Platte Canteen in the *Reader's Digest*."

I chuckled. "Seven times; amazing. Where are you coming from this time, Staff Sergeant?"

"I'm headed west, ma'am, with replacement troops we've been training. I'm not sure where exactly we're going, but somewhere in the Pacific."

I suddenly had a lump in my throat. "Good luck to you, son."

He nodded. "Thank you, ma'am." He stood for a minute, looking at me.

"Is there something else, Staff Sergeant?"

"Yes, ma'am." He looked around. "I'm looking for a Mrs. White. Do you know if she's working here today?"

I shook my head. "I'm sorry, but Mrs. White is not here today." Actually, Thelma White had received the news this week that her husband had been killed in France. She hadn't come back to the Canteen yet.

"Can I leave her a note?"

"Of course, I'm sure she'd like that." I pulled my notepad and pen from my pocket and handed it to him.

He scribbled a note, tore it out of the notebook, folded it, and handed everything back to me. "I've been writing to Mrs. White since she gave me a birthday cake on my second trip through the Canteen." His ears colored slightly.

I nodded. "How nice."

He smiled. "I knew guys who stopped in the Canteen on their birthdays got a whole cake, so I told Mrs. White it was my friend George's birthday, but he couldn't get off the train. She gave me a cake, but when I got back on the train…"

I smiled. "Where there was no 'George'?"

He nodded. "Yeah, well I guess my conscience got the better of me. I gave the cake to a couple of kids traveling with their mother. They did share a piece with me, and it was delicious. Anyway, I wrote to Mrs. White and apologized, and she's been writing to me ever since."

I put my hand on his arm. "That's a wonderful story, son. I'll stop by her house on my way home today to give

166

her this note and tell her you asked after her. But what's your name?"

He put his hat back on and saluted me. "Staff Sergeant William Harris at your service, ma'am." He gave me a quick hug. "Thank you, ma'am. She's a nice lady."

He rushed to the food table to grab some sandwiches before the announcement called him back to the train.

I put the note for Mrs. White in my pocket and watched as one group of servicemen and women rushed out while another rushed in. We were probably going to have twenty troop trains come through today.

"Maggie?" Trudy stopped in front of my table. "Can you gather some reading materials in a basket and bring it to the platform. We have a hospital train coming through next."

"Of course, Trudy." I grabbed the basket from beneath the table and filled it with a few Bibles, some books, and a large selection of magazines. Trudy was dispensing care packages, complete with toothbrushes, toothpaste, razors, and soap. The platform girls were also instructed to pass out canes that had been donated by families in town, as needed.

I liked working the hospital trains, as sad as they could be, because the wounded boys were so happy to see a smiling face. Of course, I never saw the badly wounded men, as they were not the ones who stuck their heads out of open windows to talk to us. I'm sure I reminded the boys of their mothers, and, while I knew little of nursing, it seemed to help them to talk to me.

I stopped at the doorway to one of train cars, passing my basket of reading material to the soldier manning the door. As I waited for him to return it, I spoke to a few of the wounded located near the door. "Welcome to North Platte, Nebraska, soldier. Where are you from?"

"Howdy, ma'am. I'm Private First Class John Snodgrass from Merom, Indiana," said a young man sitting on a cot.

Two other men sat next to him and one called out "I'm Sergeant Bert Hanover, from Akron, Ohio, ma'am."

"I'm from Rome, ma'am, well…Rome, New York. My name's Sergeant Francis Murray. Thank you kindly for the magazines and the new toothbrush. I lost mine and haven't had a new one in months."

She smiled. "We're happy to help, Sergeant. Where did you men come from?"

Sergeant Hanover spoke up. "We just got shipped back from the Pacific, ma'am. We were injured in the fighting in Leyte over in the Philippines."

My heart sank. "Is it bad?" My voice seemed hoarse, so I cleared my throat.

Sergeant Hanover looked at me. "You have someone over there?"

I nodded. "My fiancé. Captain Tom Carter."

Sergeant Hanover nodded, but Sergeant Murray shook his head. "It's not so bad, ma'am. We're definitely closing in on the Japs. We were simply unlucky. It's war, you know. It happens."

Private Snodgrass leaned forward, nearly coming off the cot. "Don't you worry none, ma'am. Your fiancé, a captain, don't you worry about him. He's in a right safe place, I'm sure. The tides are a turning, and it's only a matter of time now."

"Thanks to all of you. It's good to know he's got fine men like you fighting beside him." How sad must I look if these three wounded soldiers were trying to cheer *me* up from their hospital beds.

When I got home that night, I poured my shame and fears out on paper for Tom.

November 23, 1944
Dearest Tom,
I embarrassed myself at the Canteen today worrying about you, but was told by some very friendly young soldiers that the tide is turning in the Pacific and you should be home soon. These young men were

wounded in Leyte and said you, as a captain, would surely be out of the line of fire. I thought you'd get a kick out of the assessment of an officer's role in battle.

When I learned they were all wounded in the Philippines, my fear for your must have shown on my face, as they all rushed to reassure me, when I should have been buoying up their spirits. I was glad to talk to some men, even wounded ones, who had been where you are and are optimistic of our chances. Please stay out of the line of fire, as much as you can. I am anxious for you to come home.

Life continues here as usual, although we're getting more troop trains at the Canteen every time I work. A lot of servicemen are moving about the country; either replacement troops heading overseas or wounded men coming home. Surely, some of them have earned all their service points and are headed home, as well.

Our knitting circle has been so productive lately, we dropped off a whole box of hats, scarves, gloves, and socks for the Red Cross to add to their supply boxes. The ones I made are not entirely square, but I'm sure they'll be warm. I'm not a great knitter, but even so, I enjoy the time with my friends and knowing some soldier might be a bit warmer because of me.

By the way, Happy Thanksgiving. I hope you got something decent to eat, instead of just K-rations or some other Army gruel. We had turkey sandwiches and some of the fixings and the men seemed happy as can be with it. The KODY radio announcer had to send out a request for more food, but of course, the good people of North Platte showed up with more than enough. We have a good start on tomorrow already.

I'm sorry to cut this letter so short, but I'm exhausted. We served twenty-two troop trains today with well over 5,000 servicemen and women. It was a wonderful way to spend the holiday, but I have to get some sleep.

Know I am dreaming of you and seeing you step off a train in our station. Stay safe and remember how much I love you. I will always remain – Your, Maggie

CHAPTER TWENTY-EIGHT

December 15, 1944

I was so excited to receive a letter from Tom, as I'd gotten one yesterday, too. I sat down to eat my dinner at the kitchen table and pulled out the letter to read while I ate.

My Dearest Maggie,

First, let me wish you a Merry Christmas and thank you for your latest package and all the wonderful letters. I was the envy of all the officers at mail call. The cookies are delicious, as always, as is the banana bread. If you keep baking like this when I get home, I'll have to start running up and down the streets of North Platte to stay in shape.

All of your gifts and letters were wonderful and I thank you from the bottom of my heart. You make me feel loved and tie me to a little piece of home in Nebraska that keeps me working to end this war and get back to you.

Knowing how much you love me, and how excited you are for me to come home so we can be married, keeps me going when things are rough over here. I don't want to, nor can I, go into details about the fighting in the Pacific, but I will say I want it to be over, I want us to beat down those Japs once and for all, so life can go back to normal. Or, for us, begin anew.

I had a problem come up that I need your help with. I have a twelve-year-old daughter named Jane. I apologize for not telling you about her sooner.

I was married after the Great War, but only for a short time because my wife died in childbirth with Jane. I was a career Army man, so it would have been one thing for my wife to stay home with a baby while I was deployed to different bases, or even for my family to travel with me, at least when we weren't at war. But, the idea of me raising a baby on my own while in the Army was daunting. There was no way to make it work.

So, luckily, my father's sister, my Aunt Wilma, stepped in and volunteered to take Jane in to live with her. Aunt Wilma was widowed in the Great War, and her husband left her a sizable fortune, so she made a wonderful home for Jane in Chicago. I have been very lucky, and they've had a nice life together.

Unfortunately, I received a telegram yesterday telling me my Aunt Wilma passed away this week. Jane is temporarily staying with a neighbor, but that is not a reasonable, long-term solution. I've met my aunt's neighbors, but don't know the couple well. They have no children and I cannot expect Jane to go on living with them.

I need you to go to Chicago to pick her up and bring her to live with you. My plan has always been to have her live with us once I'm home and we're married, but this means we'll have to move up that time line.

I'm know it's a lot to ask you to take such a long train trip to pick her up, but Jane is young and probably worried, and I know you will be able to make her feel at home in your house. While she is not a hysterical child, she was very close to my Aunt Wilma and has lived with her all of her life. It's not fair to Jane to leave her alone for long. You can understand how distressing this must be for the child.

I wish I'd had the chance to tell you about Jane before this, but I'm sure you'll agree there's nothing else to be done at this point. You're the logical person to take care of Jane now.

I'm sure you and my daughter will get along famously. I've watched your friendship with Rose develop through your letters, and I knew you'd be the perfect stepmother for Jane. She's a bright and inquisitive girl and will take to you quickly.

I am copying Aunt Wilma's address onto the bottom of this letter, as well as the name and telephone number for the neighbor with whom she is staying. Please go as soon as you possibly can and send me a letter when she's home with you, so I won't worry about my two best girls on their cross-country travel.

I am thinking of you and kissing your picture good night.

All of my love, Tom

I dropped the letter, and it nearly landed in my soup. Luckily, I saved it at the last moment, or Aunt Wilma's address might be lost to me.

A daughter?

How could Tom have a twelve-year-old daughter he never thought to tell me about?

He was married before, and widowed, and I had no idea! I shook my head, trying to get a handle on his revelation and request. It wasn't anywhere near April 1, so it was unlikely the letter was a joke. I looked up, but there was no one there to explain this letter to me. Everything seemed slightly off-kilter.

This could not be real.

How could he really expect me to drop everything at a moment's notice, take the train to Chicago, and bring home a stranger to live in my house? I'm so disappointed and shocked by his deception—and had more than a few questions:

First, had he told Jane I was coming? What did the child know about me? Hopefully, more than I'd known about her. Like, for instance, that I existed.

Second, how was the child to live with me in this house with my mother here? Hadn't Tom been paying attention when I told him about the kind of person my mother is? I couldn't bear to expose a young girl to her fits of temper and drunkenness.

Third, how was I to enroll her in school or be her guardian? I had no relationship to this child except I was engaged to marry her absentee father if he survived the war and came back to North Platte.

Where, by the way, he'd always planned for us to all live together, but never bothered to tell me. He'd only been writing to me nearly every day for the past three years. Maybe he might have brought it up when he asked me to marry him. I might work with Rose at the Canteen and have tutored students at the library, but what did I know about living with and raising, a twelve-year-old girl?

How did I end up engaged to a man who has a secret daughter? I clearly don't know him as well as I thought I did. I stood, walked around the table, and sat back down. I picked up the letter, starting to reread it, then let it drop again. I was at a loss as to what I should do or even how to start organizing my thoughts.

Usually a list maker, I couldn't even conceive of starting a list titled "Bringing My Fiancé's Secret Daughter to Live at My House." Plus he wanted me to drop everything and catch the train to Chicago. He didn't even offer to pay for the expenses associated with *his* daughter!

I put my dishes in the sink, although I'd hardly eaten anything. I walked to the back door, slid my feet into my boots, pulled on my coat, hat, and gloves, and walked out the door. I wasn't even sure where I was headed, but I had to start walking to gather my thoughts.

CHAPTER TWENTY-NINE

December 15, 1944

When Trixie Nelson pulled the door open, her eyes widened, but she wasn't terribly successful at masking her surprise. "Why, Maggie," she said while motioning for me to enter, "how lovely to see you. Is Rose expecting you?" She looked around the parlor, as if expecting the girl to rush out to greet me.

I shook my head. "Thank you, Trixie, but no, Rose isn't expecting me. Something came up and...I need to speak with her." I looked at my watch. "I know it's late, but I hope it will be all right."

Trixie smiled, although her smile seemed shaky. "Ah, of course...let me...please have a seat." She gestured to the sofa. "I'll tell Rose you're here."

I wasn't sure how I'd gotten here. When I left the house, I'd started walking with no fixed destination in mind and found myself at her house. It never crossed my mind to go see Ann or Sue or any of the new friends I'd made at the Canteen or my knitting circle. Rose was my friend first, despite the differences in our ages, and she knew more about my relationship with Tom than anyone else.

She rushed into the parlor, her gaze on me. Her eyebrows were drawn together, and she wasn't smiling. I didn't mean to worry her before I'd even started talking. Trixie hovered in the hallway.

I stood and took her hand. "Want to take a walk?"

It was 20°, dark, and windy. Of course, she didn't want to take a walk.

"That sounds like fun." The smile pasted on her face was wobbly and she was looking at me out of the sides of her eyes. "Let me get my things."

I pulled on my coat, hat, boots, and gloves as I waited by the door. Rose joined me, layered up for the winter weather.

"Rose?" Trixie stepped forward.

"I'll be back shortly, Mom." She opened the door and walked ahead of me.

I turned and smiled at Trixie. "Thanks, Trixie, and have a good evening."

I pulled the door closed behind me, seeing Trixie's puzzled expression looming through the sheer curtains on the door.

When we got to the sidewalk, Rose put her arm through mine and said, "Which way?"

I shook my head and let her lead.

"What's the matter?" She didn't look at me, maybe sensing my embarrassment. "Is it Tom?"

She had a slightly panicked tone in her voice.

"Yes, but he's fine. It's nothing like that."

She released a breath, which I could see as well as hear. "Good." She took in a deep breath. "Then what's wrong?"

I closed my eyes and shook my head. "I...I don't even know what to think about all of this, but I knew I needed to talk it out with you. I'm sorry for dragging you out into the cold."

"Shh," she said. "Don't give it a thought. Just tell me what's going on."

I walked in silence, sentences forming and reforming in my mind.

I took a deep breath. "I got a letter from Tom today asking me to get on the next train to Chicago to pick up his twelve-year-old daughter and bring her back here to live with me."

She stopped walking, silent. Neither of us spoke for a few moments. "Please start at the beginning, but wait until we get inside."

We started walking again, nearly at the library. "You knew I'd have my keys?"

She nodded. "You've got your pocketbook, and I've never known you to put those keys anywhere else."

I smiled. "You know me well." I almost said, *I wish I knew Tom as well as you know me*, but didn't think it would help my current state of mind.

When we got inside the library, and left our wet boots by the door, we both walked through the dark to the comfy sofas in the reading area. I took off my coat and sat. She did the same.

"Okay," she said, "what is going on?"

It was easier to talk to her in the dark, even though I knew she wouldn't be judging me. It was so mortifying to be in this position, especially at my age.

"So, it seems I'm engaged to a man I don't know very well." I looked down, unable to even try to meet her gaze in the dark. "Tom was married after the Great War, but his wife died in childbirth. He couldn't take care of the baby while a career Army officer, so he left his daughter, Jane, to be raised by a wealthy widowed aunt in Chicago."

"Are his parents still living?"

I shook my head. "No, he told me some time ago they both died when he was young, so he's been on his own for a long time. Might have mentioned the daughter, though…"

She reached out a hand and laid it on my arm. "What's happened, then?"

"Tom got a telegram telling him his aunt recently passed away. Apparently, his…daughter…" I'd have to learn to say the word without tripping over it. "His daughter is temporarily staying with a neighbor until I 'take the next train to Chicago and bring her back to live with me.'"

I couldn't keep the sarcasm out of my tone, at least, not without giving into my urge to sob.

We sat quietly for a few minutes.

"I don't know him. I mean, I never would have guessed he was a widowed father, or there was this whole other part of his life he'd never told me about. How can I ever trust him again?"

She nodded, but stayed quiet.

"Plus..." I turned so I was facing her, "what kind of man leaves his daughter for years? She's never known either of her parents because her mother died giving birth to her and her father pushed his responsibility for her off on a distant relative."

"Did he tell you anything about Jane? Does she know about you? That you're engaged to her father?"

I shook my head. "I have no idea. He simply presented me with the basic facts as if I were one of the soldiers under his command. He has a daughter, I must go to Chicago on the next train, pick her up, and bring her home to live with me. No please, do me this great favor, and no real explanation for not telling me about her before. Just a 'You're the best man for the job, so go to Chicago.'"

"You're hurt and angry, and you have every right to be." She stroked my hand. "Tom has no right to spring this on you, after you've agreed to marry him, and expect you to drop everything to take care of his child."

I tried to stop the tears which threatened to spill from my lids. "Wasn't he paying attention any of the times I've written to him about my mother? How can he expect me to raise a twelve-year-old girl, a stranger to me, when my vile mother still lives in my house? I've been worried about *Tom* coming to live there after the war, and he's an Army captain."

"I'm so sorry."

"Mother is brutal on young girls. Trust me, I know. She was terrible to me simply because she was my mother. She's a dreadful, angry, spiteful person, and she'll make this girl's life a living hell when I'm not home."

She nodded. "Well, first of all, she'll spend most of her time here or at the Canteen, same as me. You've made me feel welcome here and at the Canteen, especially when I don't feel like being around my mother. We'll do the same for this girl."

I nodded. "I guess." It helped a little that Rose said "we," as if we'd be in this together.

"Are you going to go to Chicago?"

I shook my head. "I can't leave his child living with her neighbors, can I?" I sighed. "I mean, surely she'd rather come and live with a complete stranger in a place she's never heard of, waiting for the return of a father she barely knows."

The tears started silently falling from my eyes, so I closed them. She rubbed my back.

"I'll go to Chicago and bring his daughter back to live with me. I'll care for her until Tom comes home, assuming he does, but then I'm done. He'll be responsible for his own daughter and can move wherever he wants, so they can make a life together. I'll be done with him."

She slid her arm around my shoulders. "But you're in love with him, aren't you? You're engaged to the man."

I shrugged. "How can I love a man who would abandon his only child? How can I be in love with a man I know so little about?"

My heart broken, I stood and pulled on my coat. "Can you cover my shifts at the library for the next few days? I don't really know how long it will take me to get to Chicago on the train, but I expect the trip to take no less than three or four days. I'll plan to catch the first available train tomorrow morning."

Rose nodded. "The library is closed on Sunday anyway, so I'll have no trouble making sure everything's taken care of tomorrow, Monday, and Tuesday, or however long it takes. Same at the Canteen. Don't worry about it."

"Thanks." I waited as she put on her coat and we walked to the door. Even with more than twenty years between us, Rose was the best friend I'd ever had. Her help and support might actually make this crazy idea work. "Not only for covering for me. Thanks for listening. When I got Tom's letter, my mind went completely blank. I couldn't think of a next step. I put on my coat and my feet just brought me to you. Thank you for being such a good friend."

She wrapped her arm around my shoulders again. "I'm glad your feet thought of me and happy to have been able to help in any small way. I'm so sorry you have to deal with this and could kick Tom for how he's treated you."

I smiled. "Me, too."

We walked out of the library and parted ways, after a hug. I had gained a valuable friend during the course of this war, even if I might have lost a fiancé tonight.

CHAPTER THIRTY

December 18, 1944

Only a few people flew by the windows of the taxi as we drove up a tree-lined street filled with beautiful old stone and brick homes. The driver pulled to a stop in front of a lovely three-story house made of gray stone and glass.

"Here you are, ma'am."

"Thank you." I paid the driver and climbed out of the taxi. I couldn't stop from turning my head to look over all the neighboring homes until I fixed my eyes on "Aunt Wilma's" house; the tall red-brick mansion directly across the street. Tom had, at least, been truthful about Wilma being well-off.

I climbed the front steps, and the polished oak front door opened before I had a chance to even touch the brass knocker.

"Miss Parker?" An immaculately turned out dark-skinned woman in a crisp white and gray uniform eased the door open.

"Yes. I'm here for Jane Carter."

She nodded and gestured for me to come in. "We've been expecting you, ma'am. Please come in."

She helped me off with my coat. "If you'd like to have a seat," she motioned to a pair of sofas facing each other, separated by a delicate table of glass and brass. "I'll let Mrs. Wexler and Miss Carter know you're here."

The maid disappeared down the hall with my coat and I took a seat on one of the sofas. The room was luscious and calm, decorated in pale blues, greens, and a cream color. The ceilings were high and floor-to-ceiling windows ran across the front wall. Must make it difficult to heat this room, although I didn't feel cold.

It was only a few moments before a smartly dressed woman walked into the room, followed by a lanky blonde adolescent. The woman was dressed in a suit of aubergine wool with a striking pattern of contrasting swirls running from shoulder to hem on the left side. The girl wore a simple dress with her blonde hair smooth on top and curls falling from her chin line to brush her shoulders.

"Miss Parker? I'm Helen Wexler. How nice to meet you."

I rose as she approached and took the hand she held out to me. "Hello, Mrs. Wexler. I apologize for my delay in getting here. The train I was on was delayed several times to allow troop trains and trains of military equipment to pass through. I guess that's the way travel goes these days."

She nodded. Her smooth dark hair was beautifully styled; some curls sat on the top with the rest rolled into a chignon at the back.

Mrs. Wexler touched the girl's arm, bringing her forward. "This is Jane." She nodded to the girl. "Jane, this is Miss Parker."

Jane held out her hand and we shook, although her touch was light. "Hello, Miss Parker. It's lovely to meet you."

I smiled, hoping to put her at ease. "Hello. It's nice to meet you as well. And, I'm sorry to hear of your aunt's passing."

She nodded. "Thank you."

Mrs. Wexler walked to the sofa and chairs. "Please, let's sit."

I sat on one sofa, and Mrs. Wexler and Jane sat across from me. Jane's gaze fell to the floor, giving me a chance to steal glances at her unobserved. She must have favored her mother, as there wasn't much of Tom in her looks, except for her crystal clear blue eyes, so like his.

Mrs. Wexler was speaking: "…she's been no trouble at all. We've really loved having her stay with us, although I'm sure our home has been boring to her. We have no children of our own." Mrs. Wexler looked down at her hands folded primly in her lap, her serene façade slipping a bit.

I nodded. "I have never married."

She smiled. "But I'm given to understand you are engaged to Captain Carter, correct?"

I'd thought of nothing else during the past five days on the train, but I wouldn't inconvenience Mrs. Wexler with the uncertain status of my relationship with Tom. "That is correct."

Jane looked up at me, as if appraising the woman who had wrest a commitment from her father.

Mrs. Wexler looked to the doorway as the maid entered. "Yes, well, we have everything in order. Isn't that right, Jane?"

She nodded. "Yes, ma'am."

Mrs. Wexler stood; Jane and I immediately following suit. "Our driver will take you to Union Station, Miss Parker. I'm afraid she has quite a bit of luggage."

"Thank you, Mrs. Wexler, for your help and for all you've done for Jane."

The girl nodded. She stopped, turned, and leaned in to give Mrs. Wexler a perfunctory hug. "Yes, thank you and to Mr. Wexler and all the staff."

Mrs. Wexler patted Jane vaguely on her shoulder and then stepped back. She brushed her hands together and turned to the maid. "Please call Charles to secure all of Jane's luggage."

The maid went rushing out the front door and, as we walked to the entry, Jane pulled on her coat and hat. We watched the driver, Charles, carry out three large suitcases and two smaller bags in a series of trips. When he came back to the front door, he held it open for us.

We climbed into the car and saw Mrs. Wexler wave from the doorway then disappear. The maid closed the door and we were on our way. The streets of this part of Chicago were lined with snow, but enough of the center of the street was plowed to let cars take turns.

Jane was staring straight ahead.

"It looks like you've already had quite a bit of winter here in Chicago. Do you have boots packed in one of your suitcases?"

Her eyes grew large. "Yes. Do I need them now?"

I shook my head. "No, I was just checking." I pointed down at my own boots. "I don't go anywhere without my boots in the winter in Nebraska. We get a lot of snow."

She smiled. "I'm looking forward to seeing winter in Nebraska. Is there anywhere nearby for people to go snow skiing?"

I smiled. "Not really. It's pretty flat in North Platte, other than the nearby sand hills. But, if you go west toward Colorado, you'll start to find more hills. Denver is about 250 miles west and snow skiing in the Rocky Mountains outside of Denver."

Jane nodded. "Can you go sledding and ice skating in North Platte?"

"Certainly." In all my worry about having the girl living at my house, I had forgotten to think about what she would do for fun. While I'd already decided she could come straight to the library after school and home with me for dinner, I hadn't considered what she would do on weekends, other than work at the Canteen when I did, or when she made friends. What did the young people of North Platte do for fun?

"You'll make some friends at school, and they'll be full of ideas of the fun things to do in North Platte."

Her gaze met mine again. "Didn't you grow up in North Platte?"

I nodded. "Yes, but it's been a long time since I was your age, I guess." Once my father died, my childhood ended, and I don't think I ever went ice skating or sledding without him.

She smiled faintly and looked out the car window.

"Here we are, ladies." Charles pulled into a parking spot near the entrance to Union Station. I felt like I'd just been here and was not relishing getting back on a train after having no opportunity to freshen up or change clothing again. The onboard bathroom was an inadequate place for completing one's toilette.

Charles obtained a large luggage cart and followed us into the station. I stopped at the ticket window to ensure our tickets back to North Platte were correct and the train was on time. "I think we might as well find seats now, as we may not get any if we wait." I had struggled finding a seat on the train into Chicago. With so many servicemen and women traveling across the country these days, and gasoline and rubber tires so tightly rationed, every train was overflowing with passengers.

Jane and I settled in to our seats, although the train car was cold, so we didn't take off our coats, hats, or gloves. She looked at me. "Was it this cold on the journey east?"

I nodded. "Yes, but it got a little warmer once everyone was on the train." Men, women, and children, civilians and service members, were streaming past us, looking for seats. "There were so many servicemen that people were sitting on suitcases in the aisles, sitting on the floors, and even standing all the way from Omaha to Chicago."

"Amazing," she said, as she shook her head.

"I was on this train for three days, although it should be a trip of less than a day, and I saw many people with no food to eat. Now I know why the servicemen and women we serve at the North Platte Canteen are so happy and relieved to see us."

A soldier stopped in the aisle next to our seat. "Did you say North Platte? Will this train be going through North Platte?"

I smiled and nodded. "Yes, Sergeant. If you stay on this train passed Omaha, it will stop in North Platte."

He raised one arm in the air. "Hey, fellas. We're going to get to stop in North Platte."

The servicemen on the train started cheering. Jane looked at me, her eyes wide.

My heart swelled with pride. "The troops who have been through North Platte have told others about it. That way, they all know to get off at the station for our stop. Many of the men tell us when they arrive how their buddies told them not to miss it."

A sailor in front of us turned around. "Excuse me, ma'am. Are you from North Platte?"

I nodded. "Yes. I'm actually the Canteen historian. I've been working there at least once a week since it started. Have you been through the Canteen?"

He smiled and nudged his buddy, who also turned around. "I was telling Lloyd here about North Platte. I've been through three times already. You ladies are so kind and the food, well…ma'am, without out it, we'd all be pretty hungry. It's delicious."

"Why thank you, Seaman…" I tried to read his name tag over the edge of the seat.

He immediately stood, holding his cap in his hands. "Seaman Perry Benson from Hartford, Connecticut, ma'am."

He held out a hand and I shook it.

His buddy also stood, leaning over the seat. "Seaman Lloyd Font, ma'am, from Sayre, Pennsylvania." He nodded in my direction.

"It's nice to meet you both. I'm Miss Parker and this is my…my friend, Miss Jane Carter."

He nodded to Jane and then turned back to me. "The people were so nice to us, ma'am. One of the ladies helped me send a telegram to my folks, letting them know I was okay. I didn't even have enough money to pay for it, but she sent it anyway."

"I bet your parents were tickled pink to hear from you."

He smiled. "My mom wrote to tell me how much your telegram helped them. I hadn't been gone too long then, and she was really worried about me."

"I'm sure."

As they turned around to face forward, Perry told Lloyd about the pheasant sandwiches and birthday cakes. Even the small things we did for these boys made such a lasting impression. Despite all the hard work, long hours, and scrimping and saving to be able to cook for the servicemen and women, moments like this made it all worthwhile.

Jane looked at me. "Can you explain a little more about the Canteen? My father wrote to me about it, but I didn't realize what a big deal it is."

Interesting that Tom had told her about the Canteen. What had he told her about me?

I explained what we did at the Canteen and the communities who sent volunteers with food, drinks, and supplies. I told her about the early mornings and late nights, sometimes meeting as many as twenty or twenty-five trains in a single day, and being able to feed them all, without ever knowing how many souls would walk through the Canteen door on a given day. And I told her about the letters and postcards we'd been sent in thanks.

"That's amazing, Miss Parker." She shook her head. "It really is. But, if you don't mind me asking, why North Platte? It's a small place, right? What made all of you decide to take on such big job?"

I tilted my head. "The women of North Platte wanted to do our part for the war effort, to support our troops. A lot of trains stop in North Platte because it's a central location, and when those servicemen and women step off the train, they're hungry and thirsty. They're scared, too. So even though the food is good and they might pick up some reading material to take with them, they're also happy to see us, waiting for them when they arrive, and waving good-bye when they leave. They're fighting and sacrificing to help us stay the kind of country we want to be. The least we can do is thank them with some cookies and pie."

She nodded. "Who works at the Canteen?"

"Well, when it's a North Platte volunteer day, we have all ages of women working in the kitchen, at the serving tables, at our periodicals table, and even on the platform. We have younger children come to the Canteen after school to fill the platform baskets with candy, cigarettes, fruit, and reading material. Girls your age, too young to be platform girls, come to dance with soldiers during the ten or fifteen minutes before they have to get back on the train."

She smiled. "I like to dance."

"Some of these men are real dancers. Especially when we have someone good on the piano."

Her eyes were shining. "That sounds like fun. I'd like to help at the Canteen."

I nodded. "It is fun, but it's also a lot of work."

****

December 21, 1944
"Here we are, Jane."

I climbed out of the taxi in my driveway, Jane followed, and we waited as the driver carried her suitcases to the back porch. We each carried a small bag, but with so much luggage, we'd been forced to hire a taxi to get home from the train station.

The driver waited for me to open the back door and carried the suitcases into the kitchen for me. After I'd paid him, I took off my coat, hat, and boots and started moving the many bags across the kitchen to the stairs.

"Go ahead and hang up your coat, Jane. We'll take your things up to your room and then I'll make some tea and get you settled."

I brought her to the bedroom she'd be using, and we left all of her bags there before I showed her the bathroom. "My towels are the yellow ones, and my mother uses the blue ones." I took out a stack of pink towels and handed them to her. "These will be yours. I usually do the wash on Mondays after work, but try not to use too many towels."

"Okay."

I started for the stairs. "Are you hungry? We had a long ride without much food."

She nodded. "I guess so."

"Let's go downstairs, and we'll find some soup or make some sandwiches."

As we walked back into the kitchen, Mother was standing in the middle of the room with her arms crossed over her chest. "Who is this, and where have you been?"

I was too tired to deal with her tonight. "Jane, this is my mother, Mrs. Parker. Mother, this is Jane Carter. I told you I was going to Chicago to pick her up."

She threw her arms out at each side. "You really took the train to Chicago to fetch this girl?"

I went to the icebox and found cheese. "Yes, Mother. I told you that's what I was going to do." I walked past her to the pantry and found bread and a tin of tuna fish.

"Do you like tuna salad sandwiches, Jane?"

"Yes, ma'am."

"Why don't you pour us a couple of glasses of milk, Jane?" I pointed to the glasses.

"Margaret. What are you doing?"

I stopped and looked at her. "I'm making us some sandwiches. We're very hungry, Mother."

"Why is this girl in my house? Do you think she's going to live here or something? You can't just bring strangers home to live with us!"

Jane froze halfway to the table, two glasses of milk in her hands.

I walked to her, patted her on the back, and leaned close to her ear. "Ignore her."

I turned back to my mother, trying to keep my tone softer than I really wanted it to be. No use in scaring Jane her first night in the house by having a major fight with my mother.

"You know very well it's my house, Mother. Go away and leave us alone."

She turned and stormed out of the room, slamming the parlor door behind her.

Jane sank into one of the chairs at the table and looked up at me, tears in her eyes. "I'm sorry, Miss Parker. I don't want to cause trouble for you. I can go back to Chicago until my father can come to get me."

I walked to the table, pulled out the chair next to her, and sat. "Don't pay any attention to my mother. She's not well. You may as well know upfront that she drinks a lot; she's miserable and hateful, and we have to ignore her. She lives in the front bedroom and parlor and comes in here for food. I live in here and upstairs and never go in the parlor. That seems to work out best for us."

She nodded. I went to the counter, got our plates, and put them on the table with some fruit from the pantry. "Eat up, and then we'll head up to bed. We've had a long trip and I'm exhausted."

CHAPTER THIRTY-ONE

December 25, 1944

"Have you written to him? Has he written to you?" Rose stood by my side at the table, smiling at the servicemen while grilling me through her smile.

"May we please discuss this later?" My cheeks were starting to ache from the smile I had cemented there. These men were spending their holidays far from home and on their way to only the War Department knew where, and we needed to make their visit to the Canteen a happy one.

She gave me a stern look, but turned and walked toward the end of the table to help a soldier looking for a recent edition of *Life* magazine.

Jane was dancing with a sailor over near the piano. He was swinging her around like a mop handle, but she was laughing and smiling, so she must have been enjoying herself. Several other girls of a similar age were dancing with servicemen, all laughing and smiling. The Glen Miller tunes on the piano replaced the Christmas carols normally playing in the depot.

White paper snowflakes covered every window and hung from the ceiling throughout the Canteen. Several servicemen tried to stop under the mistletoe whenever a platform girl came near, but Helen was doing a good job of keeping the young girls busy.

When I spotted a tall, sandy-haired soldier leaning against the open doorway, my heart nearly stopped. Of course, it wasn't Tom, but the resemblance to the man I spotted there nearly three years ago was unnerving. After this man gathered some newspapers and moved on to the food table, I waited for my heart beat to return to normal.

How would I respond to Tom's last letter? I had no idea what I wanted to say or how I could best say it. While I could easily vent my spleen in a letter, it was hardly fair to send an angry diatribe to a man in the middle of a war. On the other hand, demanding I spend my time and money to fetch a daughter he hadn't even bothered to tell me about and bring her to live with me and my angry, alcoholic mother. That was hardly fair either.

While we surely would have many arguments over the course of our lives, should we actually get married, a fight over money or whose turn it was to make the bed was a different matter entirely than a basic disagreement on morals and values.

I couldn't write to him until my temper had some time to subside, and I knew what I wanted to say. But it also wasn't fair to leave him worried about Jane's safety.

After the troop train pulled out, I walked to the Western Union office. Telegrams were perfect for relaying short sentences of fact, which was about all I was up for right now.

December 25, 1944.
Captain Tom Carter, U.S. Army…
Jane is safe in North Platte. STOP Merry Christmas. STOP
Maggie STOP

When I got back to the table, Rose was frantic. "What's the matter? Where did you go?

I put my hand out in an attempt to calm her and get her to lower her voice. "I decided to send Tom a telegram, letting him know Jane was here."

She inhaled loudly. "Good idea. He's probably been worried about her."

Jane was sitting with a group of kids on the platform now, refilling baskets with the small, wrapped Christmas presents that had been donated. Some of the younger boys were showing off for her, pushing and tumbling around her, but everyone was having fun.

She stood at my side. "She seems to be adjusting pretty well."

"I have to admit she's an easygoing child. It has to be hard to adjust from living in her great-aunt's Chicago mansion, with butlers and maids, to my little house in North Platte, while trying to stay away from my mother. But, she has been quite good-natured about it all."

She smiled. "It looks like she's having fun, even though she's spending Christmas Day working."

I hadn't really considered that. "I can only imagine what her last Christmas was like in Chicago."

Rose turned to look at me. "How are *you* handling it all?"

I exhaled and could feel my shoulders sink. "I don't know." I picked up some magazines and started straightening the table. "I haven't written to Tom since his letter telling me about Jane. I can't find the words to say what I want without anger, which is why I sent the telegram. I want him to know she's here and safe, but, beyond that, I'm not ready to talk to him." I rubbed my forehead, trying to ease the headache that was a constant bother these days.

She put her hand on my shoulder, so I stopped shuffling papers and met her gaze. "Are you going to call off the engagement?"

I shook my head. I had no words.

"No?" She jumped in.

I held up a hand. "Well I'm not sure. It's too early, and I'm still too raw. If he walked in the door right now…" I gestured to the doorway he'd stood in three years ago, "I'm pretty sure I'd throw this ring right at his face."

She nodded, but didn't let go of me.

My wall of defenses started to weaken. "I mean, what kind of man does this? Not only did he abandon his child for twelve years, but he didn't think enough about her to tell me he even had a daughter before asking me to marry him? I don't know how to get past this problem."

Rose wrapped her arm around my shoulders. "Maybe it's for the best that he's several thousand miles away right now. The distance makes having a relationship hard, but it can also give you some time to think about how you feel."

Who knew how long it would take me to figure out how I felt or what I wanted to do about it?

As Christmas day wore on, the smiles on the faces of the servicemen and women kept my spirits up. So many were replacement troops, inexperienced, young, and scared. But, as had been true with all the all troops going through the Canteen, their spirits were buoyed by a good meal, a quick dance, or flirting with one of the platform girls.

Ann stopped by our table around 8:00 p.m., wearing her coat and hat. "I'm heading home. I want to see my kids for at least a few minutes on Christmas—at least while they're still awake." She smiled.

I nodded. "That sounds like a good idea. There are plenty of volunteers here still. Go home, enjoy your family, and get some sleep."

She put her arm around my shoulder, turning us both so we had our backs to the food tables. "How's your houseguest?"

"I think she's enjoying herself, but I don't know much about kids."

Ann nodded. "After the holidays, I'll ask my daughter Lorma to find Jane at school and make friends with her." Ann looked at me. "Jane is what thirteen? Fourteen?"

I shook my head. "She's twelve and in seventh grade."

"My," said Ann, "she must be nearly as tall as Lorma, who's in eighth grade. Well, I'm sure they can be friends. I'll get Lorma to find some nice seventh-grade girls to introduce her to, as well."

I nodded. "Thank you so much, Ann. That would be wonderful." Thank goodness for my friends. Becoming an instant guardian for an almost-teenager was more than a little overwhelming.

"And you?" Ann's eyebrows raised. "How are you doing?"

I shrugged. "So far, so good." Okay, so maybe that was an exaggeration. "I don't know how I feel about any of this, but it hardly matters right now. I want her to be comfortable and safe. Everything else will take time."

Ann gave me a quick hug, bid me good night, and headed home. I looked at my watch. Jane should probably go home, too. I shouldn't plan to work as late now that I was responsible for a young girl.

I turned to Rose, who was reading. "Rose?"

She looked up from her book. "Yes?"

I walked over to her. "Would you mind if I take Jane home now? I realized I shouldn't sign up for such long volunteer shifts with her along. I bet she's tired."

She smiled. "Don't worry about it. Go on home. I'll be fine on my own. You've got to be tired, too."

Parenting was a whole new world to me. Between the stress of every decision where Jane was concerned and the strain of my anger at Tom, I was nearly always these days. What had I gotten myself into?

On our way home, I asked Jane if she'd enjoyed her day at the Canteen.

She nodded and said, "It was a lot of fun dancing with the soldiers. I liked that best. I also had fun helping the younger children to fill the baskets and helping make sandwiches in the kitchen."

"I'm glad you had a good time. I spend a lot of time volunteering at the Canteen when I'm not working at the library."

"Will we be going to the Canteen tomorrow?" Jane kicked at the snow on the sidewalk as we walked.

"No, because another local community is providing the volunteers tomorrow. But I will need to go back to work at the library. Since school won't start again until January 2, you can either come to the library or stay at home."

She walked a while without speaking. Looking at it from her perspective, she didn't have many good choices.

"I'd rather come to the library if it's all right with you. I like reading, and it sounds like more fun to me."

I nodded. If she was a reader, we might get along quite well. "We have a nice little library. If you ever want help finding more books you might like, I can help you look for some."

She turned to look at me, a shy smile on her lips. "That'd be nice."

As we walked in the back door of my house, I put my hand out. "Oh my goodness. I don't have a Christmas present for you." I'd been so busy getting the girl and moving her in, I'd never thought to get her a present.

She shook her head. "Don't worry about it, Miss Parker." She smiled at me, looking much older than twelve. "You gave me a home to live in, so that's a pretty big present, really."

"Well, Merry Christmas, anyway." Another thing I'd missed for this child. I had a long way to go as her substitute parent.

She smiled. "And Merry Christmas to you, Miss Parker."

I smiled. "Why don't you call me Maggie, or even Miss Maggie, if you prefer. That's what Rose used to call me when she was younger. Whichever makes you feel more comfortable. We live in the same house, so it seems silly for you to call me 'Miss Parker,' don't you think?"

Jane blushed. "If you say so, Miss Maggie."

When we got into the kitchen, I warmed some milk and offered Jane some of the Christmas cookies I had donated to the Canteen. "Did you get enough to eat while you were working?"

She nodded, crumbs dripping from the corners of her mouth. "While I was in the kitchen making sandwiches, a couple of the ladies gave me some to eat."

"When I am working, either at the library or the Canteen, you're always welcome to come with me, as long as you keep yourself busy there. I'm open to help, if you're interested, or you can find other things to do." I took a drink of my milk. "After the Christmas holiday, once you're in school and I'm back to work, we'll find our rhythm."

She nodded and shoved the rest of the cookie into her mouth, taking a big sip of milk. After she swallowed, she noticed me watching and blushed. "These cookies are really good."

I smiled. "The recipe has been in my family for generations. I'd be happy to teach you how to make them sometime."

She nodded. "Maybe for next Christmas."

I paused. "Maybe."

I gathered our cups and plates and took them to the sink. The dishes could wait until morning.

"Let's call it a day. I'm ready for bed."

She tried to stifle a yawn. "Me, too, I guess."

I followed her up the stairs. After my turn in the bathroom, I changed into my nightgown and climbed into my cold sheets.

Next Christmas. How could I tell Jane I had no idea where she'd be living by this time next year, if the war ended and her father came home? Could I see myself celebrating Christmas with Tom and his daughter? Maybe, but maybe not.

Right now, I was too angry to give the future any serious thought. As Rose said, the pressure was a bit less because Tom was thousands of miles away. I didn't have to figure everything out right away. I could work through my anger, collect my thoughts, and then decide what I wanted to do. I only knew that was I wasn't going to marry an Army man who ordered me about like he did his troops, never mind a man who kept such monumental secrets from me until he needed my help.

I was too tired to think about Tom tonight. I prayed he was safe and would be home soon. Until then, I had no idea what I was going to do about him or the girl sleeping down the hall.

CHAPTER THIRTY-TWO

December 31, 1944

We'd closed the library early for New Year's Eve and because no one was there except Jane, Rose, and me. Jane and I walked into the house well before dinnertime, so I told her I was going to take a quick rest before starting to cook. She was eager to learn everything, whether it was cooking, baking, cleaning—even library cataloguing—but sometimes her enthusiasm exhausted me.

When I walked into my bedroom, I saw a letter waiting for me with Tom's handwriting on the envelope. I quickly closed my door and sat down, sliding the letter out. I closed my eyes for a moment and took a couple of deep breaths before opening my eyes again to see what Tom had to say for himself.

December 25, 1944
Dearest Maggie,

I got your telegram today telling me Jane is safe and sound and living with you in North Platte. Thank you for the update as I was going crazy worrying about whether the two of you had found each other, or if she was still on her own in Chicago. So, thank you for letting me know you're both back home safely.

But, while telegrams are expensive, I wish you'd have spared me a few more words beyond Merry Christmas to know how you are. I haven't gotten a letter from you since I wrote to ask you to rescue her. I understand you were busy on the train, both to Chicago and back, and getting her settled, but I miss you and your letters, so please hurry and write to me.

When I asked the lieutenant if mail was being held or delayed, he couldn't find any reason why my mail wouldn't be getting to me. I commented how unusual it was not to have a letter from you in more than two weeks, and he joked maybe you were angry with me.

Are you angry with me? If so, please write and tell me why.

I know I didn't send you a Christmas gift this year, and it's the first Christmas we've been engaged, but there isn't anything on this tiny island that I'd want to send to you. Besides, I know you're not the kind of woman to hold it against me if you didn't get a present.

I did receive your gift package, and thank you. The Christmas cookies were slightly melted (maybe no frosting next time, as I'm in the tropics), but still delicious. You wrapped them so well nothing else was damaged by the melted frosting. The socks are definitely needed and the talcum powder and insect repellant are exactly what I wanted. Thank you for everything.

So, if I haven't hurt your feelings by my lack of holiday gift, is it only your extended trip that kept you from writing? Or are you angry that I asked you to go pick up Jane? I know I'm not impartial, since she's my daughter, but I just know you two will get a long wonderfully. She's like you in so many ways. If you just give her a chance, I'm sure you'll fall in love with her, just as I fell in love with you.

The fighting continues here "somewhere in the Pacific." I'm getting weary of Army life and look forward to being in North Platte with both of my girls.

I'd like to say the Japs are ready to surrender, but I'm not sure it's in their makeup. From what I've seen, they think and act with such different priorities and conditioning, it's difficult for us to understand or predict. Their culture is dissimilar to ours in every way.

Sorry if I was harping on you about writing to me. I know how busy you are with work, the Canteen, and everything else. I look back at this letter and realize how much I've asked of you. Thank you for bringing my daughter into your home. It's not our home yet, although I can't wait for that to be true. But, at least now, the two girls I love most are together, and that makes me happy. I really believe you'll get along and she'll soon feel more like a daughter.

Give Jane my love and keep some for yourself. I wish even more than ever I was with you tonight. Merry Christmas! All my love, Tom

How could the man be so clueless? Of course, I didn't care he hadn't sent me a Christmas gift. And, of course, Jane is a lovely girl, and things were going well between us.

But, yes, I was angry. He had to realize how crazy it was that he hadn't told me about his daughter until he ordered me to take care of her. Maybe the Army operated on a "need to know" basis, but he was sadly mistaken if he thought our marriage was going to work that way.

****

January 7, 1945

Jane and I walked in the door from church to find Mother at the kitchen table, filling a bowl with soup. Her hands were shaking, and she had spilled soup on the table and the floor.

"Good morning, Mrs. Parker." Jane scooted up the back stairs to her room.

Mother said nothing. She'd been more irritable than usual in the last few days and sloppy drunk all the time. Even now, in the middle of a Sunday, there were several empty bottles in the trash.

I was used to her drinking, but she seemed to be worse than ever. Perhaps Jane being here had set her off. She'd never wanted anyone to visit the house. I guess she'd saved her drunken behavior for me alone.

Before church, I had put a chicken in the oven to roast. Opening the oven door, I pulled it out, basted it, and closed the oven. After getting a handful of potatoes off the back porch, I put water on to boil and started peeling the potatoes.

"How long's the girl stayin'?" Mother asked between slurps of soup.

Couldn't she just eat her darned soup and leave us alone? I'd have to mop the kitchen when she was finished.

"I don't know, but it's no concern of yours." I cut the potatoes into small chunks and dropped them in the boiling water.

"Some stranger livin' in my house is my concern." Her tone was vile, but the edge was blurred by the drink.

I picked up the cutting board and knife, walking to the sink to wash them off. "I'll invite anyone I like to live in my house, and you have no say in it. If you don't like it, move out."

She breathed in sharply. "That's no way to talk to your..."

I turned on her. "Don't say 'your mother,' as you forfeited that role long ago." Maybe my anger at Tom was fueling my outburst, but I wasn't going to fight with my mother every time I walked into my house. "I wasn't much older than Jane is now when you curled up into a bottle and left me to take care of myself. It's only because of Daddy's war pension and what I earned at the library, starting even while I was still in school, that we could even afford to stay in this house. You never lifted a hand to help or paid a dime of the mortgage. This house is mine, and you'd best keep your mouth shut about it."

Her cheeks grew red and her eyes were glazed, but instead of yelling, she got up and started shuffling toward the parlor. I was about to call after her, to tell her to pick up her own dishes, when she slid on the wet floor.

Her feet went out from under her and her head hit hard on the kitchen floor. I walked around the table and crouched down. Her eyes were closed.

"Mother? Are you all right?" I tried shaking her, but got no response.

She didn't answer, but Jane came rushing down the stairs.

"What happened?"

I looked at Jane. "My mother slipped and hit her head. Would you please call the doctor? His number is next to the telephone."

I checked my mother's pulse, as I had read about in a first aid pamphlet from the American Red Cross. Her heart seemed to be beating, but I couldn't wake her up.

"The doctor is on his way, but he said to call an ambulance as well. Since the number was on the same notepad, I called them, and one is on its way." She was very composed for a young girl in an emergency.

"Thank you. That was a big help." While my mother might be so drunk that she'd passed out again, all color had drained from her skin. "Would you go to the front door and wait for the ambulance, dear. You'll need to tell them to come to the kitchen door."

"Yes, ma'am." She went through the parlor and, shortly, I heard her speaking to the ambulance crew.

Still, my mother didn't wake.

Jane came back through the kitchen. "The doctor is here, too." She went to the back door, unlocked it, and let everyone in.

"What happened?" Doc Olson had been my doctor since I was a young girl. His hands were dry and scratchy as sand paper and his hair was nothing more than wisps of white clouds above each ear. Still, he took control of the situation just by entering the room.

As I moved back to let him get closer to Mother, I found my hands were starting to shake. He checked her pulse and eyes, pulled out his stethoscope, and listened to her heart. Finally, his kind and caring eyes met mine.

I swallowed the lump in my throat. "She slipped, Doc. She'd splashed soup all over the floor and wasn't too steady to begin with, but when she took a step, she went down like a sack of cement. She may have passed out from the alcohol, and it wouldn't be the first time."

He nodded. We'd discussed my mother's drinking issues many times. "Has she come to since the fall?"

I shook my head. "I don't think so. I couldn't get her to answer me or open her eyes."

The ambulance crew loaded Mother onto a stretcher. When they rolled her out of the kitchen, there was blood on the floor where she'd hit her head.

Dr. Olson took my hand. "Why don't you..." He looked at Jane and added, "Why don't the two of you ride with me to the hospital?"

I nodded and turned to Jane. "Get your book or homework or whatever. We may be there a while." I started for my coat, but turned back to her. "Unless you'd rather stay here?"

She shook her head. "I'll be right back."

Doc Olson helped me on with my coat and I started to walk with him to the back door. At the last moment, I ran back to turn off the oven and stove top, and then followed Jane out the back door to the doctor's car.

****

January 8, 1945

Rose walked right to the sink, filled the teapot, and put it on to boil. She pulled down three cups, some tea, and even the well-hidden and little-used sugar bowl.

After hanging up my coat, I wasn't sure what to do next. My headache was overwhelming, and I couldn't think straight.

Jane directed me to a chair at the kitchen table and then ran upstairs. She was back down in a flash and started rummaging through the icebox, pulling out last night's chicken.

"I'm starving," Jane said. "You must be too, Miss Maggie."

Rose added sugar to one of the tea cups and pushed it to me. "Drink your tea and eat the sandwich. You need something to sustain you before you head upstairs for a nap."

I looked at the food in front of me. These two young women were taking good care of me, although I wasn't sure I could swallow one bite. I sipped the tea and looked first at Jane and then Rose.

"I'm fine, you two. Sure, I'm tired, as we were at the hospital all night. But, really, my mother and I were barely roommates, never mind close. I'm fine."

Rose nodded. "Right."

Jane said nothing, but wolfed down her sandwich. I picked at half of the one she made for me, but passed her the second half. "I can't possibly eat it all, dear."

She bobbed her head, her gaze meeting mine, and then wolfed down the other half to my sandwich, too. She'd also had a long night.

Once we were done eating, Rose stood, taking the plates to the sink. "Why don't you two go lie down and see if you can sleep?"

I shook my head, although it seemed to be on the edge of bursting open at the seams. "I have to call the undertaker and make arrangements for Mother's funeral."

Rose pulled up a chair next to me and wrapped her arm around my shoulder. "You got no sleep last night and need to get some rest. You'll have a lot of responsibilities over the next few days, and you don't want to be sick. Surely, it won't matter if you call the undertaker this evening or tomorrow?"

I wasn't sure I could sleep, although I was exhausted and a little nauseated. "Maybe you're right. It's not like Mother had a lot of friends who will be rushing to the door with casseroles or anxious to find out when the services will be."

Rose smiled. "How about this? I brought my knitting and a good book. I'll stay here while you sleep. I'll answer the telephone, or the door, if anyone stops by."

I nodded. "Thank you. I'll rest much easier knowing you're here to handle anything that comes up." I turned to Jane. "Before I go upstairs to lie down, I'll call the school and let them know you won't be in school, at least for the next few days." Turning back to Rose. "Would you mind calling Mrs. Tenney to see if Lorma would pick up any homework for Jane and bring it to us?"

She nodded. "Of course, and why don't you let me call the school as well. Just put everything out of your mind for now, both of you," she nodded at Jane. "I'll take care of the details."

I hugged Rose and followed Jane up the stairs. As I walked passed her bedroom door, I stopped, leaning on the doorframe. "Thank you for staying with me last night, Jane."

She nodded, her eyes wide. "Of course, Miss Maggie. And I'm so sorry about your mother."

I smiled. "She was not a pleasant woman. We had plenty of problems between us, but I'm not sure it was her time to die."

Jane stepped closer to me, wrapping her thin arms around me silently. She let go, stepped back, and smiled.

"Get some sleep, Jane. We had a long night."

Doc Olson said Mother had fractured her skull when she hit the floor. She never woke up. Of course, we were fighting when she died. We were always at each other's throats. I didn't spend time with her, share meals with her, or even like her. Why did it feel as if the world was slightly off-kilter today?

Tears began trailing down my cheeks. I was exhausted, my defenses were low, and I needed some sleep. Everything would be better tomorrow, and by the time the funeral was over, life would go back to normal. I probably wouldn't even notice she was gone.

CHAPTER THIRTY-THREE

January 9, 1945

I'd slept all day, according to the clock on my bedside table which clearly said 5:00.

Rose was asleep on the sofa in the parlor, so I tiptoed back into the kitchen to pull together some dinner. The icebox was full of dishes I'd never seen before. I pulled out a glass bowl and saw some type of jellied salad. Behind that, there appeared to be a fried chicken. After supper, I'd make lists of everything to serve anyone who came back to the house after the funeral to determine whose dishes these were.

Glass was clanking at the back door, so I walked to it and opened the door. Our milkman, Herbert, was replacing empty milk bottles with full ones.

"Herbert, what are you doing here?"

He looked up at me, his eyes narrowed briefly, but then he glanced at his watch. "I might be a few minutes late, Maggie. My apologies."

I looked at my watch again. "It's five o'clock. Aren't you more like twelve hours late? Or twelve hours, early, I guess."

He handed me the milk bottles. "I always deliver the milk at this time of morning. Now, if you don't mind, I'm going to be late for the rest of my route."

I started to turn, shaking my head, but then stopped in my tracks. "Did you say *morning*, Herbert?"

He chuckled now. "Yes, ma'am. Have a nice Tuesday." He walked down the back steps and back to his truck.

I hurried into the kitchen, putting the milk in the icebox, although I had to remove some casseroles to get it in there. I pulled out a chair and sat. Rose had left a note for me on the table:

Maggie – I guess you were very tired, which is perfectly understandable. I called Mr. Turner at the funeral home and he's going to take care of everything. He said to call him or stop by when you can. I called the school. I spoke with Ann, who is sending Lorma over tomorrow with Jane's homework. I called in some library volunteers to handle our shifts for Monday through Wednesday and have more on backup if you need more time. Several women from the Canteen stopped by with food. I hope you don't mind, but I decided to sleep on your sofa in case anything came up in the night. Jane was awake for supper, but went back to bed early. Please wake me if you need anything. Love, Rose

At the bottom of the note, she'd jotted a postscript: *P.S. Jane sent Tom a telegram.*

I got up to make some coffee, but was at a loss as to what to do now. Nothing made sense. When my father died, I'd been devastated. I'd lost my first best friend and knew, even then, life with Mother would never be fun.

When Fred died, I'd been devastated again. I'd lost my second best friend, my fiancé, and my chance at a new life away from my mother. Mother had been cruel and reveled in my loneliness.

So, with Mother's death, I expected to feel relieved and vindicated. I was hopeful for a future without the strife of navigating life in half a house, avoiding her and her drunken rage, and dealing with my constant resentment of her. Whether or not that future included Tom and Jane, I was free of the bickering and nastiness my mother spewed whenever she showed her face.

But in addition to relief and all of the positive feelings that came with not having to deal with Mother any more, I also felt alone. I hadn't expected to feel so lost.

I looked up at a tentative knock and saw Rose standing in the doorway to the parlor. "How are you doing this morning?"

She walked to the cupboard, got two cups, and poured us the coffee I'd made but ignored.

I shook my head. "I'm amazed I slept through the whole day yesterday. Why didn't you wake me?"

She smiled. "Because there was no need to. I figured you'd wake up when you were rested. Are you?"

I looked at her. "Rested? I guess so, although I feel a bit as if I'm wrapped in cotton batting." I looked around the room. "I still have a headache, and, you know, it's like I'm removed from everything a little." I motioned toward the icebox. "A lot of people dropped off food, I see."

She nodded. "You have quite a few friends. Ann and Sue will coordinate the luncheon for after the funeral, so let them know what the plans are."

I sipped the coffee, hoping it would eat a way through the fog in my head. "That's so kind of them, of everyone who brought food. One less thing to worry about, I guess." I shook my head. "I don't know…"

"What?"

"How do I mourn a woman I hated? I can't see myself standing by her casket, receiving condolences from people." I shrugged. "I didn't wish her dead, but I didn't want her to be a part of my life. Now, she won't be, and I can't pretend to be sad about it, but I'm not sure how I feel." Despite all the sleep I'd just had, I mostly wanted to go back to bed.

Rose looked up, her eyes wide. "Are you somehow blaming yourself for what happened?"

I didn't speak at first, the images from Sunday going through, in my mind. My feelings were a jumble, but didn't include guilt over my mother's death. "No," I shook my head. "She died because she was so drunk she made a mess and was too drunk to stop herself from falling in it. It wasn't my fault."

She nodded. "Good." She took my hand and gave it a gentle squeeze before releasing it again. "So what's going round in that head of yours?"

I smiled. "I don't really know. I'm tired, overwhelmed, and dreading the funeral."

"You know, anyone who comes to the funeral is coming to support you, right? Not to mourn your mother. I don't know it for a fact, but I suspect she didn't have a single friend. Your friends will come out of respect and love for you. Just let them comfort you and absorb all those good feelings they have for you."

Rose was the sister, daughter, and girlfriend I'd never had, all rolled into one. Despite the age difference, she was dearer to me than anyone. I leaned over and hugged her. "Thank you. That's the perfect way to look at it."

I stood up, as did she, and we hugged. "Now, go home." I chuckled.

"Kicking me out?" Rose laughed.

"I have a lot of cleaning to do in the parlor and front room, and I think I need to do it by myself."

Her smile dimmed. "Are you sure you want to start on it now?"

I nodded, pointing to our lists. "We planned how the luncheon will be here after the funeral, and I'm not letting anyone else into the parlor until I take it back."

She shook her head. "Take it back?"

I smiled. "My mother held the front of the house hostage for all these years. It'll be nice to live in more than two rooms again. She had the front room and the parlor as her private domain, leaving me the kitchen and my bedroom. It'll be nice to sit on the sofa, listen to the radio, and even let people into my house through the front door. I'm going to enjoy airing things out and setting it up how I want it to be."

She nodded. "Okay, then. I'm going home to wash up and change. If you need anything, give me a call."

I gave her a hug as she left. I looked around the kitchen, pulling out cleaning supplies, and heating water. There was nothing like scrubbing the house to clear my head.

By the time Jane came downstairs several hours later, the parlor was clean, the drapes open, the lights on, and the furniture rearranged.

"Oh my goodness," she exclaimed. "This room looks wonderful."

Smiling, I put my hands on my hips, working a little kink out of my back. "It does, doesn't it?"

She shrugged, bowing her head. "You should have woken me. If I'd known you were cleaning like this…"

I held up a hand. "I needed to do it by myself. It was cathartic." My gaze met hers. "My mother and I had a terrible relationship and, even if I didn't wish her dead, I won't pretend I'm going to miss her. But with her gone, I'm sort of declaring my independence again. Taking back the whole house. We'll be much more comfortable this way."

She ran up the front stairs and back down. "There so much space now." She stopped suddenly, her eyes going wide and her mouth forming a circle. "I'm so sorry. I'm excited about the space, but you just lost your mother. I'm being insensitive."

I shook my head. "As I said, I didn't wish her dead, but there's no reason we can't enjoy having the whole house to ourselves now, is there?"

She nodded. "Until my dad comes home, then there will be the three of us."

Jane gave me a quick hug, skipped back through the parlor and pulled open the pocket doors to the kitchen. "We should keep these open all the time now."

I looked around at my clean, reclaimed house and tried to picture Tom there. When we'd first become engaged, I had no trouble picturing myself living with Tom. It wasn't clear in my mind how it would work with Mother there, but the thought of Tom and me living together was easy to see.

Now, Mother was gone. I felt like the house, and my life, was mine again, to do with as I pleased. So, what did I want to do?

What was I going to do?

I loved Tom, even though I was angry with him. The anger I could get over, although he had to understand that he couldn't order me about. If we were going to be married, he was going to have to show me more respect than that. And no more secrets. I certainly didn't appreciate being deceived for so long, even though Jane is a lovely girl.

I didn't want to spend my life angry, like my mother did. I also didn't want to be alone if I didn't have to be, but I wasn't willing to compromise my values simply to be married.

We'd have to talk about what had caused my anger, and he'd need to see why he owes me an apology. Many things would need to change. But, if change were possible, if he truly regretted how he'd treated me, maybe we could start over.

But, what if he *couldn't* change? And given that he'd walked out on Jane, could I reconcile myself with the idea of being married to an "Army man" who doled out orders for the rest of my life? How could he give his only child to Aunt Wilma and disappear? I wasn't sure anything could excuse that kind of behavior.

CHAPTER THIRTY-FOUR

January 14, 1945

"I'm going to finish my homework so I'm ready to go back to school tomorrow." Jane hung her coat in the hall closet and looked at me, her eyebrows raised.

I nodded. "Sounds like a good idea." Thank goodness I didn't have to nag the girl to do her homework.

She bounded up the stairs to her room. She hadn't needed to take the whole week off school, but it was nice to have more time together. We'd set up the house the way we wanted and were getting comfortable in our new space.

Every day, I was more thankful for Jane. She saw the good in every person and every situation. She was comfortable speaking to adults and entertaining herself. Our time together was productive with cooking, reading, working, knitting, or even simply talking about our days. We had fun playing cards and games together, but also working at the Canteen. I wasn't really sure how to be a mother, especially to a twelve-year-old girl, but she was making it seem easy. She'd be particularly helpful this past week.

I was definitely getting used to having her around, although I still had no idea what to say to her father, so I just didn't write.

There had been a lovely turnout for the funeral. I was humbled by the number of people who showed up for me, as I don't think any of them knew my mother. While I'd been on leave from the library, Rose had stopped by every day with gifts of food and flowers, as well as cards, which had been delivered there for me. It may have taken all of my life, but I had friends in this town and it made everything about this week easier.

In the kitchen, I pulled out a casserole that had been delivered after the funeral, trying to resurrect it for one more meal. After putting it in the oven, I took a book I was reading to the sofa to relax. I may have dozed off, as the next thing I heard was Jane coming down the stairs.

"Is something burning?"

"Oh, no." I jumped up and raced to the kitchen. When I pulled the casserole out of the oven, it was black.

"Excellent." She chuckled. "It wasn't good to begin with," Jane said, peering over my shoulder. "Who would ever have thought to mix tuna and canned fruit?"

I chuckled. "It wasn't very good, but I hated to waste it."

She nodded. "That's why I'm glad it burned. Aunt Will would never let us waste food either, even when it was terrible. Sometimes, we'd have the same terrible dish for two or three meals in a row."

I nodded. "You don't talk about your aunt very often. Do you miss her?"

She looked up, her gaze meeting mine, and sighed. "I do miss her. She was kind, smart, and fun, even if she was a terrible cook."

I put my hand on her shoulder. "I'm glad she was able to take care of you. Did you like living with her?"

She smiled. "Yes. There weren't many kids in the neighborhood, but I had some good friends at school. Aunt Will and I would take outings around the city, visit the parks, museums, and libraries. Plus, she had a houseful of books and she let me read whatever I liked."

"I think I would have liked your Aunt Will."

She nodded. "I think so, too. She would have liked the way you take care of people, think about their feelings, and also the way you like to read."

After a bite of my sandwich, I said what was really on my mind: "Did you get to see your father often, while you were growing up?"

She shrugged. "Not as often as I would have liked, for sure. He came to Chicago whenever he got leave, but he was stationed all over the country, so he didn't get much of a chance. But, as I'm sure you know, he's a great letter writer. I have always gotten a lot of letters from him. Not quite every day, but pretty close."

"He's always written to you so often?"

She nodded. "Even when I was little. Aunt Will would have to read me the letters, but I kept them all. It was like he was with me, even if I couldn't touch him. Back then, my friends were jealous because they never got mail."

Jane ate some of her soup. "He always answered my questions, told me where he was, what he was doing, what he was reading, and asked me everything about my day. Just like he was really there."

I nodded. Tom did write a good letter. But, did he think that was enough of a substitute for a father?

"What kinds of things would you do together when he visited?"

She smiled again. "We would visit Grant Park, unless it was winter, go to the Museum of Science and Industry, or the Natural History Museum. Sometimes, we'd stay home and play card games or checkers, or even play out in the snow." She looked down at her soup, taking a big spoonful. After she swallowed, she looked back up at me. "He could never stay for long, but it was always great to have him come home."

"Did you ever wonder why he didn't leave the Army so you could live together?" I watched her face, but her smile never faltered.

"It was his job." She shrugged. "It would have been great to have him home all the time, but I had Aunt Will, and I knew he had to do his job." She ate some more soup.

I nodded, but didn't want to push. I had no idea when the war would be over or when Tom would be home, so I didn't want to stir up a hornet's nest. But, even in hard times, he could have found another job.

She looked up from her dinner. "That's why I'm so excited about you and Dad getting married and him finally retiring from the Army. It's going to be great for our family to be all together. This house is so nice, now. I'm going to like living here with you and Dad."

She seemed genuinely excited and happy, not resentful of either Tom for his years in the Army or me for staking claim to Tom. But, then again, what did I know about adolescent girls?

As I started to gather up our empty plates, the girl stood and met my gaze. "I don't know if I'm supposed to tell you this, but since you're going to kind of be my mother, I guess it's the kind of thing mothers and daughters might share."

I set down the plates and smiled. "What is it?"

She sighed. "Dad has sounded so much happier since you agreed to marry him. He's always been pretty happy, writing about the great men he works with, the good work they do, and different sorts of thing. But he is more excited about life after the war, and when he comes home to us both, since you two got engaged. It's nice. That's all. I'm happy for him and for all of us."

She wrapped me in a hug and I squeezed back. This kind and gentle child deserved a family and a happy home. I just wasn't sure I was the right person to give it to her.

****

January 9, 1945
My darling Maggie,

I got Jane's telegram saying your mother died suddenly. While I know the two of you were not close, I'm so sorry for what you're going through. I wish I could be there to hold you, to help you, to take care of you.

I'm very sorry for your loss. In my mind, I can hear you saying it wasn't a loss for you because you didn't even like your mother, but it's your loss because she was there. She gave birth to you, shared a house with you, and shared your father with you. There may have been a glimmer of hope somewhere in the far reaches of your mind that she would wake up one day, realize what a terrible mother she'd been to you, change completely, and make it all up to you.

We both know the chances of an about-face were miniscule, but with her gone now, there is no longer any chance. You have to come to terms with the loss of that possibility, and I wish I were there to help.

You can take comfort in the fact you have worked hard for years to provide a home, food, and all of life's necessities for your mother. You took good care of her, even though she never took care of you, even when you were Jane's age. You were a good daughter to a woman who was no kind of mother to you.

I haven't gotten a letter from you in a couple of weeks, but I understand why you haven't had time to write. First, the train trip to Chicago and back to get Jane, then Christmas, getting her settled in her new school, and your mother's death. You've had a lot of upheaval for such a short period of time.

I hope that's the only reason you haven't written. If there's something more going on with you, or between us, please just tell me.

Jane sounds happy in her letters, and she says she loves living with you in North Platte. She seems to be adjusting well, and I'm not worried about her doing well at school, as she's always enjoyed it. While she has been great about writing and letting me know how everything is going, I am anxious to hear from you, my love. Please, find some time to write me a letter and fill me in on how you are handling everything. Know I am thinking of you and love you more than ever.

Is it selfish of me to say I love the picture I have in my mind now of you and Jane sitting in the parlor, reading your books in companionable quiet, enjoying the warmth of the fire? And I can't wait to be the loud oaf who crashes your womanly party of two. I long for the day the three of us will putter around the house together, reading, laughing, playing cards, or even working in the garden. These are the dreams that keep a smile on my face despite the struggles around me.

While we are making strides every day here in the Pacific, and the war in Europe seems to be drawing to a close, I can't say I see a quick or easy end to the battle here. The Japanese are a completely different type of enemy than we've faced before, and I think it's taken us all a long time to realize we cannot predict what they will do in any given situation.

Picture me wrapping my arms around you and holding you tight. Know I would take on any of the pain you are going through if only I could. I love you more than I can say and wait anxiously to hear from you, as soon as you're able to find a quiet moment to write.

Until I can curl up on the sofa with you and Jane, know I am always yours, Tom

CHAPTER THIRTY-FIVE

I've never been good at deception, preferring to face my problems head-on, which worked great when you were able to speak to someone in person and work through disagreements together. Unfortunately, that wasn't so efficient when the disagreement was happening long distance.

I hadn't worked through my anger at Tom or even told him how angry I was yet. Of course, if he knew anything about me, he should have guessed how I would react to orders and secrets. But, in the meantime, I had to figure out how to write to him about Jane, keep the lines of communication open, and eventually work out our differences. If possible.

January 17, 1945
Dear Tom,

Thank you for your letter and kind words in connection with my mother's death. I appreciate your insight into my conflicted feelings at her passing.

I'm starting to understand, because my relationship with my mother was complex, and my feelings about her death are also complex.

I haven't had much time to write. You're right, things have been very hectic between the journey to Chicago and back, which took about a week, moving Jane in to the house, the holiday, and then mother's death and funeral. My life has changed a great deal in the past few weeks, especially given I'd never expected to be responsible for an adolescent girl.

Jane is adjusting nicely to living with me in North Platte. She is making friends at school and is, as you said, a good student. She comes to the library after school every day to work on her homework and read until I'm done with work.

When I volunteer at the Canteen; she does, too. She dances with servicemen who want to use a few of their precious minutes with us to dance with a pretty, young girl. She helps the younger children sort donated items into platform baskets and works in the kitchen. She's an old hand at sandwich making already. She works hard, but I think she's having fun, too.

I don't know Jane well yet, but from what I can see, she is happy. We've talked about your Aunt Will a few times and, although she is clearly sad at your aunt's passing, she likes talking about her and their life together.

I think she is thriving and wanted you to know. Take care & stay safe —

Love, Maggie

****

January 20, 1945

"I'm so tired; I may climb into bed in my clothes."

I smiled. "Me, too, Jane." I rifled through the mail as we walked into the parlor. "We had a lot of servicemen through the Canteen today."

She walked into the kitchen and poured a glass of milk. "Want anything?"

I followed her in the kitchen, turning on the heat under the tea pot. "I think I'll have some tea."

She nodded while drinking.

I pulled out a cup and tea bag and filled it when the water was hot.

"You have mail." I handed her a letter with Tom's handwriting on it.

She set down, her mail unopened. "Can I ask you something, Miss Maggie?"

"Sure."

"Are you and Dad having a fight?"

I paused. Nothing got passed this girl. "Not really a fight. Just a disagreement, but nothing for you to worry about."

She nodded. "What did he do? Did he forget your birthday? Sometimes, he's oblivious to stuff like that. I try to remind him the world keeps going when he's away, but he seems to think we're all frozen in time in the last spot where he saw us."

I rubbed my eyes but then met her gaze. "Maybe it's something like that. We're not communicating very well right now." I shook my head. "Why did I think it a good idea to have a relationship and become engaged in the middle of a war?"

Jane's smile was simple and serene. "Because that's when you met my dad."

Shaking my head, I had to smile. She had me there. "That's true." I took a sip of my tea. "But, it's hard to be a couple when we're separated by thousands of miles. A war is a tough time to get to know someone."

She nodded. "Lucky Dad's such a good letter writer. That's how he and I got to be so close, even though he was always away with the Army."

"It must have been hard on you both."

"It was," she said, as she twirled a long strand of hair which had escaped her pins. "Sometimes I would get really mad at him for not being home with me like the other dads were. But he always seemed to know when I was mad, and he'd write me a long letter, asking about what I was doing, telling me what he was doing, including me on all the little things in his life, like he wanted to know what I thought about something. I like that."

I smiled. Jane sat up, leaning forward over her tea. "He told me it was okay to be mad at him, even in a letter. He said we would also work through whatever we were mad about, as long as we kept writing to each other. So we always did."

Communication was key, but it had to go both ways. Wise words between a father and daughter. Only time would tell if that applied to us as well.

CHAPTER THIRTY-SIX

February 3, 1945

Jane came downstairs dressed in her warmest dress, tights, and sweater. When I caught her gaze, she blushed. "It was so cold at the Canteen last week. By the time we got home, I thought I'd never get warm again."

I nodded. "Why don't you bring the slacks we got for you when you work in the Victory Garden? No one will care if you slide those under your dress when you're filling baskets out on the platform. You don't have to wear them when you're dancing."

She laughed. "If I did, I might not have any willing partners."

After she got her slacks and we both bundled up in our coats, boots, hats, and gloves, we carried our baskets of apples, boiled eggs, sandwich meat, and popcorn balls to the Canteen. Once there, she rushed back to the kitchen with the eggs and meat, and I dropped the apples and popcorn balls on the platform.

"Good morning, Maggie."

I turned and saw Sue walking into the depot with a full basket in each hand. "Good morning. It's a bitter one, isn't it?"

She smiled, putting down her baskets and unwrapping the many lengths of scarf encasing her face and neck. "I felt like an Eskimo when I walked out of the house this morning. I can barely move in all these layers."

I nodded. "And with all the servicemen we have coming through here these days, the door to the Canteen is open more than it's closed."

"That won't change any time soon, will it?"

I shook my head. "With the end of the war in Europe growing closer every day, I think we'll have even more servicemen and women coming through when they start shipping people home."

Sue smiled. "And it can't come soon enough."

"I agree."

I took one of her baskets and we walked into the Canteen, closing the door behind us. It was a little warmer inside, but not when the door was open. It was going to be a long, cold day.

"Do you really think the war in Europe is almost over?" Sue's husband, Martin, was "somewhere in Europe."

"I do, Sue." I put my hand in hers. "Just yesterday, the *New York Times* reported the Russians liberated one of Hitler's death camps in Poland. They murdered more than a million and a half people there."

She shook her head. "Horrible."

I nodded. "But the good news is that the Allies are clearing a path to Berlin and dismantling the Nazi war machine. It won't be long now."

"From your lips to God's ear." She squeezed my hand and took back her second basket. She walked to her spot on the dessert table and started unloading pies.

I saw my friend Ann setting out sandwiches as quickly as Lorma and Jane brought them out from the kitchen.

I walked over to her, giving her a hug. "Good morning."

She shivered. "It's a cold one, but I guess it's good." Ann took a big sip of her coffee. She was not a morning person.

I walked to my table and found Ann had followed me, leaning close.

"Have you heard from Tom lately?"

I shook my head. "Not in the last few days. It's hard to know what's going on in the Pacific, but it sounds like there is a lot of fighting where I think he is." As the war progressed, we had a better idea where loved ones deployed to Europe were or, at least, where they were headed as all roads seemed to lead to Berlin now. But in the island-filled Pacific, it was harder to know where our servicemen might be.

She nodded. "I got a letter from Joe on Wednesday, but I have no clue about where he is either. Of course, because he's in the Navy, at least I know what ship he's on. With Tom in the Army, he could be on any little scrap of land, a ship, or anywhere." She quickly took hold of my hand. "I'm sorry, I didn't mean..."

I squeezed her hand. "I know what you mean, and I agree."

She nodded. "I can't wait until Joe gets home. I'm starting to lose my mind. This war has been going on too long."

"Right, and I don't even have four kids to handle all on my own."

She smiled. "Lorma's the easy one. It's the boys who are making me crazy."

Back at home after a long day, Jane pulled our mail out of her pocket. "I grabbed this when you were getting the wood. In addition to some bills and letters she had received from friends in Chicago, there were two letters from Tom. The first had her name on it, but the second one was mine.

"Oh, good. A letter from Dad." She grabbed her letters with a delighted squeal. "And one for you." She pushed the envelope toward me and added, "I'm going to bed." She dragged herself off the sofa, toward the stairs. "I can't keep my eyes open." At least she was still smiling, if nearly walking in her sleep.

"Goodnight, Jane. Thanks for all your hard work today."

She waved briefly as she climbed the stairs. Despite how tired I was, I slid my finger along the envelope seam and opened the letter.

January 18, 1945
Dear Maggie,

Thank you for your letter and the updates on Jane's transition into life in North Platte. I can't thank you enough for your kindness to her. Her letters are upbeat and happy, so I agree, she seems to be adjusting well. She was always an easygoing child, and I'm hoping that doesn't change as she gets older.

But what of you, Maggie? How are you doing? How is it to be back at work? I expect a lot of people in town have shown you kindness, given your warm heart, following the death of your mother. Jane told me how many people attended the funeral and luncheon afterward, and it sounds like they couldn't do enough for you. I'm sure it makes you uncomfortable, knowing you, but I hope you can finally see how important you are to the town and how universally loved you are.

We are seeing a lot of action these days, but I hope it is moving us closer to victory. I don't care if I ever come back to the South Pacific in my life. The heat and humidity are overwhelming, and everything is moldy. I have to hound my men to drink enough water and constantly change to dry socks. Any suggestions on how to keep mosquitoes away at night? We don't need more malaria, that's for sure. While it is beautiful here, at least where it's still untouched by war, but unlike McArthur, I will never return.

I have to call it a day and get some sleep. We never know when things will get stirred up here, so I have to catch sleep whenever I'm able. Please give Jane a hug for me and then write me long letters of what you are doing and how you are feeling. If we're to have a wonderful life together someday, Maggie, we have to keep talking, or at least writing, to each other. Please keep the lines of communication open and let me back into your heart and mind.

Please know I picture you and Jane on the sofa together, reading your books, and it brings a smile to my face every time. Keep my "girls" happy and healthy. All my love, Tom

****

February 24, 1945

"Jane?"

She looked up from her schoolwork. "Yes?"

I crouched down and spoke softly out of habit, as there was no one else left in the library. "I got a call saying more volunteers are needed at the Canteen. Do you want to go on home or would you rather come with me?"

She didn't hesitate. "I'll come to the Canteen."

"Okay. We'll leave in about five minutes." I went back to my office to close up and get my things.

As we headed out and locked up behind us, she caught my gaze. "Why do they need more volunteers tonight?" We didn't usually work on Thursdays.

I shrugged, juggling my pocketbook and work bag as we walked. "I believe the towns covering the Canteen today are fairly small, so they don't have enough people with them. Also, there are a great many hospital trains coming through."

When we got to the Canteen, Jane skipped off to refill platform baskets, while I found Clara Wells, the woman in charge of the evening's volunteers. She asked me to help on the platform, particularly with the hospital trains.

"So many wounded men are coming through today. It's taken a toll on some of our volunteers. I'd like to bring them inside to hand out food and drinks."

I nodded. "That's fine, Mrs. Wells. Do you know why there are so many more hospital trains?"

She looked around and then leaned in close. "I was told, quite confidentially by one of the MPs that the Army has liberated Corregidor and Bataan in the Philippines. Many of the wounded are headed east to hospitals near their homes."

I nodded. "I'm happy to help."

She raced off to the kitchen, and I walked to the platform as another train pulled in. I grabbed my basket full of care kits for the wounded and approached one end of the train.

A soldier guarded the door, which was an uncommon a sight on a hospital train. We were used to seeing this on POW trains, but we didn't serve the prisoners. On hospital trains, we usually talked to nurses or orderlies, passing our baskets of gifts for the wounded. The soldier stepped off the train and stood at attention at the door.

"We'd like to pass our baskets through the hospital car, offering care kits to the wounded servicemen," I said.

"Do you have care kits for women?" he asked.

I paused for a moment. Wounded women? "Well, everything in the care kit is applicable to women. We have combs, toothbrushes, toothpaste, razors, and similar toiletries, as well as magazines, cards, and cigarettes."

He nodded. "I'll pass the baskets into the wounded then."

I handed him the basket, but held the handle for a moment, until his gaze met mine. "These are wounded women?"

He stood even straighter. "They are some of the Angels of Bataan and Corregidor, ma'am. You may have read about the seventy-nine Army and Navy nurses held prisoner in the Philippines since the start of the war. They were liberated a few weeks ago."

My right hand flew to my chest, and I held it against my heart. "I heard about those brave women. Please send the basket through, but I'm going to rush into the Canteen for a moment, and I'll be right back."

I hurried into the Canteen and pulled my lipstick and face powder out of my pocketbook. I waved to Mrs. Wells.

"The nurses who were held prisoner in the Philippines for the last four years are on the hospital trains. If anyone wants to donate cosmetics, I'm sure they'd appreciate it."

Every woman there donated something from her pocketbook, including cosmetics, perfume, hair pins, combs, and even jewelry. I hurried back to the train and gave them to the guard.

"Please pass these out to the 'Angels,' as well, with the compliments and thanks of the women of North Platte."

He looked at the small bag of donations and nodded, his eyes a little red. "Thank you, ma'am. I'm sure the girls will appreciate you kindness. They sure deserve it."

I waited for the care package basket to be returned to me and stood at the train door as the soldier disappeared into it. Within moments, gaunt, smiling faces peered out the windows.

"Thank you," many called to me, and more were waving from within the train.

I whispered, "You're welcome," because I couldn't make my voice any louder. My throat was tight, and my eyes watery. I couldn't begin to imagine what these women had been through. The fact that any of them was able to smile over a lipstick or face powder moved me.

As the train started to pull away, I stood, waving with tears running down my face, as the Angels of Bataan and Corregidor pulled away. When I looked around the platform, the MPs and service members stood at attention, and everyone else was waving. Most of the women were crying. Those nurses had gone out of their way to tend the men entrusted to them and worked hard to survive, even when they were prisoners themselves.

CHAPTER THIRTY-SEVEN

March 28, 1945

"I want to stop by the Canteen on our way home tonight," I said, as I pulled the library door closed behind us.

Rose, Jane, and I were leaving the library. Rose was working full-time at the library these days, in addition to helping her mother at the boardinghouse, and volunteering at the Canteen. She was still writing to several soldiers, although her heart definitely belonged to only one.

"Do they need volunteers?" Rose fell into step beside me, and Jane followed behind us.

I shook my head. "I haven't heard anything, either by phone or on the radio. I got a call from Helen Christ saying I should stop in and pick up a very important letter."

She smiled. "I got a pretty important letter yesterday."

She was clearly bursting to tell me about it, so I smiled. "What was so important about it?"

She pulled it from her pocket. "Harry is doing well. His foot is completely recovered, which is good, because he has, apparently, marched to Germany in nearly one long stretch, and he is ready for the war to be over, so he can get some rest." She giggled.

"He told you he's in Germany?" Jane piped up from the rear.

Rose shook her head. "No, silly. He uses words that will get by the sensor like: "near our ultimate goal" and "to the bull's-eye." I know what he means, though."

I nodded. "I'm sure everyone is ready for the war to be over."

"Except the Germans," said Jane.

I looked at her over my shoulder. "No, I expect the Germans are ready for the war to end, too, at least, everyone except Hitler and his high command."

Rose nodded. "Harry did tell me how hard it is, now that they are near their ultimate destination, to be conquering the locals instead of liberating them. Especially since the French and Belgians they liberated were starving and barely hanging on, but the locals they are conquering now, in other words: the Germans, are well fed, clean, and their homes are not even bombed out. It makes Harry and his buddies angry to see how well the Germans have survived the war compared to the places the Nazis had occupied."

I exhaled deeply. "I hadn't really considered that, but it must be very hard for the soldiers to deal with what they are uncovering as they move across the continent."

Rose held out her hands, shaking them in excitement. "Anyway, the fun part of the letter is he's already making plans for after the war. He says the Army will want to discharge as many men as possible as soon as possible so they can stop feeding and paying them. So, Harry's going to volunteer to be one of the early ones out, since he's got his points. He's going to get on a train to North Platte and come straight to me."

I smiled. "That sounds wonderful." I prayed it worked out just as she said for both their sakes.

She lowered her voice. "Harry says he'll send me a telegram to let me know he's on his way, so I can meet him at the station. He wants to sweep me off my feet, kiss me senseless, and then get me to a church to get married." Rose's voice got higher and softer and her smile was a wide as it could get.

I wrapped my arms around her. "Congratulations. I'm so happy for you. Harry is a lucky man."

Jane hugged Rose, too. "That's great!"

When we were walking again, Rose clearly had something else on her mind. "What's wrong?"

She looked at me quickly, then focused again on the sidewalk in front of her. "He really doesn't want to live in the city again. He says he wants a quiet life, having had enough of cities after all the time he was stationed in London."

"Well, he was there through much of the bombing, right?"

She nodded. "Yeah. He said the people were ever so kind, but there were too many of them, and the city was dirty and smelly. He definitely doesn't want to live in a city again."

I nodded. "And you want to get out of North Platte still?"

She straightened her spine and turned to look at me. "Well, I'd rather not live too near my mother, as you well know, although I'd miss you terribly."

I reached out and took her hand. "Thank you. I would miss you, too."

"Do you think I'm wrong to want to get away from the boarding house and my mother?" She looked as young as the day we met.

I squeezed her hand. "Only you know what feels right to you." I took a deep breath and released it. "I wish you would talk things over with your mother, tell her how you feel, and let her tell her side of the story, whatever it might be, before you make any life-changing decisions, though."

She nodded. "I don't know how to talk to her about it."

"I understand. I certainly didn't have any wonderful, life-changing conversations with my mother either, but now that she's gone, we never will. Who knows, maybe I would have felt better if we had."

Rose looked at me, her eyes suspiciously red. "I guess I'll think about it some more. I could give it a try. Especially since it seems so important to Harry to live in North Platte."

I smiled. "Thatta' girl."

When we walked into the depot, Jane rushed to the circle of kids hanging around the piano. Rose and I continued to the kitchen to find Helen.

"Oh, Maggie," Helen smiled when she saw me. "I'm so glad you were able to stop by. This is one of the most important pieces of mail the Canteen has ever received." She pulled a long envelope out of her pocketbook.

The envelope was a heavy, cream-colored linen paper and the handwriting was sleek and elegant. Rose looked over my shoulder as I unfolded the matching letterhead inside.

"It's from the White House!" Rose exclaimed, practically in my ear.

I chuckled. "I can see that: from Mrs. Roosevelt." So I read it aloud.

"From Eleanor Roosevelt, The White House, 1600 Pennsylvania Avenue, Washington, D.C., dated March 23, 1945. To the Volunteers of the North Platte Servicemen's Canteen. I am delighted to hear about the North Platte Canteen. I congratulate all of you on the splendid job you are doing. I feel sure you have great satisfaction in knowing that you give so much pleasure and help to our young servicemen and women. My best wishes to all of you in this work and for your own boys who are in the service... Sincerely, Eleanor Roosevelt."

"Wow." Again, Rose spoke directly into my ear.

But I had to agree. "Yes, wow." I smiled. "It's wonderful she's heard of our efforts here and very kind of her to write us this note."

Helen was wringing her hands. "This should go in a special place in the scrapbook. Along with the note President Roosevelt sent us when he mailed the five-dollar bill."

I nodded. "I agree, Helen. I'll make sure the two notes are kept together."

****

March 29, 1945

When Rose came into work on Friday morning, she was smiling despite her droopy eyelids. After dropping her coat and bag in the employee break area, she walked into my office.

"You must have been up late last night. Did everything go well?"

She smiled shyly, looking at me from the side of her eye. "Good, thanks." Rose sat in one of my guest chairs.

I smiled. "And...?"

She shrugged. "You were right, as always. Don't you ever get tired of that?" Her brief smile didn't reach her eyes. "My mother doesn't blame me for what...you know, for what *he* tried to do. She sorta' seemed embarrassed, and when I asked her why, she said she should have known something like that would happen."

Rose's father had served in the Great War, but came home with shell shock. Apparently, Trixie wanted to give him time to be the man she married again, but he was angry, erratic, and violent. She didn't realize how much the war had changed him, though, until she walked in on him with Rose.

"She said she's sorry she didn't make him leave earlier. But, really, how could she have known?"

I shook my head. "You're right. She was in a terrible situation, both legally and morally. He was her husband, after all. But you're her little girl."

Rose nodded, tears pooling in her eyes. "That's what she said. She couldn't let him hurt me like that. He'd already scared us both enough with his terrible temper."

My heart ached for the young girl Rose had been. "She's a strong woman, both for making him leave and handling the boarding house on her own for all these years—with your help, of course."

Rose looked down at her hands. "She told me she made him sign over the house to her and me, so he couldn't come back and take it from us. I guess he was so afraid she was going to call the police or something that he just did what she told him."

I walked around my desk and sat next to Rose, resting my hand on her shoulder. "You are very lucky your mother is such a smart woman."

"The boardinghouse is ours, you know. I mean, it used to belong to my father's family until he signed it over to us. There's not even a mortgage. It's ours."

"That's wonderful. You have a secure home, no matter what, and an income." I tilted my head. "How do you feel about all of this?"

Rose looked up, her gaze meeting mine. "I've been pretty angry with her. I feel bad about how I treated her. She did it all to protect me. If only I'd talked to her about it before, we could have made up a long time ago." She dissolved in tears.

I pulled her into my arms and let her have a good cry.

When she calmed, I pulled back, met her gaze, and smiled. "I'm sure she understands how you feel, and how you acted towards her, Rose. She was probably beating herself up about the whole thing, too."

Rose nodded, but said nothing.

I patted her back. "Besides, there's always a certain amount of tension between mothers and daughters. I'm just glad you talked to her about it."

She wiped her face on her handkerchief and took a few calming breaths. "Me, too."

After repairing her face in the washroom, Rose took her place at the circulation desk just in time for me to unlock the front doors. When I turned back to look at her, she was smiling and the smile went all the way to her eyes. She was going to be okay.

CHAPTER THIRTY-EIGHT

April 8, 1947

When the man walked into the library, his posture gave him away as quickly as his limp as one of the many servicemen who had so recently returned from war.

"May I help you, sir?" I walked up to him, hoping to help him avoid more steps than necessary.

He nodded. "I hope so, ma'am. I stopped in at the train station, and they sent me here to talk to someone about the Canteen you all ran here during the war."

I smiled. "I believe I'm the woman you're looking for. I'm the Canteen historian." I motioned to a nearby table. "Please, won't you have a seat?"

He nodded and held out a chair for me before sitting.

"I'm Staff Sergeant William Harris. You probably don't remember me, but I came through your Canteen eight times."

I chuckled. "No wonder you look familiar to me, Staff Sergeant. My name when we met would have been Miss Margaret Parker, but you can call me Maggie now."

He shook my hand. "I believe we spoke on at least one or two occasions, Maggie."

I nodded. "I'm so glad you decided to stop in today, Staff Sergeant. It's wonderful to see you. Is there something in particular I can help you with?"

He nodded and withdrew an envelope from his jacket. "I live over in Auburn, Nebraska, now. It's down south of Omaha, right near the Missouri line. I'm married to the cutest little lady, and we have a real nice life. I was able to go back to college on the GI Bill. I only have one more year or so before I graduate. I'm going to be an engineer."

These were the kinds of stories I lived for. "That's wonderful. Congratulations."

"I wanted to come here because you all were so good to me during the war. After the last time I went through North Platte, in November of '44, I went off to the Pacific with four of my buddies. We were replacement troops, you see, for boys who were wounded or killed in action." He looked down at the envelope in his hand, sitting silently for a moment. When he spoke again, his voice broke. "Within nine months of getting to the Pacific, two of my friends were killed, and the other three of us were injured." He cleared his throat and continued. "I was hit on Mother's Day, 1945, same time as my buddy Jasper was killed. Anyhow, my last time through North Platte was on the hospital train that brought me home."

I put my hand on his for a moment, sharing a piece of his pain for his lost friends.

"When I came through that day, I was too out of it to even realize we were in North Platte until later, when I woke up. I asked when we'd get there, and the nurse told me I slept right through it."

"I'm sorry we missed seeing you then, Staff Sergeant."

He slid the envelope to me. "To Mrs. White" was written on the front.

"I came today to say thank you to Mrs. White. She wrote to me throughout the war, all because I tricked her out a birthday cake on my second time through the Canteen. She was really good to me, sending me packages and letters during the war, and I wanted to see her today and give her my thanks in person. But, I stopped at the address I had for her, and no one was home."

I smiled. "Mrs. White's husband was killed in action, Staff Sergeant. When the war was over, one of her neighbors came home injured, and she started helping him with chores he couldn't handle anymore. They were married a couple of months ago, so her name is Mrs. Snyder. She lives in the house across the street from where she used to live."

He started to rise. "That's great."

I put my hand out. "I can call her, if you like, and make sure she's home before you walk over there."

He nodded and sat back down. "That's very kind of you."

I called the Snyder house and returned to the table, smiling. "She's so happy to hear you're in town and want to see her, she's driving over here to pick you up. Apparently, the Snyders got a new car."

He stood and pushed in his chair. "Thank you so much for your help, both now and at the Canteen."

I shook his hand. "And thank you, Staff Sergeant, for everything you did for our country and for making the trip to North Platte a ninth time. That is such a nice thing for you to do."

He shook his head. "This town has cornered the market on nice, Maggie. Everything you people did for us, the food, letters, cakes, and morale boost, that was your own special miracle, and those of us guys who benefited from it will never be able to thank you all enough."

He pulled me into a rough hug, released me, and headed outside.

****

August 2, 1948
"Good morning, Maggie"

I looked up from the newspaper I was reading at my desk. "Oh, good morning, Rose. What brings you two in today?"

She stepped into my office, her daughter on her hip. "We came to town to pick up some decorations for Shirley's birthday party. The three of you are still planning to come over tonight, right?"

I nodded. "Definitely. We're looking forward to it." I smiled. "I don't get invited to many parties for two-year olds."

Shirley wiggled in her mother's arms until Rose set her down. Shirley toddled over to my desk, and I helped her up onto my lap. She started pushing papers around on my desk.

"Hold on, there, sweet pea. This one's important."

Rose looked over my shoulder. "What's important?"

I pointed to an article in the *Chicago Tribune*. "I have to add this to the Canteen scrapbook."

Rose read the headline. "Wisconsin Army Nurse awarded Silver Star posthumously." Her gaze caught mine. "Did you know her?"

I shrugged. "Not well. Nurse Ellen Cogsworth came through the Canteen in '42 on her way to the 56th Evac. Hospital in North Africa. She signed the guest book, and I asked her to write to let us know how she was doing. She wrote to me from Tunisia when she was about to be moved. She assumed they'd be going to Italy, although they didn't know it at the time. I never heard from her again. Now I know why."

Rose nodded. "What happened?"

I bounced Shirley on my knee, giving her a ring of my library keys to keep her occupied. "Ellen was sent to Anzio, where the Germans bombed their field hospital. She was one of four nurses awarded the Silver Star for bravery when they moved their patients to safety despite the artillery attack. Ellen was hit herself and died four days later from her wounds."

She laid a hand on my shoulder. "What a brave woman."

I nodded. "So many more servicemen would have died in the war but for those heroic nurses, whether they were Army, Navy, or from the Red Cross." I leaned in and kissed Shirley's head, breathing in the sweet smell of her soft brown baby curls. "Remember those nurses who were Japanese prisoners of war throughout the whole war in the Philippines? They kept working, in the POW hospital and probably saved some of the Americans who survived the Bataan Death March—despite the fact those nurses were being starved and abused themselves. Remarkable."

Rose scooped Shirley off my lap and gave me back my keys, much to the child's dismay. She plopped Shirley on her hip and started bouncing, like mothers of young children always seemed to do. "That will make an important addition to the scrapbook about Nurse Cogsworth. A sad but incredible end to her story."

I stood to give Shirley another kiss and pull her mother into a hug. "We'll see you tonight. I'm excited to watch this one's face when she digs into her cake and presents."

Rose smiled. "Me, too. See you tonight."

CHAPTER THIRTY-NINE

April 13, 1945
My dear Maggie,

The news reached us late last night of President Roosevelt's death yesterday. I have to say, our country will miss him and all his great works. I'm not blind to his faults, nor did I agree with all of his decisions, but he was a great man. It's a shame he didn't live to see the end of the war.

While I agree the end of the war seems imminent in Europe, we are not there yet in the Pacific. We are bringing the battle closer to the enemy, but there is a vast amount of real estate in this part of the world. Everything is so far apart, which makes it hard to drive to the finish line like what is happening in Germany. I hope we can convince the Japanese they have no chance of winning, and their country will be obliterated if they don't surrender. I'm not sure it'll happen or, if it does, how long and how many American lives it'll take.

Did you read the book recommended to me on Japanese culture by G.B. Sansom? I requested a copy from the American Red Cross and finally got it. I wanted to ask what you thought about it, as I found it fascinating. Please write with your impressions, if you are able to obtain a copy.

Thank you for your latest update on Jane. I'm glad to hear her school year is going so well. She loved school even as a tiny child. She's inquisitive and interested in the world around her, plus pretty bright. I think she got it from her mother.

Also, thanks for the account of her illness. I'm glad it turned out to be nothing more than a bad cold.

How are you, though, my dear Miss Maggie? Jane has written more about you than you have in months. She says you and I are having a long-distance disagreement and that I should apologize. Yet, I've heard nothing about it from you.

Talk to me, Maggie. Let me know what's going on in your head, what's troubling you, what feelings are in your heart. If you're upset with me, don't love me anymore, or have changed your mind about marrying me, please write to me about it. We need to talk about it, and letters are the best we can do right now. If everything is okay and you're just incredibly busy, which is hopefully what is keeping you from writing me the long, expressive letters I'd gotten used to, tell me that, too.

While I understand I have put a great deal responsibility on your shoulders by asking you take care of Jane, I also know you are the perfect woman for the job. And, from everything Jane tells me, you are incredible with her. So, again, thank you for stepping up when she, and I, needed you.

As with nearly every man in this war right now, my thoughts keep turning to what life will be like after the war. I notified my CO that I will be retiring as soon as I possibly can. He's a lifer, a West Point grad, so while he doesn't plan to retire until at least his mid- to late-fifties, he said he can understand my desire to settle down and spend time with my wife and daughter. He has begun the paperwork on my behalf, although nothing will be approved by Command until the war is over.

I will be entitled to the GI Bill when the war is over, which is supposed to provide inexpensive college tuition and mortgages, among other benefits. Since you own your house, we won't need a mortgage, unless you would like to move into a larger or newer house. Think about it—I want you to have everything you want or need in life. You have helped millions of service members, and I want to be the service member who is able to do things for you. We can shape our lives together however we choose, so please give it some thought.

I never asked if you want to stay in North Platte, but always assumed it. However, there's no reason we have to stay there other than it's a nice town. Give some thought to moving, too. I'm starting fresh, but will have my Army pension, so we can live wherever we want to.

I thank God for the stop in North Platte three-and-a-half years ago. I would never have made it through this war without your letters, packages, love, and support. I never thought I'd find a woman to love, who could love me in return, until I laid eyes on you that December day. You wanted nothing to do with my flirting, but didn't want to be rude to me either. You resisted my charm and charming letters, but thank you for giving in, writing me back, sending me countless packages of food and supplies, and, most of all, for falling in love with me and agreeing to be my wife.

You are what I'm fighting for, you and Jane both. I stay alive and keep my head down because I want to come home to you more than I've ever wanted anything in my life.

Okay, enough of this mushy stuff. I want you to know you mean the world to me, the entire world. I love Jane and can't wait to be there to see her grow into womanhood, but you, you are my heart.

All my love for you forever — Tom

****

May 8, 1945

When we walked into the depot, the whole town must have been there. Music was blasting from the PA system. Someone had hung bunting and flags all over the platform. The celebration was in full swing.

"Holy cow!" Jane's eyes went wide, and her mouth hung open.

Smiling, I put my arm around her shoulder. "Holy cow is right. This is a day we will always remember."

She nodded. "V-E Day. Sounds pretty good, doesn't it?"

"Definitely." I took my spot at the periodicals table, but so many people were celebrating the end of the war in Europe, I wasn't sure the servicemen and women could get to my table even if they wanted to. It was really all about victory today: victory in Europe and impending victory in the Pacific with all kinds of desserts to celebrate it.

Rose came rushing to me in a hug so fierce it nearly knocked me to the ground. "It's over! The war in Europe is finally over!"

As happy and relieved as I was for our troops and my friends whose loved ones were there, I had trouble really letting go to celebrate. Tom was still in danger. So many conflicting emotions swirled in my mind.

As the troop trains came in all day, soldiers were in a party mood. Jane and her friends must have danced with almost twenty soldiers each during every fifteen-minute stop. Sandwiches, milk, and coffee were still popular, but it was the cookies, cakes, pies, and popcorn balls the servicemen couldn't get enough of. I don't know how many popcorns balls they actually ate, but many of them were thrown around the station.

I didn't know exactly where in the Pacific Tom was these days, but the news was full of heavy casualties in Iwo Jima, Burma, Borneo, and Okinawa. While it meant our troops were getting closer to the Japanese mainland, it was more frightening for those of us with loved ones in the Pacific theatre.

I smiled and laughed and celebrated with everyone who came through the Canteen on V-E Day, but it wasn't quite real to me. How could we celebrate when the war wasn't completely over?

I was happy for Sue because her husband, Martin, would be coming home. I was very happy for Rose. Harry would be on his way home to marry her and start their life together. But I was still worried for Ann, whose husband, Joe, was in the Pacific. And I was, of course, worried about Tom.

Ambiguity had never been easy for me, and I chafed with it now.

I wanted to join in the V-E Day celebrations, but felt torn by my concern for the battles still raging in the Pacific.

I loved Tom, but could I still respect him? I wanted him safe and the war over, but did I want him to come home to North Platte? I wanted Jane in my life, but could I step into the job of stepmother? What was the right path for me going forward?

That night, when I climbed into bed, I was exhausted from a wonderful if exhausting day, but I couldn't quiet my mind for sleep. Tom was still in danger. If the worst happened and he was killed in action, what would that mean for me?

Jane was becoming the daughter I never had. A dear, sweet, smart, and funny girl; she was a treasure to have around. I was not her legal guardian or even a stepparent, so what if someone tried to take her away from me? I doubted Tom had updated his will to list me as her guardian. But that's what I'd want if he wasn't coming home.

I had my job at the library and, after my work at the Canteen, I had some good friends in town. Although Rose, Sue, Ann, and the other women would be busy with their husbands when they came home, we'd still have time to get together, occasionally. Jane and I would be a family together, too. So I wouldn't be alone.

If he didn't come home, I probably would never marry. I thought I'd lost my chance when Fred died, along with so many men of my generation. I had resigned myself to life as a spinster before Tom came along. It would be harder to go back to the future I'd begun to imagine, after I'd allowed myself to fall in love with him, but I could do it if he wasn't coming home.

As I drifted asleep, one last question floated through my mind. I had a good idea what my life would look like if he didn't come home from the war, but what about if he did?

CHAPTER FOURTY

May 19, 1945

"Good news!" Rose was running toward Jane and me as we walked into the Canteen. She was waving a yellow scrap of paper that looked like a telegram, so I'm glad she said it was good news.

Rose thrust the telegram into my hands, her eyes bright and her smile big. "I got this telegram yesterday. Harry's on his way to North Platte."

I read the telegram, shaking my head. "He's injured again?"

She nodded. "Yeah, but it doesn't sound bad. It means he was back in the hospital in London for V-E Day and got to be one of the first ones shipped out. I told you he'd earned his 85 points a while ago because of the work he did in London when he was injured earlier."

I handed her back the telegram. "It doesn't say when he'll be here. Any idea?"

She linked one of her arms through mine. "I don't know, but I'm hoping soon."

I nodded. "Me, too, Rose. I'm so happy for you."

From what I'd read, many of the servicemen in Europe were being prepared to go to the Pacific, so it was definitely lucky for Harry and Rose that he'd earned his 85 points.

"Me, too," said Jane. "I can't wait to meet him."

Rose and I straightened the table and put out more donations of books and magazines. "When do you think the Canteen will close? As soon as we have peace in the Pacific? Or will it stay open for a while?"

I looked up from the table. "Well, we have to win the Pacific, but, given how many servicemen and women will be crossing the country again to get home, I suspect we'll keep it going. The service members will have as much need for food on their train trips home as they did when shipping out."

She nodded. "That's true. I didn't think about how long they'd be on the trains."

The first troop trains of the day started arriving. Some of the soldiers were returning home, although the vast majority were young replacement troops heading to the Pacific.

After she'd been quiet a moment, Rose rested her hand on my arm. "I'm sorry if I'm being insensitive. I know the war is still raging in the Pacific, and Tom and everyone over there is still in danger. I'll keep him in my prayers."

I smiled and patted her arm. "Thank you, Rose. And I don't want you to think I'm not celebrating V-E Day and Harry's impending return. I couldn't be happier for you and everyone whose loved ones are safe and coming home soon."

She leaned in, placing her cheek on my shoulder. "I love you, Maggie. I want you to know that in case I sometimes don't always show it. You mean the world to me, and it was my lucky day when Rae Wilson asked me to help you at this table."

I kissed her head. "Thank you, Rose. I love you, too. You were a sweet girl then and have grown into a warm and wonderful young woman. We were both lucky things worked out as they did here at the Canteen."

As the day wore on, we'd had twenty troop trains and over four thousand service members come through the Canteen by six p.m. We were all exhausted but happy to help so many soldiers, sailors, marines, WACs, and WAVEs. When Helen told us another troop train was arriving, we brightened up our smiles and took our places.

"Can I help you, Sergeant?"

A tall, dark-haired soldier turned from the guest book and held out his hand, so I shook it. "I'm Sergeant Andrew Hannel of Seattle, ma'am. This is my second time through North Platte, so I wanted to sign in again and give someone my thanks."

I smiled. "You're quite welcome, Sergeant. Where are you coming from?"

"I was originally sent to training out in Denver and then east to deploy to North Africa. From there, we landed in Anzio and fought our way north through Italy and into France. After the Battle of the Bulge, we kept right on into Germany. But I got my points, and I'm heading home. After, of course, all the Army paperwork and such in Colorado."

I leaned in and gave the young man a hug. "Thank you for all you've done, Sergeant. You fought in some of the toughest battles of this war."

He blushed. "I just did what they told me to, ma'am."

"Help yourself to some food, Sergeant Hannel. It's still a long way to New York."

He bobbed his head. "Yes, ma'am. I don't want to miss out on the great sandwiches and cookies like I had last time."

As Sergeant Hannel moved on to the food table, another soldier in an Army uniform stepped up to sign the guest book. He wore the insignia of a Master Sergeant.

When he turned to face me, my breath caught. "Harry?"

He did a double take. "Do I know you?"

I laughed. "I'm sorry, Master Sergeant. When I saw your face, I was taken aback. Rose and I are very close and she's shown me your pictures many times. I'm Maggie Parker." I held out my hand to him, but he crushed it as he pulled me into a bear hug.

"I'm sorry, ma'am." He stepped back. "I feel as if we've known each other for years. I've heard so much about you, Mag...uh, Miss Parker. It's great to finally meet you."

Shaking my head, I said, "Why don't you call me Maggie, and I'll call you Harry, as we're going to be family very soon, if I'm not mistaken."

He blushed. "Where is she?" He looked around the room. "She told me she worked at the Canteen on Saturdays. I really hope she's here right now."

"She is." I pointed to the kitchen door just as Rose stepped through it, carrying a tray of sandwiches. After she set them on the table, she looked at me and froze.

Before I could say a word, Harry was striding across the room, parting the crowd like a hot knife through butter, and picking Rose up off the floor. He swung her around and set her down, pulling her into a passionate kiss right there in the Canteen. Several of the other servicemen were hooting and clapping, but Rose didn't seem to hear or care.

I couldn't take my eyes off the happy couple, tears streaming down my face. Rose had grown so much from the not-quite-sixteen-year-old girl I'd met more than three years ago. I loved her like a daughter, was relieved she'd made peace with her mother, and wished her every happiness in her marriage to Harry. I hoped he was good enough for her, would treat her well, and do everything to keep her happy.

Rose and Harry walked hand in hand to the periodicals table, smiling. When Rose turned to speak to me, I was practically blinded by the brilliance of her smile and the sparkle in her eyes. "Harry says you met."

I smiled and nodded to Harry. "Yes, we bumped into each other while he was looking for you."

Rose blushed. "He swept me off my feet just like he said he would."

I chuckled. "I saw." She was just glowing, and it was a good look on her.

"We're…" she hesitated, looked at Harry and when he nodded, she began again. "We're getting married." She smiled. "Now."

I couldn't hide my surprise. "Now?"

She nodded. "Harry got a special license, which I guess isn't too hard for the returning soldiers. He called ahead and made an appointment with a judge. So, we're going there now."

I pulled her into my arms. "My best wishes to the bride. I'm so happy for you, honey."

When she pulled back, her tear-filled gaze met mine. "I want you to be my maid of honor. Will you come?"

Touched, my eyes filled with tears again. "Of course. Let me tell Helen that someone else will have to cover our table."

She nodded. "We'll go tell Jane. I want her there, too."

After I talked to Helen and got my pocketbook, I met Jane, Harry, and Rose on the platform. The bride was radiant, and the groom looked nervous. Jane seemed excited to be included.

"Let's go," said Harry, taking Rose's hand again.

We all walked to the judge's home, where he would prefer the ceremony. Rose had called Trixie from the Canteen, so she was waiting for us when we arrived. Trixie handed Rose a small bouquet of flowers she'd picked in her garden.

The ceremony was short and incredibly sweet. Rose looked up at Harry like the sun and stars rose in his eyes. Harry held Rose as if she were made of spun glass, but he couldn't bear to stop touching her. Trixie and I both cried throughout the ceremony, and Jane clapped when the judge pronounced them man and wife.

After kissing the happy couple and catching the bouquet Rose threw directly to me, I invited everyone back to our house for tea and cake. Luckily, I'd made a cake to donate to the Canteen, but kept a smaller one from the same batter for Jane and me to eat at home.

Rose smiled. "That'd be lovely. Thank you so much."

When we walked into the parlor, Jane hurried to the kitchen to cut slices of cake while I made the tea. Everyone was seated when we returned.

"Here's a toast to the happy couple," Trixie said, holding up her tea cup. "Sorry I don't have any champagne to toast with."

Everyone sipped their tea. "Don't worry about it, Mom." Rose said, leaning her head on Harry's shoulder. "We'll toast with champagne on our first anniversary. Right?"

Harry nodded. "On every anniversary." At that, everyone laughed.

"That sounds like a great idea," I said, putting my tea cup down and cutting into the cake. "And always eat cake." I held up my fork with a piece of cake on it.

Everyone "toasted" again with a forkful of cake.

As we ate, Harry told us about his journey to get to North Platte. "Because my foot gave out again in Frankfurt, the doctors in the field hospital decided I needed to go back to London to see a specialist. They were afraid it would keep giving me trouble. The timing was perfect, as I was in London for V-E Day and now, here I am." He took a sip of his tea. "You would not believe how crowded it was on the Queen Elizabeth when we sailed." He looked at Rose, whose adoring gazed was glued on him. "Anyway, the voyage was smooth and fast, since there were no U-boats to worry about, and I jumped on a train headed west. I'll have to go back to my unit next week, but I got a week's furlough to get married."

"You're still in the Army?" Rose sounded worried.

Harry wrapped his arm around her shoulders. "I won't be gone long. Basically, the Army just has to complete our paperwork, and then we'll be discharged."

I nodded. "I'm sure there's always a lot of paperwork in the Army."

Harry laughed. "That's for sure. Everything must be filled out in triplicate."

When the cake and tea were done, it became obvious the happy couple wanted to spend their evening alone. Trixie stood. "I hate to call an end to this lovely evening, but I have guests waiting for me at the boarding house."

We all stood.

"We'd better be on our way as well," Harry said. "I reserved us a room at the Pawnee Hotel for tonight."

"Wow," said Jane. "That's a beautiful hotel. We had tea there once and got to take a peek at the Crystal Ballroom."

I opened the front door and stood in the doorway, hugging Rose once more as she left.

Harry stepped forward and I pulled him into a hug. "Congratulations, Harry. Take good care of our girl."

He smiled. "I promise."

I wrapped my arms around Rose. "Best wishes, Mrs. Gates."

She giggled and pulled back, her gaze meeting mine. "It sounds wonderful, doesn't it?" She linked her arm through Harry's.

"Yes, it does."

Trixie followed the happy couple out the door, so I watched them all leave. I turned to close it, but someone was walking up the porch at just the same moment.

It was the Western Union delivery boy.

My heart fluttered in my chest and my blood ran cold. "May I help you?" My voice sounded low and strangled, even to my own ears.

He nodded, but didn't smile. When he met my gaze, I could tell it wasn't good news.

"Telegram for Miss Jane Carter." He handed me the yellow envelope, tipped his hat, and retreated off the porch.

I closed the door and stood, frozen in my place, unable to talk. Jane starred at me, her eyes wide and her lips stretched tight.

"Would you like me to read it for you?"

She nodded. My hands shook slightly as I slid my finger under the thin yellow envelope flap. I slid out the folded telegram and opened it.

"He's not dead." I had to say that right away, to reassure us both. "The Army says Tom was declared missing in action in the Battle of Okinawa, which is still ongoing. They will send us additional information when they have it."

She ran into my arms, tears already streaming down her face. "Oh, Daddy…"

I patted her back, trying to keep my voice even. "We have to hang on to the fact that he's only missing, not worse. We have to pray for him and keep hoping."

She nodded, crying onto my shoulder. I held her tight and let myself give way to tears. *Oh, Tom…*

CHAPTER FORTY-ONE

June 24, 1945

"I'm going to get changed; don't start without me." Jane raced up the stairs to get out of her Sunday best, while I walked to the kitchen to put a kettle on.

I would need to change my clothes as well before we began making the popcorn balls, but first, I needed tea.

Everyone at church meant well, but I couldn't take much more of this. I needed a chance to renew my soul, share some quiet time with the Lord, and believe my prayers were heard. I couldn't do that when everyone felt the need to tap me on the shoulder through the service to whisper questions about Tom or share words of support. I poured a cup of tea and sank into a chair, feeling as old as the Earth. I hadn't moved by the time Jane came downstairs, ready to cook.

"Feeling sad today, Miss Maggie?"

I was going to protest, but decided against it. The girl was smart, observant, and didn't deserve a lie. "Yes. I'm having a tough time today."

She sat beside me. "I thought you got a little sad when Mrs. Schmidt asked you about Dad."

I nodded and took a sip of tea. When I put my cup down, I met her gaze. "How are you feeling about your father being MIA all these weeks? You don't seem to get down too often. How do you do it?"

"Sometimes I get sad. The first few days after I got the telegram, I cried myself to sleep every night." I placed my hand on top of hers. "I couldn't imagine what we'd do if we lost him. But then, after a few weeks, I felt that he's going to be okay. I know it sounds a little crazy, but I truly believe we'll get a telegram any day now telling us they found him, he's fine, and he's coming home."

"We could get a much worse telegram, too." I had to balance keeping hope alive with preparing her for the worst. I didn't want to think about it either, but we needed to be prepared.

She shook her head. "I don't know how to explain it, but I don't believe that's going to happen. He's coming home to us soon." She took my hand in hers. And said, "It's okay. You can believe it, too. He's going to be all right."

I smiled. "I would love to believe what you're saying, but I'm afraid."

"Here's what I know. You love my father, although you're angry with him and not sure you want to marry him anymore. You're worried about him and afraid he won't make it home. You never talk about what it will be like when he gets home because you haven't decided whether you're going to marry him or not, but you're still in love with him, and now you love me, too."

I stared at her. How could she know all of that? Had she overheard conversations between Rose and me?

Jane held up a hand. "No, I don't read your mail or eavesdrop on you, but I'm not blind or stupid, either. You wouldn't worry about my dad the way you do, even getting upset with friends and neighbors, if you weren't in love with him. You wouldn't treat me like your daughter, instead of someone else's, if you didn't love me. You're mad at my dad for something, but when it comes down to it, he'll come home, and you'll get married. You love us too much to turn him down."

She laid her head on my shoulder and wrapped an arm around my waist.

I tried to digest everything she'd said and figure out how a girl of thirteen could know me so well. How was it all so clear to her, but such a mess of conflicting emotions to me? I wasn't sure I dared to believe what she said was true.

I kissed the top of her head. "I'll admit to at least one part of all that. I do love you, Jane."

She lifted her head and smiled at me. "I love you, too."

"And I'm praying that your father is well and will come home soon." I pushed back from the table and stood. "Let me get changed, and we can start our popcorn balls."

When I walked back downstairs after getting changed, someone knocked on the door. These days, the sound always made my heart stop. "I'll get it," I yelled to Jane.

A shadow of the Western Union delivery boy shown through the etched glass of the front door. Ice ran through my veins, and I had to resist the urge to run back upstairs and shut myself in my bedroom. I just stood there, unable to touch the door knob.

"Who is it, Miss Maggie?" She walked into the parlor while I stood frozen at the door.

I shook my head, as if clearing away shards of ice, and pulled the door open. "Yes?"

He handed me the hated yellow envelope again. "Telegram for Miss Carter." He turned and headed back to his bicycle.

I closed the door behind him and turned toward her. "Do you want to read it or should I?"

She walked forward, braver than she'd been a few weeks ago, and took the telegram. She ripped it open and read it quickly. "Dad's fine."

We both exhaled, taking a moment to hug before she continued: "He was injured in battle and has been in a hospital, but he's coming home." She looked up at me, beaming. "See, I told you so. He's on his way home."

The room grew hot, my legs were shaking and weak, and the next thing I knew, Jane was sitting on the floor beside me.

"Miss Maggie? Are you okay?" She was patting my hand, but when I couldn't seem to speak, she dropped it and ran to the phone.

I tried to tell her I was fine, but the words wouldn't come out. I had no breath, no voice. I blinked a few times, trying to bring everything into focus, and took a few shallow breaths. "Would you please help me to the sofa?"

She pulled me to a sitting position, but my neck seemed to be insufficient to hold up my head, and I felt myself listing to the side. "Let's move slowly," she said.

After a few moments, or it could have been hours, my head had cleared enough to be able to move. I leaned heavily on her and we slowly got me on my feet long enough to sort of dive onto the sofa. When I felt the soft cushions beneath me, I closed my eyes again just for a moment.

"I'm okay, honey. Really, I simply got dizzy."

She shook her head. "I'm sorry."

"For what?"

A single tear escaped her right eye lid. "I should have been quicker. I didn't catch you before you hit the floor. You'll probably have a bad headache."

I leaned up on my right elbow, pulling her into my embrace with my left arm. "It's not your fault. I'm fine. Really, don't worry about it. We can make the popcorn balls in a bit."

"I'm going to make you some fresh tea and bring you a snack. Just sit here for a while, and I'll be right back."

After she left, I pulled out a piece of stationary to write to Tom.

June 24, 1945
Dear Tom,

We received the telegram telling us, despite the fact you were wounded, you're going to be all right, and you're on your way home. Thank God. I can't tell you how relieved Jane and I are you are no longer listed as MIA and are well enough to travel.

The telegram didn't tell us much, and we haven't received any letters, so we are anxiously awaiting more news from you, the Army, or any source. What happened? How bad was your injury? How about the rest of your men? Are you recovered?

Jane has been very strong throughout this whole ordeal. She serenely believed you would be fine and would soon be home with us. And she was right. I wish I had been able to blindly believe that as much as she did.

I've been worried about you and am so relieved you are coming home. In fact, I'm sure she will tell you I fainted when we got the telegram, but it was no big deal. I hadn't eaten my lunch yet and the sight of the Western Union delivery boy is enough to shake the nerves of anyone these days.

This whole time you've been listed as missing, I've thought about what would happen if you didn't come home. I'm sorry to have even considered it, but with responsibility for her now, I couldn't stop myself.

I also came to realize I'm ashamed of how I've treated you the past six months.

I've been angry with you, although I'm sure this is not news to you. I've never been good at deception. I was angry to learn my fiancé had been married before and had a twelve-year-old daughter he neglected to tell me about. Why didn't you tell me any of this during the three years we were writing to each other and before we got engaged? Didn't you think was something I not only would want to know, but deserved to be told if I was going to be your wife and your daughter's stepmother? Why would you keep her a secret, even from me?

And while I'm happy to help you, and Jane is a lovely girl, I didn't appreciate you assuming I could drop everything, go immediately to Chicago, and bring her to live with me. I'm not saying I wouldn't have done it if you'd asked, but you didn't ask. You told me to do it and do it instantly. You ordered me around like I was one of the enlisted men under your command.

I am not. Aren't we supposed to be partners?

You just assumed I would do as I was told. I had a lot to rearrange in terms of my work and volunteer schedules, paid a lot of money for trains and taxis, and changed my life to raise a girl I knew nothing about. You should have both told me about her much earlier and simply asked to help you with her.

Your lack of respect for me in this instance has made me question what our life would be like together after the war was over. Maybe because I've been taking care of myself for thirty-some years now, or maybe it's just who I am, but I don't take well to being ordered around. This is not the kind marriage I'm interested in, and I hoped you would have known me better by now.

Jane is a well-mannered, intelligent, and sweet girl, and I've grown to love her. She is a great help around the house and at the Canteen. She even seems to enjoy spending time at the library. We get along wonderfully, and I'm happy to have her in my life, but why couldn't you have told me about that part of your life and realized how much it would affect me?

I have been conflicted about writing this type of letter because everything and everyone, all the advertisements in ladies magazines, newspapers, posters, and newsreels, and even the government, tell us not to upset our fighting men with angry letters. The life-and-death issues you have been facing are more important than my anger and hurt feelings.

I don't want you to think I'm still angry. I realized, when faced with that dreaded telegram, that my pride had been wounded, but no real harm had been done. When I had to consider the possibility you might not be coming home to me and Jane, I realized my anger is gone. I am in love with you and want to be your wife. All I want is for you to come home safe and sound.

I hope we will hear soon about when you are going to arrive, but I understand transportation is inconsistent at best and beyond your control. I hope you are healthy enough so your arrival in North Platte is not delayed. Hurry home, Tom; we are waiting for you.

All my love, Maggie

CHAPTER FORTY-TWO

June 30, 1945

"I can't believe how many servicemen have come through here today." Sue walked over to where I stood, wiped her hands on the edge of her apron before starting to slice a new batch of pies.

"The War Department is moving men all over the place, and many are coming through North Platte." I smiled. Newspapers had become the most requested item as men returning home tried to catch up on the latest news.

"You're probably tired of people asking, but have you heard anything about Tom coming home?"

I shook my head. "Nothing new." I straightened some piles that were already straight. "Did you talk to Ann this morning? How's she doing?"

Sue turned her back to the room, giving us some privacy. "I'm not sure how she's holding on. I spoke to her late last night and she was a wreck."

I nodded. "I dropped off a casserole two days ago, and she was putting on a good front. I don't know how she's going to manage alone with four kids."

Sue shook her head. "Joe was great with those kids, too, especially the boys. They fell apart when the telegram arrived."

"My heart is breaking for her. She thought he'd be safe; that the Seventh Fleet was pulling out of the Philippines."

"That much was true, apparently, but not before the ship he was on took a lot of artillery. Joe was hit and died instantly from what Ann was told."

We both stood quietly, knowing it could have been the men we cared about who were never coming home. I put my hand on Sue's arm. "I'm going to organize meals for them for the next few weeks. I'm sure most of the ladies here would be willing to take a day."

She nodded. "That's a good idea. Put me down for any open time slots."

I gave Sue a quick hug and walked back to my table.

"Were you talking about Mrs. Tenney?" Rose walked over to where I was.

"Yes. Sue talked to her last night, so I wanted to see how she's is doing."

Rose nodded. "This war can't end soon enough. We have to stop ripping families apart."

I nodded. "I hope we all get some good news about the war in the Pacific soon, but I don't know how we get to V-J Day. The Japanese premier just declared that they will never surrender. I hope that doesn't mean we'll have to invade Japan."

Rose shuddered. "I hope not. I can't imagine the number of Allied servicemen who would die."

Later that afternoon, Jane came running over to my table, an envelope in her hands. Thankfully, it was not yellow.

"I ran home to change shoes, since I finally wore through the sole of my favorite pair." She giggled. "Too much dancing, I guess."

I said, "We'll have to see if there are any shoes available to buy in your size."

She nodded. "Yeah. But, anyway, this letter was in the mailbox when I got home." She handed me the envelope from Tom.

"I wonder when he had time to write this." Hopefully, there was more information about when to expect him. The waiting was getting to me. My skin felt two sizes too small.

She smiled. "I got one, too. He said he was in transit, but didn't seem to know when he'd get here."

She ran back to the piano to be ready to dance with the next group of servicemen coming in. I walked down to Rose.

She looked up. "Did you hear from Tom?"

Holding up the envelope, I nodded. "Jane ran home and got the mail. Do you mind keeping an eye on things while I duck outside to read this?"

Rose gave me a gentle shove, shaking her head. "Don't be silly. Go find a private spot and read your letter."

June 26, 1945
My darling Maggie,

First, I wanted to let you know I'm fine and am on my way to North Platte. I was injured in the fighting on Okinawa, but mostly just messed up my knee really bad. It's not life threatening and will hopefully heal okay, but I'm walking with a cane and am useless to my unit. Since my CO had already put in for my retirement, the Army is sending me stateside for rehab, and then I'll be done. I should be getting to North Platte by early July, but won't be there for long before I'm sent on to a VA hospital.

Now, let me say I'm so sorry that I'm an idiot. Of course, you already know that, but I'll get it out there right at the start, so you know I understand it, too. I've spent too many years in this man's Army, or maybe I got too many knocks on the head. Whatever the reason, I'm an idiot and I don't deserve a woman like you. I know you're not one of my enlisted men, and I never should have given you orders as if you were.

I am incredibly, supremely, humbly sorry for taking you for granted, ordering you around, acting like a boorish prick [excuse my language], and being an overall horse's ass.

I'm sorry I didn't tell you about Jane and her mother before asking you to marry me. Jane is part of me, part of my heart, so I rarely talk about her to anyone. Even the men closest to me don't know I have a daughter, only that I write several letters every night.

When her mother died, I was devastated and petrified. First, I had been so in love with her mother, Virginia, that I had no idea how I could go on without her. I was overwhelmed with sadness and despair, yet had a newborn infant daughter depending on me.

I knew nothing about raising babies, especially girls, and had no idea how to be an Army officer and a father at the same time. I wanted to take Jane with me when I went back to the base, knowing I could get a house or apartment, and raise her there. It would have been a lot of work and involved getting a lot of help, but that's what I planned to do.

My Aunt Wilma—Aunt Will as we called her—took me aside and told me that an Army base was no place for my motherless daughter. She volunteered to help me and said leaving the baby with her would be the best option for Jane. I couldn't imagine not having Jane with me, but Aunt Will insisted the baby needed to stay in one place (with her), rather than traipse around the country with me.

Leaving Jane with my aunt was the hardest decision I'd ever made, and I struggled with it for a long time. I nearly went AWOL from my unit after my compassion leave expired because I couldn't abandon her. Finally, my aunt convinced me that she could have a safe, stable, comfortable life in Chicago and that I could visit as often as I got leave.

I made up for missing her so much by writing to her every day, even when she was tiny. I wanted to be a part of her life, especially when I was deployed to the other side of the country. And I wanted to know what she thought about life, what she liked or disliked, and be the keeper of her secrets.

You're probably thinking I should have left the Army and gotten a different job to be with her. I gave it serious thought, but when Virginia died in 1932, we were deep in the Depression, and I couldn't find anything else. Probably should have kept trying, but, with my aunt's encouragement, I made the decision to stay in the Army. It all seemed to be working well, and I was so rarely in Chicago, I didn't keep looking for other jobs.

I will not deny that I loved my job, at least, during the time between the Great War and this one. I enjoyed training young men, teaching them, and molding them into strong, resilient soldiers. Unfortunately, the training of men I was doing in the '30s bears little resemblance to the work I do now. After a few weeks of boot camp or other basic training, we throw them into the fire and hope the other men in the unit will help keep the new guys from burning to death. I don't love my job now, but it's more important than ever because what I teach these young men, boys, really, might be what they need to know to keep themselves alive. At least, that's what I pray for when I lay my head down at the end of the day.

So, regardless of the fact that the situation worked for Aunt Will, Jane, and me as a family, that still doesn't explain why I didn't tell you about her or the fact I was married before.

When I first started writing to you, I wasn't sure I could get you to write back. I was mesmerized by you from the first time I saw and spoke to you, and I wanted to get to know you better. I never thought I'd find someone to love after losing Virginia, but knew you were special from the moment we met. I had to convince you to get to know me, and I didn't think telling you about my late wife and young daughter would help me entice you to get to know me better.

Honestly, while I'm proud of Jane and of the relationship we've been able to develop, I'm not too proud of myself for abandoning my daughter. While it was easier for me to believe my aunt that Jane was better off with her, I've always believed that I should have tried harder to keep my daughter with me. I can't go back and change it now, but it was not my finest hour.

Once you started to warm up to me and we fell in love, and certainly before I asked you to marry me, I should have told you about Jane and sent you her address at Aunt Will's, so you could get to know her, too. I guess I was too used to keeping each part of my world separate. I talked to my fellow officers about orders, plans, and strategies. We shared some personal information, but nothing too deep.

I issued orders to the men underneath me and took orders from my CO. I wrote to Jane about her life, to Aunt Will about Jane, and to you about everything else.

Again, if I'm being honest, which I'm sure you agree it's long past time that I am, I was afraid you'll call me out on it; that you'd change your mind about me if you knew.

I can't imagine you ever shirking your responsibility to someone. Even with as difficult as your mother was and how hard it was for you to share a house with her, you never turned her out. You never abandoned her the way I did Jane, and I was too ashamed of myself to let you see what I'd done.

As I mentioned previously, I'm an idiot.

Please forgive me for my "military" approach to problem solving, too. When Wilma died, the next hurdle was to move her into her new home. I'm afraid I treated you a bit like my lieutenant, rather than my partner, and issued the orders I knew were necessary to accomplish the objective. I will work very hard to change my approach when it comes to our life together, but feel free to remind me about being an idiot when I mess up.

Thank you for your forgiveness. All I think about is when I get to take you in my arms, marry you, and make you my wife. I'm looking forward to our life together with Jane in North Platte, and acknowledge I'm a lucky man that you are willing to marry an idiot like me. I love you more than life itself. Please don't give up on me.

I can't wait to see you and hope it will be soon. I'll call from the depot when I arrive, as I'm not going to be able to walk to your house. Thank you for giving me another chance to be the man you deserve —
Tom

I pulled a tissue from the pocket of my apron and wiped my eyes. The man did write a good letter. While I had never had children of my own, I could imagine how torn he must have been when faced with the uncertain life he could provide his child in the Army or the stable, loving home his aunt would provide. As a newly widowed father, he must have been overwhelmed and panicked. My heart ached for the tough decision he was forced to make.

Understanding what he went through helped me to forgive him, yet again. I was going to be Tom's wife. We were getting married, and soon. Tom would move into my house, well, it would be our house then, and I'd be Jane's stepmother.

The family that had always been out of reach for me was going to be real. I walked back to the Canteen and through the kitchen again, despite the controlled chaos happening in there, to regain my spot at the table.

As I passed Rose, she took my arm. "Well?" She was grinning so much, she looked like she knew what I was going to say.

I smiled. "It was a good letter."

She prodded my ribs with her elbow. "Is he forgiven?"

I nodded. "Yes. I can't wait for him to get here so I can tell him so myself."

Rose smiled, tears spilling from her eyes. "Then turn around."

Her words took a split second to sink in, but when I turned, I had to blink repeatedly and not only to clear the tears filling my eyes, too.

Tom stood, albeit on crutches and with a huge cast on his left leg, staring at me from the doorway where I first saw him. He wasn't up to sauntering or even leaning suggestively at this point, but his gaze was still filled with bits of mischief and insolence. Mostly, it was filled with love.

Jane was hovering slightly behind him, her arms spread wide. I wasn't sure if she was showing me he was here or if she was preparing to catch him if he fell.

When my gaze met his, I felt the breath leave my chest. My heart was pounding as I ran to him, carefully wrapping my arms around him, while still holding him tight so he could stay upright.

"Oh, Tom." Tears started falling in earnest, and I began to sob.

Tom wrapped his arms around me, leaning on me, and buried his face in my neck. "Maggie. My God, Maggie, I've missed you so much."

His right hand came up, tilted my chin back, and he captured my lips with his.

Our first kiss.

His ring was on my finger, his daughter stood to my side, and hundreds of servicemen raced around us. It didn't matter. I slid into this kiss as if we'd been doing this for years. My toes curled in my shoes, and my skin tingled in my clothes.

Tom was home, he was alive, and he was mine.

When we finally came up for air, Tom reached his right arm back and pulled Jane into our hug, too. She burrowed between us, also careful not to tip Tom over, and the three of us shared a private moment.

We were a family. My family.

Rose tapped me on the shoulder. "Why don't you three go home? I think you can be excused from Canteen duty this afternoon."

Tom released Jane and held out his right hand, although he still had an arm over my shoulder. "Captain Tom Carter, soon to be U.S. Army, retired. You must be Mrs. Gates."

Rose smiled, taking his hand. "Please call me Rose, Captain. We're practically family."

Tom pulled Rose in to kiss her cheek. "Then call me Tom, Rose. It's nice to finally meet you."

She nodded. "You, too. I'm glad you made it home," she said looking down at his cast, "mostly in one piece."

Tom laughed. "Thanks. The pieces are all there; they just don't fit together exactly the way they used to."

"You're right, Rose. We're going to go home. Thanks for covering for me." I turned back to Tom. "I didn't bring my car today, so let me get us a taxi."

My heart was racing and my ears were ringing. I have no idea if the station was full of people or completely empty. There was no one for me besides Tom and Jane.

I left Jane to walk with her father while I hurried off to get a taxi. Once Tom was carefully loaded into the back seat, I climbed in the other door, and she took a seat in the front. Tom reached across the seat, lacing his fingers with mine. His skin was cool and warm and felt wonderful next to mine.

I couldn't stop smiling, but at least I'd stopped sobbing.

The taxi driver, Bert, pulled into my driveway and got Tom's bags out of the trunk while Jane and I helped Tom out of the car and up the front steps. While she unlocked the front door, I turned to pay the driver.

He shook his head. "It's taken care of, Miss Parker. Have a lovely day."

"Oh," I shook my head. "Who paid you?"

Bert smiled. "Just never you mind. Go enjoy having your man home."

When I tried to give Bert a tip, he refused that, too, and hurried down the steps. I closed the front door and turned. Tom and Jane were seated on the sofa with Tom's leg propped up on the table. The girl was snuggled into his left side, and she had the biggest smile on her face I'd ever seen.

He looked up as I closed the door, smiled, and held up his right arm. I walked to the sofa and slipped under his arm, and found the home I'd been seeking my entire life.

CHAPTER FORTY-THREE

June 25, 1945

Tom only had a three-day furlough before he had to report to the VA hospital to begin his treatment, so I took the next three days off work to be home with him. We promised Jane she could stay home from school on Wednesday, his last day, to spend time with her father before he boarded the train to Omaha.

"Good morning, sleepyhead." I eased open the guest room door to bring Tom a glass of water and the pills he was supposed to take every morning.

He rolled over and his eyes popped open. A smile filled his face. "I love waking up to the sight of you." He propped himself up on his right elbow.

I giggled. "Sure, after I've had time to do my hair and put on some lipstick." I handed him the pills, he popped them in his mouth, and took a long swallow of water before setting the glass on the nightstand. His Adam's apple bobbed as the water worked its way down his throat. As my eyes traveled down from his throat to his chest, I quickly made myself stop and look him in the eyes again.

His color was back and his gaze didn't show as much exhaustion and pain as it had when I helped him into bed last night. "You're one of those crazy people who wakes up instantly and happy, aren't you?"

He laughed, reaching up and grabbing me around the waist. "Yes!" He pulled me into the bed with him, lifting me over his left leg.

I shrieked. "Your knee. I'm going to hurt you."

He plopped me down on my back and leaned over me. "You could never hurt me. Not unless you stopped loving me." Tom leaned down and kissed me like I'd never been kissed like before. My eyes drifted closed, and my arms wound around his neck.

Tom's hands roamed over my arms, my sides, into my hair, and then down my torso. As his right fingertips skimmed the edge of my ribs and breast, I felt my body tighten and arch.

Tom took a deep breath, broke the kiss, and leaned his forehead onto mine. "I have to stop. Otherwise, I'll have us racing to the wedding, and I'd be making promises my body isn't up to delivering quite yet."

He smiled, but the frustration was clear in his gaze.

"You need to regain your strength and get your health back. There'll be time for us to be together once you're healed."

He kissed my forehead. "And we're married."

I nodded. "Yes, and we're married."

He slid back down and pulled me against his shoulder. "Do you want a big wedding?"

I shook my head. "No. I'd like to invite Rose and Harry, the minister, Jane, you, and me."

"None of your other friends?"

"I don't think so." The smile in his gaze calmed my nerves. "Everyone is stretched thin, waiting for loved ones to return, celebrating those who have made it home, or mourning the ones who didn't. I don't need a big party, only the people I love the most."

He kissed me. "Sounds good to me."

He pulled his arm from beneath my neck, pretending to push me out of the bed. "Come on, woman. I can't lay around all day simply to satisfy your prurient desires. I need some breakfast!"

I shook my head, laughing, and climbed out of bed. This was what my life was going to be like from now on. I could definitely get used to this.

****

August 6, 1945

"What time did you and Jane get back from Omaha yesterday?" Rose was sitting in the guest chair in my library office during a quiet moment in the afternoon.

"Our train was delayed getting home, so we didn't get to the house until almost 10:00 p.m. I was beat this morning, but she is like her father. She pops up, smiling and awake, without my need for coffee."

Rose laughed. "Thank God Harry is like me: slow, groggy, and a little cranky in the morning. On Sundays, we flip a coin to see who has to get up first to make the coffee."

I smiled. "I've always enjoyed the slow start to our day in the library, starting the coffee, unlocking the cabinets, taking our time before we open the front doors." I held up one hand. "I mean, I love when are patrons are here, making use of our great facilities, but it's nice to have the quiet, too."

Rose nodded. "I agree. I still like having some time during the day to read, so I know what to suggest when a patron asks."

The telephone interrupted our quiet. "Hello?"

"Okay, thanks." I jumped up and turned on the radio. President Truman's voice came on.

"Sixteen hours ago, an American airplane dropped a bomb on Hiroshima, an important Japanese army base. That bomb has more power than 20,000 tons of TNT... The Japanese began the war from Pearl Harbor. They have been repaid many fold and the end is not yet. With this bomb we have added a new revolutionary increase in destruction to supplement the growing power of our armed forces…"[1]

Rose had gone pale. Her eyes were rimmed in red. "Oh my God."

What have we done? A shiver ran down my spine, spreading a cold chill throughout my body.

Rose looked at me, already shaking. "The Japanese will have to surrender now."

I walked over to her chair, putting my hand on her shoulder. "Yes, please, let this bring an end to the war."

---

[1] Harry S. Truman, "August 6, 1945: Statement by the President Announcing the Use of the A-Bomb at Hiroshima," UVA Miller Center, https://millercenter.org/the-presidency/presidential-speeches/august-6-1945-statement-president-announcing-use-bomb.

CHAPTER FOURTY-FOUR

September 1, 1945

"They're going to broadcast President Truman's speech over the PA system, so everyone can hear it." Helen stopped at our table to tell us what to expect.

"Thanks, Helen. Do we know for sure the war is over?"

She shrugged. "That's what everyone says. The MPs said they heard the Japanese surrendered today."

I clasped my hand to my heart. "I pray it's true. It's long past time for this to be over."

Helen moved on to the next group of women. I turned to Rose and said, "If this is really over, we're going to have even more troops coming through the station every day, making their way home."

She nodded. "It'll mean more work and definitely more food, but I couldn't be happier."

I nodded. Rose looked at me, holding up her crossed fingers.

The voice of the radio announcer came over the PA: "Please stand by for the president."

Truman began: "The thoughts and hopes of all America—indeed of all the civilized world—are centered tonight on the battleship Missouri. There on that small piece of American soil anchored in Tokyo Harbor the Japanese have officially laid down their arms. They have signed terms of unconditional surrender.

"Four years ago, the thoughts and fears of the whole civilized world were centered on another piece of American soil—Pearl Harbor. The mighty threat to civilization which began there is now laid at rest. It was a long road to Tokyo—and a bloody one. We shall not forget Pearl Harbor.

"The Japanese militarists will not forget the USS Missouri. The evil done by the Japanese war lords can never be repaired or forgotten. But their power to destroy and kill has been taken from them. Their armies and what is left of their Navy are now impotent.

"To all of us there comes first a sense of gratitude to Almighty God who sustained us and our Allies in the dark days of grave danger, who made us to grow from weakness into the strongest fighting force in history, and who has now seen us overcome the forces of tyranny that sought to destroy His civilization."[2]

I rushed into Rose's arms amid an explosion of cheers and hoots from every corner of the depot. Women openly wept, as did many men, and the servicemen stopped in North Platte exploded in celebration. Canteen volunteers were pulled into kisses by servicemen who were complete strangers. The war was finally, completely over.

The scene was surreal, as if already captured in a Norman Rockwell print. While it seemed too good to be

---

[2] Harry S. Truman, "Radio Address to the American People After the Signing of the Terms of Unconditional Surrender by Japan, September 1, 1945," Harry S. Truman Presidential Library and Museum, https://www.trumanlibrary.org/publicpapers/index.php?pid=129.

true, the shouting, laughing, and prayers surrounding me assured me the war was really over. A sense of new beginning took root in my heart.

Now to get everyone back home safe and sound.

****

September 1, 1945
Dear Tom,

I couldn't get a long-distance telephone line today; I'm sure everyone was trying to make calls across the country and even around the world. What a day for celebration!

I'm so relieved all of our troops will be coming home and praying their return is speedy and safe. Thank God you got out when you did, even if it meant you had to be injured to do so. I keep thinking of my friend Ann and her husband, Joe, who was killed in the Philippines near the end of the fighting there. It's so sad to think he made it through four years of war only to die within a few months of peace.

The Canteen committee had a meeting last week, in view of the end of the war, and decided we will keep the Canteen going as long as we think it's useful to the returning service members. While the number of troops through North Platte has risen to well over 6,000 on some days, there are clearly many more men still on their way home. I would guess we'll stay open at least another six months, but we'll see how it goes.

Did I tell you about the sailor from Maine who moved to North Platte this week? He stopped in at the Canteen to let us know it was the kindness he encountered at the Canteen that prompted him to decide to live here after the war. He's a very nice young man and will be a wonderful addition to the community.

Have the doctors given you an update on your release date yet? It's been a month since your surgery and you seemed to be recovering nicely when we visited last week. We're anxious to have you home.

Once we have an idea when you're getting released from the hospital for good, I will get the wedding plans finalized. All I need is the date for the minister and our friends. Everything is ready, as long as you're willing to be married in your uniform. I don't think we'd be able to buy you a suit right now, as there's nothing available yet in the stores.

We'll talk more when we visit on Sunday, but I needed to touch base with you today, after the news of the surrender. You worked long and hard to bring this about and I wanted you to know how proud I am of you for what you've done for this country.

All my love — Maggie

CHAPTER FOURTY-FIVE

April 1, 1946

Tom slipped his arm around my waist. "Going to start crying again?"

I poked him in the ribs. "And what if I am?"

He gave me a little squeeze. "No problem. There's not a dry eye in the house today."

The ring on my finger sparkled and, again, I sent up my silent thanks to God and the universe for bringing my husband home to me.

He'd looked so handsome on our wedding day, even with the crutches he'd needed to help support him after his surgery. I still smiled at the sight of Harry standing by his side as his best man. Rose was my matron of honor and Jane our flower girl. It had been a wonderful day.

We stood on the platform of the North Platte train depot as Rae Wilson and Helen Christ, with the help of the station director and a maintenance man, took down the sign that read *North Platte Canteen.*

After fifty-one months, we were closing up shop. Most of the servicemen and women had returned home in the eight months since V-J Day. It was time, but it was hard.

None of us wanted to let go of the feeling of being part of something bigger than ourselves.

Rae Wilson spoke, her voice soft: "When I first suggested we create this Canteen, I had no idea it would turn into the miracle it did. Fifty-five thousand volunteers from 125 communities within a 200-mile radius of North Platte—towns from Nebraska, Colorado, and as far away as the Kansas state line—came together to create a place for over 6 million servicemen and women to get a good meal, a warm hug, a touch of home, and a fond farewell. The true miracle of North Platte was, as with the loaves and fishes, we never ran out of food. Despite never knowing how many trains or troops we'd be serving, we never had to charge for our food, nor did we turn anyone away. The morale boost each of us was able to share with these service members was as important to the Allied victory as any other war production."

Helen Christ cleared her throat and continued, "We continue to get mail every day from soldiers, sailors, marines, and other servicemen and women, and their families, thanking us for caring for them, feeding them, and showing them love and support. This is what North Platte is truly about, and I couldn't be more proud of everything we accomplished. While we are closing our doors today, the Canteen spirit will stay a part of us for the rest of our lives. Thank you, one and all, for everything you did to make this possible."

Tom pulled me in close and whispered in my ear, "I'm so proud of you."

I blushed but smiled and linked my arm through Jane's to pull her in close. "You were a part of this, too. You should be proud of the work you did here."

She smiled and put her head on my shoulder. She was getting so tall, it would be harder for her to do that soon.

Rose stood beside Jane, with Harry by her side. I caught Rose's gaze and smiled at her, mouthing, "I love you," to her. She returned the emotion and slipped her arm through Harry's.

The Canteen had brought Tom and Jane into my life, as well as Harry and Rose. While my friend Sue stood on the platform with her husband and children, Ann was there with only her daughter. My heart ached for her but she would go on, do what needed to be done for her children.

I wrapped my arms around Tom and Jane, pulling them closer, grateful we'd come through the war relatively unscathed.

The Canteen had produced marriages for Rose and Harry, Tom and me, and Beatrice and her MP, but that had never been the point. The boxes of letters from servicemen and women, and their families were evidence of the fact we'd accomplished what we'd intended to do.

Many of the volunteers had lost husbands, fathers, sons, boyfriends, and even grandsons, but they kept coming to work at the Canteen. North Platte lost eight men in the war, and many more had returned home injured, whether the injury was physical, mental, or spiritual. The war was over, and we had made it through, but many had not been so lucky.

There was a short reception after the ceremony. Tom and I walked hand in hand a few steps behind Jane as we headed home. When we got a few blocks from the depot, a car came racing around the corner. Tom and I reached for Jane as one, but it was my hand that connected and pulled her back from the curb.

She turned to me and smiled. "Thanks, Mom."

THE END

ABOUT THE AUTHOR

Barb Warner Deane writes emotional stories about strong women and small towns. Her published novels include *On The Homefront*, *Killing Her Softly*, *And Then There Was You*, and *The Whistle Stop Canteen*.

Barb grew up in the beautiful Finger Lakes area of New York. She graduated from Cornell University and the University Of Connecticut School of Law. Barb, her husband, and family have lived in the Chicago area for the past twenty-five years, other than two years in Frankfurt, Germany and two years in Shanghai, China.

After giving up the practice of law, Barb has worked mostly as a mom, but also as a paralegal, bookstore owner, travel writer, and IT tech specialist. She has also volunteered: for Girl Scouts, the American Women's Club in both Frankfurt and Shanghai, and as President of the Windy City Chapter of Romance Writers of America.

In addition to writing, Barb is a genealogy buff, is a huge fan all things Harry Potter, and is crazy for both U.S. and international travel. Now that she and her husband are empty-nesters, she's making plans to expand on her list of having visited 47 states and 42 countries on 6 continents.